V.L. McDERMID

Val McDermid grew up in Kirkcaldy on the east coast of Scotland, then read English at Oxford. She was a journalist for sixteen years, spending the last three years as Northern Bureau Chief of a national Sunday tabloid. Now a full-time writer, she divides her time between Cheshire and Northumberland.

Report for Murder is the first of six novels featuring journalist-sleuth Lindsay Gordon (the fifth, *Booked for Murder*, was shortlisted for the Lambda award). Val is also the author of the Kate Brannigan series and four tense psychological thrillers featuring criminal profiler Tony Hill. The first of these, *The Mermaids Singing*, was awarded the 1995 Gold Dagger Award for Best Crime Novel of the Year, while the second, *The Wire in the Blood*, lends its name to the acclaimed ITV series featuring Robson Green as Tony Hill. She has also written three stand-alone thrillers: *A Place of Execution*, *Killing the Shadows* and *The Distant Echo*.

For more information see Val's website
www.valmcdermid.com

D1464156

By the same author

V.L. McDERMID

Report for Murder

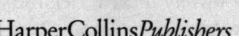

HarperCollins*Publishers*

HarperCollins*Publishers*
77–85 Fulham Palace Road
London, W6 8JB

The HarperCollins website address is:
www.harpercollins.co.uk

First published in Great Britain by
The Women's Press Ltd 1987

This paperback edition published 2004

1

Copyright © Val McDermid 1987

Val McDermid asserts the moral right to be identified as the
author of this work

ISBN 978-0-00-785804-0

Set in Meridien by Palimpsest Book Production Limited,
Polmont, Stirlingshire

Printed and bound in Great Britain
by Clays Ltd, St Ives plc

For Gill

PART ONE: OVERTURE

1

Lindsay Gordon put murder to the back of her mind and settled down in the train compartment to enjoy the broken greys and greens of the Derbyshire scenery. Rather like home, she decided. Except that in Scotland, the greens were darker, the greys more forbidding. Although in Glasgow, where she now lived, there was hardly enough green to judge. She congratulated herself on finishing the detective novel just at the point where Manchester suburbia yielded place to this attractive landscape foreign to her. Watching it unfold gave her the first answer to the question that had been nagging her all day: what the hell was she doing here? How could a cynical socialist lesbian feminist journalist (as she mockingly described herself) be on her way to spend a weekend in a girls' public school?

Of course, there were the answers she'd been able to use to friends: she had never visited this part of England and wanted to see what it was like; she was a great believer in 'knowing thine enemy', so it came under the heading of opportunities not to be missed; she wanted to see Paddy Callaghan, who had been responsible for the invitation. But she remained unconvinced that she was doing the right thing. What had made her mind up was the realisation that, given Lindsay's current relationship with the Inland Revenue, anything that had a cheque as an end product couldn't be ignored.

The fact that she cheerfully despised the job she was about to do was not a novel sensation. In the unreal world of popular journalism which she inhabited, she was continually faced with tasks that made her blood boil. But like other tabloid journalists who laid claim to a set of principles, she argued that, since popular newspapers were mass culture, if people with brains and compassion opted out the press would only sink further into the gutter. But in spite of having this missionary zeal to keep her warm, Lindsay often felt the chill wind of her friends' disapproval. And she had to admit to herself that saying all this always made her feel a pompous hypocrite. However, since this assignment involved writing for a magazine with some credibility, she was doubly pleased that it would avoid censure in the pub as well as provide cash, and that was enough to stifle the stirrings of contempt for Derbyshire House Girls' School.

Paddy, with the contacts of a life membership

of the old girls' network, had managed to persuade the features editor of *Perspective* to commission a piece from Lindsay about a fund-raising programme about to be launched by the school with a Gala Day. At that point, Lindsay was hungry for the cash and the prestige, so she couldn't afford the luxury of stopping to consider if it was the sort of project she'd actually choose to take on. Three months ago she'd reluctantly accepted redundancy when the *Daily Nation* discovered it needed fewer journalists so that it could pay its print workers their 'pound of flesh'. Since then, she had been applying for unlikely jobs and frenetically trying to make a living as a freelance. That made the call from Paddy all the more welcome because it meant a relatively quiet weekend away from the demands of the telephone – which would soon stop disrupting her life altogether if she didn't earn enough to pay the last quarter's bill.

At that unwelcome thought, Lindsay reflected with relief on the money she would receive from the Derbyshire House job. It seemed poetic justice that such a bastion of privilege should stake her. Good old Paddy, she mused. Ever since they'd met in Oxford six years before, Paddy had not only been a tower of strength in emotional crises but the first to offer help when life got Lindsay into one of its awkward corners. When Lindsay's car staged a break-down on a remote Greek mountainside it was Paddy who organised the flying out of a spare part. When Lindsay was made redundant it was Paddy who found the cousin who told Lindsay the best thing to do with her less-than-golden handshake. And when Lindsay's lover died, it was Paddy who drove through the night to be with her. The daughter of two doctors, with an education begun at the 'best' schools and polished off at Oxford, Paddy Callaghan had shaken her family by deciding to become an actress. After four years of only moderate success and limited employment, however, she had realised she would never make the first rank. Always a realist, and fundamentally unaffected by four years of living like a displaced person, she reverted to type and decided to make sure that the rising generation of public school-girls would have a better grounding on the stage than she'd had. When the two women first met, Paddy was half-way through the teacher training that would take her back to her old school in Derbyshire to teach English and Drama. It had taken Lindsay quite a long time to realise that at least part of her appeal for Paddy was her streak of unconventionality. She was an antidote to the staid world Paddy had grown up in and was about to return to. Lindsay had argued bitterly with Paddy that to go back to her old environment was copping out of reality. Though the argument never found a solution, the friendship survived.

Lindsay felt sure that part of the reason for the

continuation of that friendship was that they had never let their separate worlds collide. Just as Lindsay would never drag Paddy off to a gay club, so Paddy would never invite Lindsay to one of her parents' weekend house parties. Their relationship existed in a vacuum because they understood and accepted the gulf that separated so much of their lives. So Lindsay was apprehensive about encountering Paddy on what was firmly her territory. Suddenly all her fears about the weekend crystallised into a panic over the trivial issue of what she was wearing. What the hell was the appropriate gear for this establishment, anyway? It wasn't something that normally exercised her thoughts, but she had gone through her wardrobe with nervous care that morning, rejecting most items on the grounds that they were too casual, and others on the grounds that they were too formal. She finally settled on charcoal-grey trousers, matching jacket and burgundy shirt. Very understated, not too butch, she'd thought. Now she thought again and considered the vision of the archetypal dyke swaggering into this nest of young maidens. God help her if St George hove into sight.

If only she'd brought the car, she could have brought a wide enough selection of clothes to run no risk of getting it wrong. But her crazy decision to opt for the uncertain hands of British Rail so she could get some work done had boomeranged – you could only carry so much for a couple of days, unless you wanted to look like the wally of the weekend tipping out at the school gates with two cabin trunks and a holdall. As her paranoia gently reached a climax, she shook herself. 'Oh sod it,' she thought. 'If I'm so bloody right-on, why should I give a toss what they think of me? After all, I'm the one doing them a favour, giving their fund-raising a puff in the right places.'

With this bracing thought, the train shuddered into the station at Buxton. She picked up her bags and emerged on to the platform just as the sun came out from the autumn clouds, making the trees glow. Then through the glass doors she caught sight of Paddy, waiting and waving. Lindsay thrust her ticket at the collector and the two women hugged each other, laughing, each measuring the other for changes.

'If my pupils could see me now, they'd have a fit,' laughed Paddy. 'Teachers aren't supposed to leap around like lunatics in public, you know! My, you look good. Frightfully smart!' She held Lindsay at arms' length, taking in the outfit, the brown hair and the dark blue eyes. 'First time I've ever seen you fail to resemble a jumble sale in search of a venue.'

'Lost weight. It's living off the wits that does it. Food's a very easy economy.'

'No, darling, it's definitely the clothes. Who's the new woman, then?'

'Cheeky sod! There's no new woman, more's the pity. I went out and bought this all by myself.

8

At least six months ago, too. So there, Miss Callaghan.'

Paddy grinned. 'All right, all right. I'll take your word for it. Now, come along. I'm parked outside. I've got to pick up a couple of things from the town library then we can shoot back to the school itself and have a quick coffee to wipe away the strain of the train.'

In the station car park, they climbed into Paddy's battered Land Rover. 'Not exactly in its prime, but it's practical up here,' she apologised. 'Highest market town in England, this is. When the snow gets bad, I'm the only member of staff who can make a bid for freedom to the local pub. You still got that flashy passion wagon of yours?'

Lindsay scowled. 'If you mean my MG, yes I have.'

'Dear, oh dear. Still trying to impress with that retarded status symbol?'

'I don't drive it to impress anyone. I know it's the sort of car that provokes really negative reactions from the 2CV brigade, but I happen to enjoy it.'

Paddy laughed, 'Sorry. I didn't know it was such a sore spot.'

'Let's just say that I've been getting a bit of stick about it lately from one or two people who should know better. I'm seriously thinking about selling it just for a bit of peace and quiet from the purists who think you can only be right-on in certain cars. But I think I'd miss it too much. I can't afford to buy a new sports car. I spend a lot of time in transit and I think I've got a right to be in a car that performs well, is comfortable and doesn't get like an oven in the summer. Plus it provokes interesting reactions from people. It's a good shorthand way of finding out about attitudes.'

'Okay, okay. I'm on your side,' Paddy protested.

'I know it's flash and pretentious,' Lindsay persisted. 'But then there's a bit of that in me anyway. So you could argue that I'm doing women a favour by forewarning them.'

Paddy pulled up in a Georgian crescent of imposing buildings. 'You are sensitive about it, aren't you? Well, if it's any consolation, I've never thought you were flash. A little over the top some-times, perhaps . . .'

Lindsay changed the subject abruptly. 'What's this, then,' she demanded, waving an arm at the buildings.

'Not bad, eh? The North's answer to Bath. Not quite on the same scale. Rather splendid but slightly seedy. And you can still drink the spa water here. Comes out of the ground warm; tastes rather like an emetic in its natural state, but terribly good for one, so they say. Come and see the library ceiling.'

'Do what?' demanded Lindsay as Paddy jumped down. She had to break into a trot to catch Paddy, who was walking briskly along a colonnade turned golden by the late afternoon sun. They entered the library. Paddy gestured to Lindsay to go upstairs while she collected her books. A few minutes later she joined her there.

'Hardly over the top at all, dear,' Lindsay mocked, pointing to the baroque splendours of the painted and moulded ceiling. 'Worth a trip in itself. So where are all the dark satanic mills, then? I thought the North of England was full of them.'

'I thought you'd appreciate this,' said Paddy with a smile. 'You're in altogether the wrong place for dark satanics, though. Only the odd dark satanic quarry hereabouts. But before you dash off in search of the local proletarian heritage, a word about this weekend. I want to sort things out before we get caught up in the hurly-burly.'

'Sort out the programme, or my article?'

'Bit of both, really. Look, I know everything about the school goes right against the grain for you. Always embraced your principles so strongly, and all that. I also know that *Perspective* would be very happy if you wrote your piece from a fairly caustic point of view. But, as I tried to get across to you, this fund-raising project is vital to the school.

'If we don't raise the necessary £50,000 we'll lose all our playing fields. That might not seem any big deal to you, but it would mean we'd lose a great deal of our prestige because we've always been known as a school with a good balance –

you know, healthy mind in a healthy body and all that. Without our reputation for being first class for sport as well as academically we'd lose a lot of girls. I know that sounds crazy, but remember, it's usually fathers who decree where daughters are educated and they all hark back to their own schooldays through rose-tinted specs. I doubt if we'd manage to keep going, quite honestly. Money's become very tight and we're getting back into the patriarchal ghetto. Where parents can only afford to educate some of their children, the boys are getting the money spent on them and the girls are being ignored.' Paddy abruptly ran out of steam.

Lindsay took her time to answer while Paddy studied her anxiously. This was a conversation Lindsay had hoped would not have had to take place, and it was one she would rather have had over a drink after they'd both become accustomed to being with each other again. At last she said, 'I gathered it was serious from your letter. But I can't help feeling it wouldn't be such a bad thing if the public schools felt the pinch like everyone else. It seems somewhat unreal to be worrying about playing fields when a lot of state schools can't even afford enough books to go round.'

'Even if it means the school closing down?'

'Even if it means that, yes.'

'And put another sixty or seventy people on the dole queue? Not just teachers, but cleaning staff, groundsmen, cooks, the shopkeepers we patronise? Not to mention the fact that for quite a lot of the girls, Derbyshire House is the only stable thing in their lives. Quite a few come from broken homes. Some of their parents are living abroad where the local education isn't suitable for one reason or another. And others need the extra attention we can give them so they can realise their full potential.'

'Oh, Paddy, can't you hear yourself?' Lindsay retorted plaintively, and was rewarded by scowls and whispered 'shushes' from around the reading room. She dropped her voice. 'What about all the kids in exactly the same boat who don't have the benefit of Mummies and Daddies with enough spare cash to use Derbyshire House as a social services department? Maybe their lives would be a little bit better if the middle classes had to opt back into real life and use their influence to improve things. I can't be anything but totally opposed to this system you cheerfully shore up. And don't give me those spurious arguments about equal opportunities. In the context of this society, what you're talking about isn't an extension of equality; it's an extension of inequality. Don't try to quiet my conscience like that.

'Nevertheless . . . I've had to come to the reluctant conclusion that I can't stab you in the back having accepted your hospitality. Shades of the Glencoe massacre, eh? Don't expect me to be uncritically sycophantic. But I won't be doctrinaire either. Besides, I need the money!'

Paddy smiled. 'I should have known better than to worry about you,' she said.

'You should, really,' Lindsay reproached her. 'Now, am I going to see this monument to the privileged society or not?'

They walked back to the Land Rover, relaxed together, catching up on the four months since they had last seen each other. On the short drive from Buxton to Axe Edge, where Derbyshire House dominated a fold of moorland, Paddy gave Lindsay a more detailed account of the weekend plans.

'We decided to start off the fund-raising with a bang. We've done the usual things, like writing to all the old girls asking for contributions, but we know we'll need a bit of extra push. After all, most of our old girls are the wives and mothers brigade who don't exactly have wads of spare cash at their disposal. And we've got less than six months to raise the money.'

'But surely you must have known the lease was coming up for renewal?'

'Oh, we did, and we budgeted for it. But then James Cartwright, a local builder and developer, put in a bid for the lease that was £50,000 more than we were going to have to pay. He wants to build time-share holiday flats with a leisure complex. It's an ideal site for him, right in the smartest part of Buxton. And one of the few decent sites where he'd still be able to get planning permission. The agents obviously had to look favourably on an offer as good as that. So our headmistress, Pamela Overton, got the governors mobilised and we came up with a deal. If we can raise the cash to match that £50,000 in six months, we get the lease, even if Cartwright ups his offer.'

Lindsay smiled wryly. 'Amazing what influence can do.'

Although Paddy was watching the road, Lindsay's tone of voice was not lost on her. 'It's been bloody hard to get this far,' she complained mildly. 'The situation's complicated by the fact that Cartwright's daughter is one of our sixth-formers. And in my house, too. Anyway, we're all going flat out to get the money, and that's what the weekend's all about.'

'Which is where I come in, yes?'

'You're our bid to get into the right section of the public consciousness. You're going to tell them all about our wonderful enterprise, how we're getting in gear, and some benevolent millionaire is going to come along and write us a cheque. Okay?'

Lindsay grinned broadly. 'Okay, yah!' she teased. 'So what exactly is going to happen? So far you seem to have avoided supplying me with any actual information.'

'Tomorrow morning we're having a craft fair, which will carry over into the afternoon. All the girls have contributed their own work as well as begging and scrounging from friends and relations.

15

Then, in the afternoon, the sixth form are presenting a new one-act play written especially for them by Cordelia Brown. She's an old girl of my vintage. Finally, there will be an auction of modern autographed first editions, which Cordelia and I and one or two other people have put together. We've got almost a hundred books.'

'Cordelia Brown? The chat-show queen?'

'Don't be snide, Lindsay. You know damn well she's a good writer. I'd have thought she'd have been right up your street.'

'I like her novels. I don't know why she does all that telly crap, though. You'd hardly believe the same person writes the books and the telly series. Still, it must keep the wolf from the door.'

'You can discuss the matter with her yourself. She's arriving later this evening. Try not to be too abrasive, darling.'

Lindsay laughed. 'Whatever you say, Paddy. So the book auction rounds the day off, does it?'

'Far from it. The high point is in the evening – a concert given by our most celebrated old girl, Lorna Smith-Couper.'

Lindsay nodded. 'The cellist. I've never seen her perform, but I've got a couple of her recordings.'

'More than I have. I've never come across her, as far as I know. She had left before I came to the school – I didn't get here till the fifth form. And it's not my music, after all. Give me Dizzy Gillespie any time.'

'All that jazz still the only thing you'll admit is music, then? You'll not be able to help me, in that case. I'd love to get an interview with Lorna Smith-Couper. I've heard she's one of the most awkward people to get anything out of, but maybe the good cause together with the old school ties will make her more approachable.'

Paddy turned the Land Rover into a sweeping drive. She stopped inside the heavy iron gates, leaned across Lindsay and pointed. 'See that folly on the hill over there? It's called Solomon's Temple. If you look straight left of it you can just see a corner of the stupid green acres that all this fuss is about.' There was an edge in her voice and they drove on in silence. Ahead of them stood Derbyshire House, an elegant mansion like a miniature Chatsworth. They swung round a corner of the house and dropped down into a thick coppice of birch, sycamore and rowan trees. After a hundred yards, they emerged in a large clearing where six modern stone blocks surrounded a well-tended lawn.

'The houses,' said Paddy. 'About half of the girls sleep in the main building and the more senior ones sleep here,' she pointed as she spoke, 'in Axe, Goyt, Wildboarclough and my house, Longnor. The two smaller ones, Burbage and Grin Low, are for teachers and other staff.'

'My God,' said Lindsay, 'the only thing this verdant near my school was the bloody garden of remembrance behind the local crematorium.'

17

'Very funny. Come on, Lindsay, do stop waving your origins around like a red flag and have a drink. I can feel this is going to be a good weekend.'

2

Paddy and Lindsay were stretched out in Paddy's comfortable sitting-room. It was furnished by the school in tasteful if old-fashioned style, but Paddy had stamped her own character on it. One wall was completely lined with books and the others were covered with elegant photographs of stage productions and a selection of old film posters. The chairs were upholstered in leather and, in spite of their shabbiness, they were deep and welcoming. By the window was a large desk strewn with piles of papers and exercise books and in the corner near the door was a cocktail cabinet, the only piece of furniture that Paddy had carted around with her everywhere for the last ten years.

Lindsay nursed her glass and drawled, 'So what's this one called?'

'Deep Purple.'

'Great hobby, making cocktails. Of course, I'd never have your flair for it. What's in this, then?'

'One measure Cointreau, three of vodka, blue food-colouring, a large slug of grenadine, a measure of soda water and a lot of ice. Good, isn't it?'

'Dynamite. And it goes down a treat. This is certainly the life. What time's dinner? And should I change?'

'Three quarters of an hour. Don't bother changing, you're fine as you are. Tomorrow will be a bit more formal, though; best bib and tucker all round. We'll have to go over to the staffroom shortly, so I can introduce you to the workers.'

Lindsay smiled. 'What are they like?' she asked, slightly apprehensive.

'Like any collection of female teachers. There are the super-intelligent, witty ones; the boring old farts; the Tory party brigade and the statutory radical – that's me, by the way. And a few who are just ordinary, unobjectionable women.'

'My God, it must be bad if you're their idea of a radical. What does that mean? You occasionally disagree with Margaret Thatcher and you put tomato sauce on your bacon and eggs? So am I going to like any of this bunch of fossils?'

'You'll like Chris Jackson, the PE mistress. She comes from your neck of the woods, and apart from being a physical fitness freak is obsessed with two things – wine-making and cars. You can imagine what we have in common, and it isn't overhead camshafts.'

Lindsay grinned. 'Sounds more like it. I don't suppose . . . ?'

Paddy returned the grin. 'Sorry. There's a large rugby player in the background, I'm afraid. You'll also like Margaret Macdonald, if she can spare enough time from this concert to say hello. She's head of music, and a good friend of mine. We sit up late and talk about books, politics and what passes for drama on radio and TV.'

Lindsay stretched, yawned, then lit a cigarette. 'Sorry,' she muttered. 'Train's tired me out. I'll wake up soon.'

'You better had. You're due to meet our magnificent headmistress, Pamela Overton. One of the old school. Her father was a Cambridge don and she came to us after a brilliant but obscure career in the Foreign Office. Very efficient and very good at achieving what she sets out to do. High powered but human. Talk to her – it's always rewarding, if unnerving,' Paddy observed.

'Why unnerving?' Lindsay was intrigued.

'She always knows more about your area of competence than you do yourself. But you'll enjoy her. You'll have a chance to judge for yourself tonight, anyway, before the guest of honour gets here. Ms Smith-Couper has not said when she'll be arriving. Her secretary simply said some time this evening. Really considerate.'

Paddy got to her feet and prowled round the desk, her strong, bony face looking puzzled. 'I'm sure I left myself a note somewhere . . . I've got to do something before tomorrow morning and I'm damned if I can remember what it is . . . Oh, found it. Right. Remind me I have to have a word with Margaret Macdonald. Now, shall we go and face the staffroom?' They walked through the trees to the main house. In a small clearing over to one side, a few floodlights illuminated a building site.

'New squash courts,' Paddy explained. 'We have to light the site because we kept having stuff stolen. It's very quiet round that side of the school after about ten – an easy target for burglars. Chris Jackson is champing at the bit for them to finish. Pity we can't hijack the cash for the playing fields, but the money came to us as a specific bequest.'

The two women entered the main building by a small door in the rear. As they walked through the passages and glanced into the classrooms, Lindsay was struck by how superficially similar it was to her own old school, a crumbling comprehensive. Both had had the same institutional paint job done on them; both used pupils' artistic offerings to brighten the walls; both were slightly down at heel and smelled of chalk dust. The only apparent difference at first sight was the absence of graffiti. Paddy gave Lindsay a quick run-down on the house as they walked towards the staffroom.

'This is the kitchen and dining-room. The school has been in the building since 1934. Above us are the music rooms and assembly hall – it was a ballroom when Lord Longnor's family had the house. There are classrooms, offices and

Miss Overton's flat on this floor. More class-rooms on the second floor, and the top floor is all bedrooms. The science labs are over in the woods, on the opposite side from the houses. And this is the staffroom.'

Paddy opened the door on a buzz of conversation. The staffroom was elegantly proportioned, with a large bay window through which Lindsay could see the lights of Buxton twinkling in the darkness. About twenty women were assembled in small groups, standing by the log fire or sitting in clumps of unmatched and slightly shabby chairs. The walls were occupied by a collection of old prints of Derbyshire and a vast notice-board completely covered with bits of paper. The conversations did not pause when Lindsay and Paddy entered, though several heads turned briefly towards them. Paddy led Lindsay over to a young woman who was poring over a large book. She was slim but solidly built, and seemed bursting with a vitality that Lindsay only dreamed of these days. Her jet black curly hair, pink and white complexion and dark blue eyes revealed her Highland ancestry and reminded Lindsay painfully of home.

Paddy interrupted the woman's concentration. 'Chris, drag yourself away from the exploded view of a cylinder head or whatever and meet Lindsay Gordon. Lindsay, this is Chris Jackson, our PE mistress.'

'Hello there,' said Chris, dropping her book.

She still had the accent Lindsay had grown up with but had virtually lost under the layers of every other accent she had lived amongst. 'Our tame journalist, eh? Well, before everybody else says so without meaning it, let me tell you how grateful I am for any help you can give us. We need to keep these playing fields, and not just to keep me in a job. We'd never get anything nearly so good within miles of here. It's good of you to give us a hand, especially since you've no real connection with the place.'

Lindsay smiled, embarrassed by her sincerity. 'I'm delighted to have the chance to see a place like this from the inside. And besides, I'm always glad of work, especially when it's commissioned.'

Paddy broke into the pause which followed. 'Chris, you and Lindsay are from the same part of the world. Lindsay's from Invercross.'

'Really? I'd never have guessed. You've hardly any trace of the accent. I'd have said yours was much further south. I'm from South Achilcaig myself, though I went to school at St Mary Magdalene in Helensburgh.'

The two women launched into conversation about their origins and memories of the Argyllshire villages where they grew up, and discovered they had played hockey against each other a dozen years before. Paddy drifted off to talk to a worried-looking woman seated a few feet away from Lindsay and Chris. Only minutes later their reminiscences were interrupted by raised voices from Paddy and the other woman.

'I had every right to excuse the girl. She's in my house, Margaret. On matters of her welfare, what I say goes,' Paddy said angrily.

'How could you blithely give her permission to opt out when it's so near to the actual concert? She is supposed to have a solo in the choir section. What am I supposed to do about that?'

Startled, Lindsay muttered, 'What's going on?'

'Search me,' Chris replied. 'That's Margaret Macdonald, head of music. Normally Paddy and her are the best of pals.'

Paddy glared at Margaret and retorted, 'Far be it from me to put my oar in, but Jessica did suggest the Holgate girl could perfectly well handle an extra solo.'

The other woman got out of her chair and faced Paddy. 'I make the decisions about my choirs, not Jessica Bennett. If the girl had come to me with her demands, I would not have given her permission to skulk in a corner and avoid her responsibilities. She's not the only person who has reasons for wanting to have nothing to do with this concert. But some people just have to struggle on.'

'Look, Margaret,' said Paddy more quietly, realising the eyes of the staffroom were on them, 'I'm sorry this has put you out. I know how much you've got on your plate. But in my view it would be far worse if I'd sent the girl off with a flea in her ear and she ended up throwing a fit on the concert platform. And in my view that would have been quite possible.'

Margaret Macdonald opened her mouth to retort, but before she could speak the staffroom door opened and a tall woman entered. As she moved into the room, the conversations gradually started up again. The music teacher turned sharply away from Paddy, saying only, 'Since you have told the girl it will be all right, I must abide by your decision.'

Looking slightly stunned, Paddy returned to Lindsay and Chris. 'I've never known Margaret to behave like that,' she murmured. 'Incredible. Hang on a minute, Lindsay; I'll go and bring the head across.' She walked over to the tall woman who had just entered and who was now chatting to another mistress.

Pamela Overton was an imposing woman in her late fifties. She was dressed in a simple dark blue jersey dress and wore her silver hair over her ears in sweeping wings which flowed into an elaborate plaited bun on her neck. Paddy went over to her and exchanged a few words in a low voice. The two women joined Lindsay and Chris.

Paddy had scarcely finished the introductions, with Lindsay lost in admiration at Pamela Overton's beautifully modulated but unquestionably pukka voice, when there was a knock at the door. It was opened by one of the staff who stepped outside for a moment. Returning, she came straight to Miss Overton's side and said, 'Miss Smith-Couper is here, Miss Overton.'

Pamela Overton had hardly reached the door when it was flung open to reveal a woman in her early thirties whom Lindsay recognised instantly. Lorna Smith-Couper was even more stunning in the flesh than in the many photographs Lindsay had seen of her. She had a mane of tawny blonde hair which descended in a warm wave over her shoulders. Her skin was pale and clear, stretched tightly over her strong bone structure. And her eyes shone out from her face like hard blue chips of lapis lazuli.

As Lindsay watched her sweep into the room, she was aware of Paddy turning to face the door. And she sensed her friend's body stiffen beside her. Only Lindsay was close enough to hear Paddy breathe, 'Jesus Christ Almighty, not her!'

3

After dinner, Lindsay and Paddy skipped coffee in the staffroom and walked back through the trees to Longnor House. All Paddy had said was, 'They'll be too busy with the superstar to notice our absence. And besides, we've got the excuse of having to be back in case Cordelia arrives early.' Lindsay was struggling to remain silent against all her instincts both as a friend and as a journalist. But she realised that to press Paddy for information would be counter-productive.

Dinner had not been the most comfortable of meals. Lorna Smith-Couper had greeted Paddy with an obviously false enthusiasm. 'Dearest Paddy, whoever would have expected to find you in such a respectable situation,' she had cooed. Paddy had smiled coldly in return. Her attempts to drift away from the group that had immediately formed around the cellist had been thwarted by Pamela Overton, who had suggested in a way that brooked no argument that Paddy and Lindsay should join Lorna and her at high table. Lorna had ignored Paddy from then on and had devoted herself to her conversation with Pamela Overton, after pointedly saying to Lindsay, 'Anything you hear is completely off the record, do I make myself clear?' As it happened, she said nothing that anyone could have been interested in except Lorna herself.

The meal itself had come as a pleasant surprise to Lindsay, whose own memories of school and college food had left her disinclined to repeat the experience. A tasty vegetable broth made with a good stock was followed by chicken and mushroom pie, baked potatoes and peas. To finish there was a choice of fresh fruit. She remarked on the quality of the food to Paddy, but her friend was too abstracted to do more than nod.

Back in Paddy's room, Lindsay stretched herself out in a chair while Paddy brewed the coffee. From the kitchen she called out, 'Sorry I've not been much company.'

Lindsay saw her chance to dig an explanation out of Paddy and immediately called out, 'Dinner was a bit of a strain. I could hear my accent becoming more and more affected with every passing sentence. But I thought you said you'd never met our guest of honour?'

There was a lengthy silence filled only by the sound of the percolating coffee. When Paddy eventually spoke there was deep bitterness in her voice. 'I didn't realise I had,' she said. 'I only ever knew her as Lorna. In that particular circle, first names were all we ever seemed to exchange.'

She returned to the living-room and poured coffee for them both. 'You make it sound like a John Le Carré novel,' Lindsay said.

'Nothing so dramatic.'

'You don't have to tell me about it unless you want to. No sweat.'

'I'd better tell someone before I blow up. It goes back, oh, eight or nine years. I was doing bit parts in London and the odd telly piece. Looking back at it now, the people I used to hang around with were a pretty juvenile lot, myself included. We thought we were such a bunch of trendies, though. We were heavily into night-clubbing, getting stoned, solving the problems of the world, and talking a lot about permissiveness without actually being particularly promiscuous. A depressing hangover from the sixties, our crowd was. It was all sex and drugs and rock and roll. Or at least we tried to convince ourselves it was.'

Paddy looked Lindsay straight in the eye as she spoke, not afraid to share her shame with someone she trusted. 'An expensive way of life, you see. And not easy to sustain on the sort of money I was making. But I found a way to finance it. I started dealing dope. No big-time hard stuff, you understand, but I put a fair bit around, one way or another. So there were always people coming round to my flat to score some dope. Regular customers, word of mouth, you know.'

Lindsay nodded. She knew only too well the scenes that Paddy described. 'One of my customers was a musician, a pianist. William. Came several times with his girlfriend. The girlfriend was Lorna.'

Lindsay pulled out two cigarettes from her pack and lit them. She passed one to Paddy who inhaled deeply. 'You see what this could mean?' she asked. Lindsay nodded again as Paddy went on. 'All she's got to do is drop a seemingly casual word when there are other people around and bang, that's my job gone. I mean, okay, most of our generation have dabbled with the old Acapulco Gold at one time or another but nobody talks about it now, do they? And no school, especially a public school, can afford to be seen employing a teacher who is known to have dealt in the stuff. It's no defence to say I've never so much as rolled a joint on school premises. What a story for you, eh?'

Paddy abruptly rose and poured two brandies. She handed one to Lindsay and paced the floor. Lindsay sensed her anguish. She knew Paddy had worked hard to achieve her present position. That hard work hadn't come easily to someone who was used to having the world on a plate. So it was all the more galling that even now it might come to nothing because of a way of life that hadn't seemed so risky at the time. Lindsay ached for Paddy. She tried to find words that might help.

'Why should she say anything? After all, she'd be admitting her involvement in the drugs scene and she'd surely be loath to damage her own reputation,' was all she could manage.

'No, she wouldn't do herself any damage. You see, she never used the stuff herself. Always took the deeply self-righteous line that she could feel good without indulging in artificial stimulants. As to why she should say anything – well, why not? It might be her idea of fun. She could always say she had the best interests of the school at heart.'

Lindsay was silent. She got to her feet and went to Paddy. They held on to each other tightly. Lindsay prayed Paddy could sense the support she wanted to offer. Then, relieved, she felt the tension begin to seep out of her friend.

The moment was broken by a single peal of the telephone. They smiled at each other, then Paddy went to her desk and picked up the phone, pressing the appropriate button to take an internal call.

'Miss Callaghan here . . . Oh good, I'll be right over.' She put the phone down and started for the door. 'Cordelia's arrived. I'll go and collect her from the main building. There's some cold meat and salad in the fridge. Could you stick it on a plate for me? She'll doubtless be starving. Always is. Dressing's on the top shelf, by the tomatoes.' And she was gone.

Lindsay went into the kitchen to carry out her instructions. Her mind was still racing over Paddy's problem, though she knew there was nothing she could do to improve the situation. She was also considering the more general problem of how to persuade Lorna Smith-Couper to grant her the sort of interview that would provide more than just a piece of padding for her feature on the school. Then there was Cordelia Brown. She might also be good for a feature interview to sell to one of the women's magazines.

Lindsay had never met the writer, but she knew a great deal about her from what she had read and from what mutual friends had told her. Cordelia Brown was, at thirty-one, one of the jewels in the crown of women's writing, according to the media. She had left Oxford half-way through her degree course and worked for three years as administrator of a small touring theatre company in Devon. Then she had gone on to write four moderately successful novels, the latest of which had been short-listed for the Booker Prize. But she had broken through into a more general public awareness with a television drama series, *The Successors*, which had won most of the awards it was possible to be nominated for. A highly acclaimed film had followed, which had appeared at precisely the right moment to be described as the flagship of the re-emergent British film industry. All of this, coupled with an engaging willingness to talk wittily and at length on most subjects, and an acceptable quota of good looks, had conspired to turn Cordelia into the darling of the chat shows.

As she shook the dressing and tossed it into

the bowl of salad, Lindsay had to admit to herself that she was looking forward to their meeting. She had no great expectations of finding the writer sympathetic; on the other hand, she might be considerably more pleasant than her television appearances would lead one to imagine. She heard the door opening and the sound of voices. She went to the kitchen door just as Cordelia dropped a leather holdall to the floor. The woman had her back to Lindsay and was speaking to Paddy. Her voice sounded richer face to face than it did coming from the television set which managed to strip it of most of its warmth. The accent was utterly neutral, with only the faintest trace of the drawl Lindsay had become familiar with at Oxford and with which she had renewed her acquaintance earlier that evening at dinner. 'There's four or five boxes, but I'm too bloody exhausted to be bothered with them now. Let's leave them in the car till tomorrow.'

Then she turned and took in Lindsay standing in the doorway. The two women scrutinised each other carefully, deciding how much they liked what they saw, both wary. Suddenly the weekend seemed to hold out fresh possibilities to Lindsay as Cordelia's grey eyes under the straight dark brows flicked over her from head to foot. She felt slightly dazed and weak with something she supposed was lust. It had been a long time since she had felt the first stirrings of an attraction based on the combination of looks and good vibes.

34

Cordelia, too, seemed to like what she saw, for a smile twitched at the corners of her wide mouth. 'So this is the famous Lindsay,' she remarked.

Lindsay prayed that her face did not look as stricken as she felt. She nodded and smiled back, feeling a little foolish. 'Something like that,' she answered. 'Nice to meet you.' She found herself desperately hoping that what she'd heard about Cordelia's taste in lovers was true.

She was spared further conversational efforts just then by the demands of Cordelia's stomach.

'I say, Paddy, any chance of some scoff?' she demanded plaintively. 'I'm famished. It took much longer than I thought to get here. The traffic was unbelievable. Does the entire population of London come to Derbyshire every weekend? Or are they simply all desperate to see the new one-act play by Cordelia Brown?'

Paddy laughed. 'I knew you'd be hungry. There's some salad in the kitchen. I'll just get it.' But before Paddy could make a move, Lindsay had vanished into the kitchen. Cordelia shot a look at Paddy, her eyebrows rising comically and a smile on her lips. Paddy merely grinned and said, 'I'll fix you a drink. What would you like?'

'A Callaghan cocktail special, please. Why the hell do you think I was prepared to come back to this dump?' As Paddy mixed the drinks, Lindsay returned with Cordelia's meal. She promptly tucked in as though she had not eaten for days.

Paddy strained a Brandy Alexander out of the

shaker and passed it to Cordelia, saying, 'Lindsay is writing a feature about the fund-raising.'

'Poor old you. But you're not an old girl, are you?'

'Do I look that out of place?' asked Lindsay.

'No, not at all. It's simply that I knew that I'd never seen you before either at school or at any of the old girl reunions. I'd have remembered. I'm good at faces. But you're not one of us, are you?'

'No. I know Paddy from Oxford. I was up when she was doing her teacher training. And she talked me into this. I'm freelancing at the moment, so it's all grist to the mill.' Lindsay's response to the assurance of the older woman was to adopt the other's speech pattern and to polish up her own accent.

'And what do you make of us so far?'

'Hard to tell. I haven't seen enough, or talked to many people yet.'

'A true diplomat.' Cordelia resumed eating.

Paddy chose a Duke Ellington record and put it on. As the air filled with the liquid sounds, Lindsay thought, I'm always going to remember this tune and what I was doing when I first heard it. She was embarrassed to find she could hardly take her eyes off Cordelia. She watched her hands cutting up the food and lifting the glass; she watched the changing planes of her face as she ate and drank. She found herself recalling a favourite quotation: 'A man doesn't love a woman because he thinks her clever or because he admires her but because he likes the way she scratches her head.' She thought that perhaps the reason her relationships had failed in the past was because she hadn't looked for such details and learned to love them. She was surprised to find herself saying rather formally, 'I was wondering if there was any chance you could be persuaded to give me half an hour during the weekend? I'd like to do an interview. Of course, I can't guarantee that I'd be able to place the finished feature, but I'd like to try if you don't mind me asking on a weekend when you're intent on having fun with your old friends.'

Cordelia finished eating and put her plate down. She considered her glass for a moment. She turned to Paddy and said in a tone of self-mockery familar to her friend, 'What do you think, Paddy? Would I be safe with her? Is she going to lull me into a false sense of security and tempt me into indiscretions? Will she ask me difficult questions and refuse to be satisfied with easy answers?'

'Oh, undoubtedly!'

'Very well then, I accept the challenge. I will place myself in your hands. Shall we say Sunday morning while the school is at church?' Lindsay nodded agreement. 'And don't feel guilty about dragging me away from old friends. The number of people here I actually want to see can be counted on the fingers of one thumb. And there are plenty of others I'll be glad of an excuse to avoid. Such as our esteemed guest of honour.'

'You're not alone there,' said Paddy, struggling unsuccessfully to make her words sound light-hearted.

'You another victim of hers, Paddy?' asked Cordelia, not waiting for a reply. 'That Smith-Couper always had the charm and rapacity of a jackal. But, of course, she'd left before you arrived, hadn't she? A fine piece of work she is. Beauty and the Beast rolled into one gift-wrapped package. Do you know what the bitch has done to me? And done it, I may say, in the full knowledge that we were both scheduled for this weekend in the Alma Mater?' There was a pregnant pause. Lindsay recalled that Cordelia had started her career in the theatre.

'She's suing me for libel. Only this week I got the writ. She claims that the cellist in *Across A Crowded Room* is a scurrilous portrait of her good self. Though why she should go out of her way to identify herself with a character whose morals would not have disgraced a piranha fish is quite beyond me. That aside, however, she is looking for substantial damages, taking into account the fact that the bloody thing made the Booker list and is about to come out in paperback. If she was going to get in a tizz, you'd think it would happen when the book came out, wouldn't you? But not with our Lorna. Oh no, she waits till she's sure there's enough money in the kitty. Infuriating

38

woman.' Having let off steam, Cordelia subsided into her chair, muttering, 'There you are, Lindsay, there's the peg to hang your feature on. The real-life confrontation between the Suer and the Sued. By the way, Paddy, I hope I'm not bedded down within a corridor's length of our Lorna. The temptation to get up in the night and commit murder most foul might be altogether too much for me!'

Through her infatuated daze, even Lindsay could detect the acrimony behind the self-mocking humour in Cordelia's voice. 'Luckily not,' Paddy replied quickly, 'she's in Pamela Overton's flat.' She went on to explain that Cordelia was to occupy the guest room in Longnor, while Lindsay was to have the room next door, its occupant having volunteered to give up her room to the visitor in return for the privilege of sharing her best friend's room for the two nights.

'Fine by me,' yawned Cordelia. 'Oh God, I must have a shower. I feel so grubby after that drive, and I need something to wake me up. Okay if I use yours, Paddy?' Paddy nodded. Cordelia opened her holdall and raked around till she found her sponge-bag, then headed for the bathroom, promising to be as quick as possible.

'Another drink?' Paddy demanded. 'You look as if you could use it. Quite a character, isn't she?'

'Wow,' said Lindsay. 'Just, wow. How do you expect me to sleep knowing she's only the thickness of a wall away?'

'You'll sleep all right, especially after another

Brandy Alexander. And if you're really lucky, maybe you'll dream about her. Don't fret, Lindsay. You've got all weekend to make an impression! Now, just relax, listen to the music and don't try too hard.'

With those words of wisdom, Lindsay had to be content until Cordelia returned, pink and glowing from her shower. She apologised for her lack of manners in dashing off. 'If I hadn't taken drastic action, I'd have been sound asleep inside five minutes. Which would have been remarkably rude. Besides, I did want to talk,' she added with a disarming grin, as Paddy announced that, since it was ten o'clock, she was going on her evening rounds of the House to check that all was well and everyone was where they should be. Left alone with Cordelia, Lindsay found herself at a complete loss. But Cordelia was too generous and perceptive to let the younger woman flounder, and before long they were talking avidly about the theatre, a shared passion. By the time Paddy returned half an hour later, Lindsay's nervousness had been subdued and the two were arguing with all the affectionate combativeness of old friends. Paddy was quickly absorbed into the conversation.

In the small hours of the morning, she eventually saw her two friends to their respective rooms and made a last circuit of the house before she headed back to bed. Cocktails and conversation had driven away her earlier fears about Lorna.

But as she prowled the dark corridors on her own, her thoughts returned to the cellist. Somehow Paddy would have to make sure that Lorna's presence could not leave a trail of wreckage in its wake.

4

Lindsay was drifting in that pleasant limbo between sleep and wakefulness. A distant bell had aroused her from deep and dreamless slumber, but she was luxuriating in her dozy state and reluctant to let the dimly heard noises around her bring her up to full consciousness. Her drifting was abruptly brought to an end by a sharp knock on the door. Her nerves twitched with the hope that it might be Cordelia and she called softly, 'Come in.'

But the door opened to reveal a tall young woman carrying a tea-tray. She was wearing a well-cut tweed skirt and a fisherman's sweater which engulfed the top half of her body. 'Good morning Miss Gordon,' she said brightly. 'Miss Callaghan asked me to bring your tea up. I'm Caroline Barrington, by the way, second-year sixth. This is my room. I hope you've been comfortable in it. It's not bad really, except that the window rattles when the wind's in the east.' She dumped the tray on the bedside table and Lindsay struggled into a sitting position. Caroline poured out a cup of tea. 'Milk? Sugar?' Lindsay shook her head as vigorously as an evening of Paddy's cocktails would permit.

Caroline walked towards the door, but before she reached it, she hesitated, turned, and spoke in a rush. 'I read an article in the *New Left* last month about women in politics – that was by you, wasn't it?' Lindsay nodded. 'I didn't think there could be two of you with the same name. I enjoyed it very much. I was especially interested, you see, because I might go into politics myself after university. It's rather given me a boost to realise that there are other women out there with the same sort of worries.'

Lindsay finally managed to get her brain into gear. 'Thanks. Which party do you favour, by the way?'

Caroline looked extremely embarrassed, shifting from one foot to the other. 'Actually, I'm a socialist,' she said. 'It's something of a dirty word round here. I just think that things ought to be changed – to be fairer. You know?'

Half an hour later, Lindsay felt she had been put through an intellectual mangle. Never at her best in the morning, she had had to struggle to keep one step ahead of Caroline's endless stream of questions and dogmatic statements about everything from student politics to the position of women in Nicaragua. Trying to explain that things

43

were never as simple as they seemed without bruising the girls idealism or patronising her had not been easy, and Lindsay wished they'd been having the conversation over a cup of coffee after dinner, the time of day when she felt at her most alert. Finally, the buzz of a bell made Caroline start as she realised that this was neither the time nor place for such a discussion.

'Oh help,' she exclaimed, leaping off the end of the bed where she had settled herself, 'that's the breakfast bell. I must run. You don't have to worry – staff breakfast is pretty flexible, and Miss Callaghan's waiting to take you across. Blame me if she moans on at you about being late – I'm always in trouble for talking too much. See you later.'

'Thanks for the tea, and the chat. Oh, and the use of your room. Maybe we'll have the chance to talk again. And if we don't, enjoy the weekend anyway,' said Lindsay, wondering to herself how quickly she could manage to wash and dress. She almost missed Caroline's words as she dashed through the door.

'Sure. But don't ask me to join the fan club for our concert star.' And she was gone, her footsteps joining the general background clamour that the bell had released.

Over a breakfast of scrambled eggs and mush-rooms, Lindsay told Paddy about her early morning visitor. Paddy laughed and said, 'She's full of adolescent fervour about the joys of

44

socialism at the moment. She was always an ideal-istic child, but now she's found a focus, she's unstoppable. Her parents' marriage broke up last year, and I think we're getting a bit of referred emotion in the politics.'

Lindsay sighed. 'But she's not a child, Paddy, and her views are perfectly sound. Don't be so patronising.'

'I'm not being patronising. But in a closed world like ours, I don't believe the opinions of one individual make a blind bit of difference.'

Lindsay, who should have known better after six years' friendship with Paddy, allowed this red herring to set her off into a familiar fight about politics. It was an argument neither would ever win, but it still had the power to absorb. In spite of that, Lindsay found herself continually glancing towards the door. Paddy finally caught her in the act, grinned broadly and relented.

'She's not coming in for breakfast. She always does an hour's work first thing in the morning, then goes for a run. She even did it when we went on holiday to Italy four years ago. You won't see her much before ten-thirty, I'm afraid,' said Paddy.

'What makes you think I'm looking for Cordelia?'

'Who mentioned Cordelia?' asked Paddy inno-cently. Lindsay subsided into silence while Paddy started reading her morning paper. Lindsay felt fidgety, but was not certain if this was simply because she was in an alien environment, or because of Cordelia's disturbing effect on her. She found herself studying the half-dozen or so other women at breakfast. Chris Jackson was deeply engrossed in a book about squash, and the two other women at her table were also reading. Lindsay's gaze moved to Margaret Macdonald who was sitting on her own. A magazine was open by her plate, but although she kept glancing at it, she was obviously not reading. She was not eating either, and the eggs and bacon on her plate were slowly congealing. A bright red sweater emphasised the lack of colour in her face. Every time someone passed her or entered the room, she started, and her eyes were troubled.

As they rose to leave, Lindsay quietly remarked, 'She looks scared stiff.'

'Nervous about tonight, I suppose. Who wouldn't be? There's a lot hanging on it,' Paddy replied in an offhand way before bustling off to put her cast through their paces one more time before the afternoon's performance. Left to herself, Lindsay thought again about Margaret Macdonald. Paddy's explanation didn't seem to go far enough. Not knowing the woman, however, there was nothing Lindsay could do to find out what was troubling the teacher so.

She strolled back to Longnor House, revelling in the magnificent colours of the changing trees against the grey limestone and the greens and browns of the moorland surrounding the school.

There were even patches of fading purple where the last of the heather splashed colour on to the bracken. Lindsay decided to run upstairs for her camera bag so she could take some photographs before the day became too crowded. After all, if she waited till the quiet of Sunday, she might miss the sunshine and the extraordinary clarity of the Derbyshire light.

A few minutes later, she was wandering through the grounds, pausing every now and again to change lenses and take a couple of shots. She took her photography seriously these days. It had started as a hobby when she'd been a student, and she had gradually built up an adequate set of equipment that allowed her to work on all sorts of subjects in most conditions. She had also picked the brains of every photographer she had ever worked with to the extent that she could now probably do the job as well as many of them. Her favourite work was portraiture, but she also enjoyed the larger challenge of a landscape. Now, looking at the contours of the land, she realised that a short scramble up the hillside would give her the perfect vantage point to catch the main building, its gardens, and the valley leading down to Buxton. Thankful that she was wearing jeans and training shoes, she began the steep climb up through the trees. After ten minutes' brisk walking, she was out of the woods and on top of a broad ridge. From there, it was all spread before her. She took several shots, then, just as she was about to descend, her eye was caught by a splash of colour and movement in a corner of the gardens. In a sheltered nook, invisible from the school, two women were standing. Lindsay recognised the vivid scarlet of Margaret Macdonald's sweater.

Hesitating only for a moment, she quickly grabbed her longest lens and slotted it into the camera body. She flicked the switch from manual to motor drive and set her legs apart to give herself more stability. Swiftly she focused and began to shoot. She could see clearly who was with the teacher now. Margaret looked as if she was pleading with Lorna Smith-Couper, who suddenly threw her head back in laughter, turned and stalked off. The music teacher stood looking after her a moment, then stumbled blindly into the wood. Lindsay had been surreptitiously photographing people without their awareness or consent for a long time. Journalists called it 'snatching'. But for the first time she felt she had behaved shabbily – had in fact spied on what did not concern her.

Before she could ponder further on what she had seen, her attention was distracted once again. She had caught the flash of a running figure in the direction of the main gates. She swivelled round and could tell even at the distance of half a mile or so that the runner was Cordelia. She waited till Cordelia was nearer, then swung the camera up to her face again and steadily took a couple of pictures. Like the earlier photographs, they would be no great shakes as portraiture – they'd be too grainy for that. But as character studies, they'd do very well. Even the familiar barrier of the camera, however, could not distance Lindsay from the surge of emotion she felt at seeing Cordelia. There was nothing for it but to go back down the hill and hope the craft fair would bring the chance to talk to her. Lindsay knew that Paddy wouldn't be there this time to interrupt because she would be busy with her dress rehearsal. And she also knew that Cordelia would not be watching the run-through. One of the last things she had said to Paddy the night before was that she never attended rehearsals. 'I always prefer to wait for the finished product,' she had said. 'Any changes or cuts I can sort out with the director. But I've served my time dealing with the bumptious, egocentric shower of know-alls that make up such a large part of the acting profession. There is one in every cast who always knows better than you how the damn thing should be written.'

Her rich laughter echoed in Lindsay's memory as she scrambled quickly down the hillside. She noticed she wasn't as nimble as she used to be and resolved to start going to the gym again as soon as she got back to Glasgow. She was back in her room with twenty minutes to spare before the start of the craft fair. She had just slipped out of her jeans and into a skirt when there was a knock at her door. She called out permission to come in as she squeezed into a pair of court shoes, expecting Caroline to breeze in. But when the door opened, it was Cordelia who appeared.

'Hi there,' she said. 'I heard you come in as I was changing. Are you coming down to the hall to have a look round ahead of the hordes? The front drive's already filling up with cars. I suppose the locals can't resist the chance of a good poke around. Amazing how curious the great unwashed are about the supposed mystique of public schools.'

'Yes, aren't we, though! That's part of the reason why I agreed to come. I feel extremely curious about how the other half is educated,' said Lindsay wryly, smiling to take the sting out of her words.

'But you went to Oxford! Surely that must have given you some idea, even if you didn't have the misfortune to spend your childhood in one of these institutions,' Cordelia remarked as they walked down the corridor.

'Yes, but by that stage, one is well on the way to being a finished product. You forget, I'd never come across people like you before. I wanted to see how young you'd have to catch kids before their assumptions and preconceptions become ingrained. How much comes from schooling and how much from a general class ethos imbibed at home along with mother's milk and Château Mouton Rothschild.'

'And how much of what made you the woman you are comes from home rather than education?'

'I suspect about equal amounts from each. That's why I'm a mass of contradictions.' By now they were walking through the woods and Lindsay was well into her stride. 'Sentimental versus analytical, cynical versus idealistic, and so on. The only belief that comes from both home and education is that you have to work bloody hard to get what you want.'

'And do you?'

'Sometimes – and sometimes.'

They fell silent as they entered the main building, neither willing to pursue the conversation into more intimate areas. A large number of people were milling around the corridors, ignoring the arrows pointing them towards the main hall. Lindsay and Cordelia struggled through the crowds and nodded to the girls as they slipped into the hall. But even here there was no peace. All the stalls were laid out in readiness, and behind most of them schoolgirls were making last-minute adjustments to the displays. Lindsay looked around and from where she stood she could already see stalls of embroidered pictures, knitted garments, stained-glass terrariums and hanging mobiles, hand-made wooden jigsaws and pottery made in the school's kiln. As Lindsay and Cordelia stood admiring a stall of patchwork, the senior mistress called out from her vantage point by the doors, 'Two minutes, girls. Everyone get ready.'

Lindsay had moved on to look at a display of wooden toys when she saw Chris Jackson hurrying through the hall. She made straight for Lindsay and spoke to her in a low voice. 'Do you know where Paddy is?'

'She's rehearsing with the cast in the gym.'

'No, they're having a half-hour break. I thought you might have seen her. I've got to get hold of her now.'

'Hello Chris, long time no see. Hey what's up?' asked Cordelia, joining them.

'I've got one of the sixth in floods of tears behind the stage. She's just had a stand-up row with a couple of other sixth-formers. The girl is absolutely hysterical, and I reckon Paddy's the only one who can deal with her. There'll be chaos if we don't sort it out. And soon.'

Immediately, Cordelia took control. She grabbed a couple of passing juniors and said, 'I want you to find Miss Callaghan for me. Try Longnor, or her classroom or the staffroom. Tell her to come to us at the back of the hall as soon as possible, please.' The girls scuttled off at top speed. 'I wasn't Head of House for nothing,' she added to the other two. 'Wonderful how they respond to the voice of authority. I say, Chris, sorry and all that, I hope you didn't think I was trying to usurp you?'

'No, you were quite right. I lost my head for a moment when I couldn't find Paddy.'

'But what on earth happened?' asked Cordelia,

putting the question that Lindsay was longing to ask.

Chris said, 'Sarah Cartwright's father is the developer who's trying to buy the playing fields. Apparently she said something about it being a real bore to have to give up Saturday morning games for this, and the others rounded on her and told her straight out that if it wasn't for her rotten father we wouldn't have to do it at all. That set the cat among the pigeons and it ended with Sarah being told that her classmates take a pretty dim view of what has happened; she's more or less universally despised, they informed her. So she's weeping her heart out. Paddy's the only one who can help; she's the only one that Sarah lets near enough. In spite of the fact that I spend hours in the gym with the girl, I may say.

'She's gymnastics mad. She wants to teach it, but you need temperament as well as talent for this job. Mind you, this is the first time I've seen her lose her cool. I'd better get back there now till Paddy comes, in case the girl makes herself ill. Besides, I've had to leave her with Joan Ryan, who is neither use nor ornament in a crisis.'

'Do you want either of us?' asked Cordelia. 'No? Okay, we'll wait here for Paddy and send her through to you as soon as she appears.' At that moment, the doors opened and people surged into the hall, separating Lindsay from Cordelia. She saw Paddy arrive and be hustled off to the rear of the hall. It seemed to Lindsay as she browsed round the stalls that there was no need for Cordelia's play; there were altogether too many mini-dramas taking place already. So much for her quiet weekend in the country.

PART TWO: EXPOSITION

5

The play was an unqualified success, Cordelia had used the limitations of cast and sets and turned them into strengths in the forty-five minute play which dealt wittily, sometimes even hilariously, with a group of students robbing a bank to raise money for a college crèche. As the audience sat applauding, Cordelia muttered to Lindsay, 'Always feel such a fraud clapping my own work, but I try to think of it as a way of praising the cast.' There was no time for more. Even before Lindsay could reply, the young local reporter intent on reviewing the play was at Cordelia's side.

'Any other plans for this piece, Cordelia? Are we going to see it again?'

'Certainly are,' she replied easily, switching the full glare of her charm on him. 'Ordinary Women start rehearsing it in a fortnight's time. They're doing it for a month as half a double bill at the Drill Hall. Though I doubt if even they will be able to give it more laughs. That was a remarkable performance, wasn't it?' And she drifted off with the young man, giving Lindsay no chance to produce the detailed critical analysis of the play she had been preparing for the past five minutes.

She couldn't even discuss it with Paddy who, with her young cast, was surrounded by admiring parents and friends from the nearby towns. So she perched in a corner of the hall as the audience filed out and scribbled some notes in her irregular shorthand about events and her impressions. So far, she had no clear idea of the shape her feature was going to take but, by jotting down random thoughts, she could be reasonably sure of capturing most of the salient points. She had also found that this method helped her to find a hook for the introductory paragraphs and, in her experience, once the introduction was written, the rest fell neatly into place. The problem here was going to be striking the right tone, she mused as she stared out of the window into the afternoon sunlight. Beneath her was the flat roof of the kitchen block, surrounded by a sturdy iron railing which enclosed tubs of assorted dwarf conifers. She admired the mind that could appreciate details such as the decoration of an otherwise depressing expanse of flat roof. Beyond the roof, the woods stretched out, and she caught a glimpse of one of the other buildings as the breeze moved the trees.

Lindsay was roused from her reverie by Cordelia's voice ringing out over the public address system. 'Ladies and gentlemen, please take your seats. The book auction is about to begin and you really mustn't miss any of these choice lots.'

The hall was filling rapidly again. Paddy wove through the crowds and made her way to Lindsay's side. 'We're doing very well so far,' she said. 'And I recognise at least a couple of book dealers among that lot, so perhaps we'll get some decent prices. There are one or two real rarities coming up. Shall we find ourselves a seat?'

Bidding was slow for the first few lots, all newish first editions by moderately successful writers. But it soon became brisk as the quality began to improve. An autographed first edition of T.S. Eliot's *Essays Ancient and Modern* fetched a very healthy price, and a second edition of Virginia Woolf's *Orlando* with a dedication by the author climbed swiftly and was bought for an outrageous amount by the doting mother of one of Paddy's fifth-formers. Paddy whispered in Lindsay's ear, 'That woman will try anything to get her Marjory to pass A level English.' Lindsay bid for a couple of items, but the things she really wanted were beyond her means. After all, she reasoned, it was crazy to spend more than she would earn this weekend on one book. Her resolution vanished, however, when it came to lot 68.

Cordelia grinned broadly and said, 'Ladies and gentlemen, what can I say? A unique opportunity to purchase an autographed first edition of a priceless contemporary novel. *The One-Day Summer*, the first novel of Booker prize nominee, yours truly. A great chance to acquire this rarity. Who'll start me at a fiver?'

Lindsay thrust her arm into the air. 'Five pounds I am bid. Do I hear six? Yes, six. Seven over there. Ten from the gentleman in the tweed hat. Eleven pounds, madam. Eleven once, eleven twice . . . twelve, thank you, sir. Do I hear thirteen? Yes, Thirteen once, thirteen twice, sold for thirteen pounds – unlucky for some – to Lindsay Gordon. A purchase you'll never regret, I may say.'

An embarrassed Lindsay made her way over to the desk where the fourth-formers were collecting the money and wrapping the purchases. She didn't feel much like facing Paddy's sardonic grin right away, so she slipped down to the end of the hall by the stage and crossed through the heavy velvet curtains to the deserted backstage area where all the music rooms were situated. As she rounded the corner of the corridor, she saw Lorna Smith-Couper coming up a side corridor. The cellist did not notice Lindsay, because she was turning her head back to talk to someone coming round the corner of the corridor behind her. Without thinking, Lindsay slid through a half-open door and found herself behind the heavy backdrop of the stage. She could hear every word of the conversation in the corridor. Lorna Smith-Couper was speaking angrily.

'I don't know how you could have the nerve

to put such a proposition to me. I may be many things, but shabby I'm not – and to let this place down now would be shabby in the extreme. You think money can buy anything. That's astonishing for a man your age.'

The reply was muffled. But Lorna's retort came over loud and clear. 'I don't care if your life depends on it, never mind your pathetic little business. I intend to play tonight and no amount of money is going to change my mind. Now, take yourself out of here before I have you removed. Don't think you've heard the last of this, I'm sure the world will be delighted to hear how you conduct your business affairs.'

The man stormed off furiously down the corridor, past Lindsay's hiding place. She leaned against the wall, exasperated with the melodramatic excesses that the weekend seemed to be producing. All Lindsay wanted to do was to get inside the skin of this school to write a decent piece. But every time she thought she was making some headway, some absurdly histrionic confrontation spoiled her perspective. Either that or, as happened even as the thought came into her head, Cordelia Brown appeared out of nowhere and reduced her to a twitchy adolescent.

Cordelia had just finished the auctioneering and had decided to slip out through the backstage area and down the back stairs behind the music rooms. 'Hey,' she said when she saw Lindsay, 'the only reason I came through this way was to avoid you journos. But here I am, caught again.'

'Sorry, it's my nose for a scoop. I just can't help it. But I wasn't actually looking for you, honestly. Simply poking around,' said Lindsay contritely.

'Don't apologise. I was only joking. You must never take me seriously; I'm incorrigibly frivolous. Lots of people hate me for it. Don't you be one, please.' Cordelia smiled anxiously, yet with a certain assurance. She was sharp enough to see the effect she had on Lindsay, but was trying not to exploit it; she never found it easy to guard her tongue, however. 'By the way,' she went on, 'what on earth possessed you to spend all that money on my book? I'd have given you a copy if you'd asked.'

Lindsay mumbled, 'Oh, I don't have the book – though I've read it of course. It seemed to be for a good cause at the time.'

'Oh-oh, the young socialist changes her tune!' A glance at Lindsay's face was enough to make her add, 'Sorry, Lindsay, I don't mean to be cheap. Look, hand it over and I'll stick a few words in it if you want.'

Lindsay gave the book to Cordelia who fished a fountain pen out of her shoulder bag. Above the scrawled signature on the flyleaf, she scribbled something. Then she closed the book, embarrassed in her turn, said, 'See you at dinner,' and vanished down the side corridor where Lorna and the man had come from. Lindsay opened the book, curious.

There she read, 'To Lindsay. Who couldn't wait. With love.' A slow smile broke across her face.

Twenty minutes later, she had changed into what she called her 'function frock' for the evening's activities and was again firmly embedded in Paddy's armchair, clutching a lethal-tasting cocktail called Bikini Atoll, the ingredients of which she dared not ask. Paddy had relaxed completely since the previous evening. After all, she had argued to herself, the day had gone off well: much money had been raised and no one had so much as mentioned the word dope. Now she was gently teasing Lindsay about Cordelia before an early dinner. The meal had been put forward to six because of the evening's concert, and Cordelia bounced into Paddy's room with only ten minutes to spare. She looked breathtaking in a shiny silk dress which revealed her shoulders. She was carrying a shawl in a fine dark blue wool which matched her dress perfectly.

'Hardly right-on, is it, my dears?' she said as she swanned across the room. 'But I thought I'd better do something to bolster the superstar image.'

'We'd better go straight across; you've missed out on the cocktail phase, I'm afraid. We've been invited by my House prefects to sit with them tonight, so we'll be spared the pain of eating with dear Lorna,' said Paddy.

'Terrific,' said Cordelia. 'I've managed to avoid her so far. If it weren't for the fact that she plays a heavenly cello, I'd give this concert a miss and make for the local pub for a bit of peace. Oh, by the way, Paddy, how is the Cartwright girl?'

As they walked through the trees, Paddy said that Sarah was feeling somewhat embarrassed after her earlier outburst. She had decided to go to bed early. 'I popped up earlier with some tea and I'll take a look later on,' said Paddy. 'She's very overwrought. I worry about that girl. She keeps too much locked up inside herself. If she'd let go more often, she'd be much happier. Everything she does is so controlled. Even her sport. She always seems to calculate her every move. Even Chris says that she lacks spontaneity and goes too hard for perfection. I think her father is probably very demanding, too.'

The subject of Sarah was dropped as soon as they entered the main building by the kitchen door. Cordelia remarked how little it had changed in the thirteen years since she had left. She and Paddy were deep in the old-pals-together routine by the time they arrived at the dining hall; it was only the presence of the Longnor House prefects and their friends which changed the subject. On sitting down to eat, Lindsay was immediately collared by the irrepressible Caroline who demanded, 'Do you mostly work for magazines like *New Left*, then?'

Lindsay shook her head. 'No, I usually write for newspapers, actually. There's not a vast amount of cash in writing for magazines – especially the heavy weeklies. So I do most of my work for the nationals.'

'Do you write the things you want to write and then try to sell them? Is that how it works?'

'Sometimes. Mostly, I put an idea for a story to them and if they like it, either I write it or a staff journalist works on it. But I also work on a casual basis doing shifts on a few of the popular dailies in Glasgow, where I live now.'

Caroline looked horrified. 'You mean you work for the gutter press? But you're supposed to be a socialist and a feminist. How can you possibly do that?'

Lindsay sighed and swallowed the mouthful of food she'd managed to get into her mouth between answers. 'It seems to me that since the popular press governs the opinions of a large part of the population, there's a greater need for responsible journalism there than there is in the so-called "quality" press. I reckon that if people like me cop out then it's certainly not going to get any better; in fact, it's bound to get worse. Does that answer your question?'

Cordelia, who had been listening to the conversation with a sardonic smile on her face, butted in. 'It sounds awfully like someone trying to justify herself, not a valid argument at all.'

A look of fury came into Lindsay's eyes. 'Maybe so,' she retorted. 'But I think you can only change things from inside. I know the people I work with, and they know me well enough to take me seriously when I have a go at them about writing sexist rubbish about attractive blonde divorcees. What I say might not make them change overnight but I think that, like water dripping on a stone, it's gradually wearing them down.'

Caroline couldn't be repressed for long. 'But I thought the journalists' union has a rule against sexism? Why don't you get the union to stop them writing all that rubbish about women?'

'Some people try to do that. But it's a long process, and I've always thought that persuasion and education are better ways to eradicate sexism and, come to that, racism, than hitting people over the head with the rule book.'

Cordelia looked sceptical. 'Come on now, Lindsay! If the education and persuasion bit were any use do you think we'd still have topless women parading in daily newspapers? I know enough journos to say that I think you're all adept at kidding yourselves and producing exactly what the editor wants. You're all too concerned about getting your by-line in the paper to have too many scruples about the real significance of what you are writing. Be honest with yourself, if not with the rest of us.'

Her remarks had the salutory effect of injecting a little reality into Lindsay's attraction towards her and she scowled and said, 'Given how little you know about the work I do and my involvement in the union's equality programme, I think that's a pretty high-handed statement.' Then, realising how petulant she sounded, she went on, 'Agreed, newspapers are appallingly sexist. Virginia Woolf said ages ago that you only had to pick one up to realise that we live in a patriarchal society. And the situation hasn't changed much. But I'm not a revolutionary. I'm a pragmatist.'

'Ho, ho, ho,' said Cordelia hollowly. 'Another excuse for inaction.'

But Caroline unexpectedly sprang to Lindsay's defence. 'Surely you're entitled to do things the way you think is best? I mean, everybody gets compromises thrust upon them. Even you. Your books are really strong on feminism. But that television series you did didn't have many really right-on women. I don't mean to be rude, but I was . . .'

Whatever she was was cut off by Paddy interjecting sharply, 'Caroline, enough! Miss Brown and Miss Gordon didn't come here to listen to your version of revolutionary Marxism.'

Caroline grinned and said, 'Okay, Miss Callaghan, I'll shut up.'

The conversational gap was quickly filled by the other girls at the table with chatter about the day's events and the coming concert.

As they finished their pudding, Pamela Overton came over to their table. 'Miss Callaghan,' she said, 'I wonder if I might ask for your help? Miss Macdonald and the music staff are extremely busy making sure that everything is organised for the girls' performances in the first half of the concert.

I wonder if, since you seem to know Miss Smith-Couper, you could help her take her cello and bits and pieces over to Music 2 so that she can warm up during the first half?'

Paddy swallowed her dismay and forced a smile. 'Of course, Miss Overton.'

'Fine. We'll see you in my flat for coffee, then. Perhaps Miss Gordon and Miss Brown would care to join us?' With that, she was gone.

Caroline sighed, 'She's the only person I know who can make a question sound like a royal command.'

'That's enough, Caroline,' said Paddy sharply. The three women excused themselves from the table and walked through the deserted corridors to Miss Overton's flat, Paddy muttering crossly all the way. Fortunately, Lorna was in her room changing, so coffee was served in a fairly relaxed atmosphere. Miss Overton reported on the success of the day and revealed that, by the end of the evening, she hoped they would have raised over £6,000. Lindsay was impressed, and said so. Before anything more could be said, Lorna appeared and announced she was ready to go over to the music room. Paddy immediately rose and grimly followed her out of the room, as Pamela Overton apologetically revealed that she too would have to leave, to welcome her special guests. Lindsay and Cordelia trailed in her wake and made their welcome escape up to the gallery where they settled in among the sixth form and those of the music students who were not directly involved in the concert.

Cordelia said, 'That woman makes me feel like a fifteen-year-old scruff-box, I'm so glad she wasn't head when I was here; if she had been, I'd have developed a permanent inferiority complex.'

Lindsay laughed and settled down to enjoy the concert. In the hall below she saw Margaret Macdonald scuttling through the side door to the music rooms. Members of the chamber orchestra were taking their places and tuning up their instruments. Caroline and several other seniors were showing people to their seats and selling programmes which, Paddy had told Lindsay, had been donated by a local firm of printers. Caroline also slipped through the curtains, returning five minutes later with a huge pile of programmes. Cordelia leaned over and said to Lindsay, 'I'm going to the loo, keep my seat,' and off she went. Lindsay absently studied the audience below, and noticed a girl with a shining head of flaming red hair go up to Caroline, who pointed to the door beside the stage. The redhead nodded and vanished backstage. About eight minutes later, she re-emerged with Paddy. They left the hall together. 'One damn thing after another,' thought Lindsay 'I wonder what's keeping Cordelia?'

The lights went down and the chamber orchestra launched into a creditable rendering of Rossini's string serenade No.3. Half-way through it, Cordelia slipped wordlessly into her seat, Lindsay surfaced from the music and smiled a greeting.

Then the senior choir came on stage and performed a selection of English song throughout the ages, with some beautifully judged solo work conducted by Margaret Macdonald. The first half closed with a joyous performance of *Eine Kleine Nachtmusik* and the audience applauded loudly before heading for the refreshments. Lindsay and Cordelia remained in their seats.

Cordelia leaned over the edge of the balcony. Suddenly she sat upright and said, 'Hey, Lindsay, there's something going on down there.' Lindsay followed her pointing finger and saw Margaret Macdonald rushing up the hall, looking agitated. The velvet curtains were still swinging with the speed of her passage. She headed straight for Pamela Overton and whispered in her ear. The headmistress immediately rose to her feet and the two women hurried off backstage.

'Well, well! I wonder what that's all about? Something more serious than sneaking a cigarette in the loos, by the look of it.' As Cordelia spoke, the bell rang signalling the end of the interval, and the audience began to return to the hall. Meanwhile, Miss Macdonald came scuttling back through the hall, gathering Chris Jackson and another mistress on her way.

'Curiouser and curiouser,' mused Cordelia. At that moment, Pamela Overton emerged on to the stage. So strong was her presence that, as she stepped towards the microphone, a hush fell on the hall. Then she spoke.

'Ladies and gentlemen, I am deeply sorry to have to tell you that Lorna Smith-Couper will be unable to perform this evening as there has been an accident. I must ask you all to be patient with us and to remain in your seats for the time being. I regret to inform you that we must wait for the police.' She left the stage abruptly and at once the shocked silence gave way to a rumble of conversation.

Lindsay looked at Cordelia, who had gone pale. When she met Lindsay's eye, she pulled herself together and said, 'Looks like someone couldn't stand any more of the unlovely Lorna.'

'What do you mean?'

'Come on, Lindsay, you're the journalist. What sort of "accident" means you have to stay put till the police get here? Don't you ever read any Agatha Christie?'

Lindsay could not think of anything to say. Around them, the girls chattered excitedly. Then Paddy came down the gallery to the two women. Her skin looked grey and old, and she was breathing rapidly and shallowly. She put her head close to theirs and spoke softly.

'You'd better get backstage and see Pamela Overton, Lindsay. We've got a real scoop for you. Murder in the music room. Someone has garrotted Lorna with what looks very like a cello string.

Pamela reckons we should keep an eye on our journalist. You've been summoned.'

Lindsay was already on her feet as Cordelia exclaimed, 'What?'

'You heard,' said Paddy, collapsing into Lindsay's seat, head in hands. 'No reason to worry now, Cordelia. Dead women don't sue.'

6

Lindsay hurried on down the hall, aware that eyes were following her. She pushed through the swathes of velvet that curtained the door into the music department. Uncertain, she listened carefully and heard a number of voices coming from the corridor where she had seen Lorna quarrelling with the unknown man earlier. She turned into the corridor and was faced with a door saying 'Music Storeroom'. The passage turned left, then right, so she followed it round and found Pamela Overton and another mistress standing by a door marked 'Music 2'. Beyond them was a flight of stairs.

Even in this crisis, Pamela Overton was as collected as before. 'Ah, Miss Gordon,' she said quietly. 'I am afraid I have to ask another favour of you. I was not entirely truthful when I said there had been an accident. It looks as if Lorna has been attacked and killed. I don't quite know how the press operates in these matters, but it seemed to me that, as you are already with us, it might be simpler for us to channel all press dealings through you. In that way we might minimise the upheaval. Does that seem possible?'

Lindsay nodded, momentarily dumbstruck by the woman's poise. But her professional instinct took over almost immediately and she glanced at her watch. 'I'll have to get a move on if I'm going to do anything tonight,' she muttered. 'Can I see . . . where it happened?'

Miss Overton thought for a moment then nodded. She walked to the door and, with a handkerchief round her fingers, delicately opened it, saying, 'I fear I may be too late in precautions like this, since others have already opened the door. By the way, it was locked from the inside. The key was on the table by the blackboard. There was some delay while Miss Macdonald searched for the spare key.'

Lindsay crossed the threshold and stood just inside the room. What she saw made her retch, but after a brief struggle she regained control. It was her first murder victim, and it was not a pleasant sight. She realised how wise she'd been to avoid it in the past when she'd reported on violent death. Then, there had always been someone else to take over that aspect of the job. But this time it was up to her, so she forced herself to look, and to record mentally the details of the scene. There had been nothing peaceful about Lorna Smith-Couper's end. She had been sitting on a chair facing the door, presumably playing her cello. Now she was slumped over her instrument on the floor, her face engorged and purple, her tongue sticking grotesquely out of her mouth like some obscene gargoyle. Round her neck, pulled so tight that it was almost invisible amidst the swollen and bruised flesh, was a wicked garrotte. It did indeed seem to be a cello string, with a noose at one end and a simple horn duffel-coat toggle tied on to the other end to enable the assassin to tighten the noose without tearing the flesh on his – or her – fingers.

Lindsay dragged her eyes from this horror and forced herself to look around with something approaching professional detachment. She noticed that all the windows were shut, but none of the casements appeared to be locked. Then she turned, revolted and overcome, and went back to the corridor. 'Where can I find a quiet telephone?' she demanded.

'You'd be best to use the one in my study,' said Miss Overton. 'Ask one of the girls to show you the way. I must stay here till the police arrive. Is there anything else you need?'

'To be perfectly blunt, I need a comment from you, Miss Overton,' Lindsay replied awkwardly.

'Very well. You may say that I am profoundly shocked by this outrage and deeply distressed by the death of Miss Smith-Couper. She was a very distinguished woman who reflected great credit on her school. We can only pray that the police will quickly catch the person responsible.' With that, Miss Overton turned away. Lindsay sensed her disgust at the situation in which she found herself and understood it very well.

She walked back down the corridor towards the hall. Just before she re-emerged into the public gaze, she paused and took out her notebook. She leant on the window ledge to scribble down the headmistress's words before her memory of them became inaccurate. For reasons which she didn't understand at all, she was more determined than usual to be completely precise in quoting the head-mistress. Then she stared briefly out into the night. The last thing she had expected was to find herself caught up in a murder and part of her resented the personal inconvenience. She was also aware of her own callous selfishness as she thought to herself, 'Well, this is really going to screw up any chance I might have had with Cordelia.'

Then Lindsay pulled herself together, gave herself a mental ticking-off for her self-indulgence, reminded herself that as sole reporter on the spot she stood to make a bob or two, and resolutely shoved the vision of the dead musician to the back of her mind. There would be time later to examine her personal feelings. She glanced up at the gallery, but Cordelia and Paddy were no longer there. Lindsay looked around her for a face she recognised and spotted Caroline half-way up the hall. She went over to her and asked to be shown the way to Miss Overton's study. Caroline nodded and set off at a healthy pace. Half-way down the stairs, she turned and said conversationally, 'I say, not wishing to talk out of turn and all that, but what has happened to the Smith-Couper person? I mean, everyone staff-wise is running around in circles like a bunch of chickens with their heads cut off. What's all the fuss in aid of? And why are the police coming?'

'Sorry, Caroline, it's not for me to say. I'd like to tell you, but I'd be breaking a confidence.'

'Oh, I see, grown-up conspiracies, eh? Anything to protect the kiddiewinks,' the girl retorted, smiling.

Lindsay laughed in spite of herself. 'Not quite. It's just that it's not right for me to pass on what I've been told in confidence.' A little white lie, she thought, and that's not going to fool Caroline.

'I see. So you're not actually dashing to the phone to tell the world's press about murder most foul, then?' Caroline said mischievously. They had reached Pamela Overton's quarters, so Lindsay managed to avoid giving an answer by vanishing through the door indicated and into the study with only a word of thanks. Caroline shrugged expressively at the closed door then took herself off. Lindsay turned on a side-light and sat down at a desk which was fanatically tidy. All that adorned its surface was a telephone, a blotter and a large pad of scribbling paper. Lindsay pulled the paper towards her and roughed out two introductions. 'A brutal murderer stalked a top girls' boarding school last night (Saturday). A star cello player was found savagely murdered as she prepared to give a concert before a glittering audience of the rich and famous,' read the first, destined for the tabloids. The other, for the heavies, was, 'Internationally celebrated cellist Lorna Smith-Couper was found dead last night at a girls' public school. Her body was discovered by staff at Derbyshire House Girls' School, just before she was due to perform in a gala concert.' Then she jotted down a series of points in order of priority; 'How found? When? Why there? Overton quote. No police quote yet.'

Within minutes she was on to her first news-desk and dictating her copy to one of those remarkably speedy typists who perform the inimitable and thankless task of taking down the ephemeral prose of journalists out on the road all over the world. It was well after ten when she finished. A good night's work, she thought, but tomorrow would be a lot tougher. She'd have to file copy again with more detail to all the dailies, and act as a liaison for Pamela Overton, her staff and the girls. And some time within the next few hours, she would somehow have to develop the roll of film in her camera. Someone would pay a good price for what were almost certainly the last photographs of the murder victim. She would, of course, have to crop Margaret Macdonald right out of the frame. No one wanted a photograph of an unknown music teacher.

She sat smoking at Pamela Overton's desk, using the waste-paper bin as an ashtray. She was strangely reluctant to return to the centre of events where a good journalist should be. The police would be here by now, and she would have to get a quote from the officer leading the investigation. But that could wait. The police would be too busy at present to be bothered with her questions. She was jotting down a few notes to herself about her course of action in the morning when there was a knock at the door. Before she could answer, it opened and Cordelia came in.

'I hoped I'd find you here,' said Cordelia. 'Paddy reckoned Pamela Overton would have sent you here to do your stuff. I'm not interrupting you, am I?'

'No, I'd just finished phoning copy over. It's debatable how much any of the newspapers will be able to use at this time of night. But the radio news will give it plenty of airtime, and I'm afraid that by tomorrow morning we'll have the whole pack of journos on the doorstep. And how Pamela Overton imagines I'm going to cope with that lot, I do not know,' Lindsay replied wearily.

'Paddy says the boss will probably ask you to stay for a couple more days.'

'Not beyond Monday, I'm afraid. I've got a dayshift on Tuesday on the *Scottish Daily Clarion*, and I can't afford to let them down since they are my major source of income at the moment.

Still, tomorrow will be the worst, the fuss should have died down by Monday, especially if they make a quick arrest.'

Cordelia sat down on the window seat and looked out into the darkness. She spoke quietly. 'The police are here now. Going into their routines. They've got a batch of coppers on the door of the hall. Taking down the names and addresses of all the audience, and then letting them go off. They've pulled Paddy and Margaret Macdonald and Pamela Overton off to one side and a very efficient-looking Inspector is questioning them one by one. They'll be tied up for a while yet, I suspect. Another bunch of plain-clothes men are questioning girls and staff. Anyone who's got anything interesting to contribute will no doubt be winnowed out and sent through to the Inspector. Pamela Overton still hasn't turned a hair. But then you probably guessed all that anyway.'

Lindsay said nothing. She went over to the window and gave Cordelia a cigarette. She noted with a clinical eye that the hand that took it was shaking. Cordelia slowly smoked the cigarette. When it was burned half-way down, she gave a nervous laugh and said, 'It's not always like this, you know. Most of the time it's pretty civilised. We don't go around killing old girls on a regular basis, no matter how obnoxious.'

'I didn't for one moment think you did.'

There was another pause. Then Cordelia said,

'Lindsay – I've got to ask a favour. Or, rather, ask your advice.'

'Ask away.'

'You know when we were sitting together before the concert and I went off to the loo?' Lindsay nodded. 'Well, I didn't only go to the loo. You probably noticed I was gone for quite a while. You see, I thought that just before the concert might be the best time to tackle Lorna. You know, I thought she'd have her mind on what she was about to do and might just be a little less vindictive than usual.

'I know one is supposed to leave all that wheeling and dealing to the lawyers, but I simply thought that a few words, woman to woman, appealing to the old better nature and all that, might do the trick and we could come to a civilised agreement that would avoid going to court.'

Cordelia nervously stubbed out her cigarette. She ground it so fiercely that it broke and shreds of tobacco scattered in all directions. She went on, her voice rising. 'I ducked down the stairs, through the ground floor, down to the back stairs beyond this flat. I knew she was in Music 2 and I knew I could get there without being seen. I went up and knocked on the door. There was no reply, so I tried the door handle. It was locked. There was nothing else I could do but come back. I swear that's all. I didn't hear a sound. I didn't call out to her or anything.'

A sudden coldness gripped Lindsay's chest. With

icy clarity she realised that she could be listening to a murderer laying down her first line of defence. But surely not Cordelia? Lindsay broke the silence that followed Cordelia's outburst, forcing herself to speak calmly and quietly. 'You're going to have to tell the police. I think you knew that really.'

'But nobody saw me. I'm sure of that.'

'You can't be certain. At the very least, there must be other people in the gallery who saw you leave and return later. And remember, you tried the door. There's an outside chance that your prints are still on the handle, though that's been handled enough since to make that unlikely. Also, it is material evidence. At the time you say you knocked, it was all quiet in there. So presumably she was dead by then, or there would either have been music or some response from Lorna. You can't withhold evidence like that, Cordelia.'

She put her hand on the other woman's shoulder. Cordelia gripped it tightly. 'I'm afraid,' she said. 'I'm afraid they'll think I did it.'

Lindsay replied quickly, trying to convince herself as much as Cordelia. 'Don't be silly. How on earth could you have got into the room, killed Lorna and got back to your seat, having locked the door behind you, replaced the key and not shown the slightest sign of upheaval? At the very least you'd have been out of breath and I'd have noticed that. Besides, whoever killed her must have had the weapon ready, and you couldn't hide anything in that dress,' she ended, realising even as she spoke that the garrotte could easily have been hidden in the music room in advance. But she desperately didn't want to consider seriously the proposition that a woman she'd fallen for could have murdered someone. So she wanted to offer what reassurance she could. When the police made any move towards Cordelia, that was the time to worry. Not before.

'Look, it's okay. Don't worry. Nobody could think for a moment that it was you. You've hardly got a motive, after all. Oh, I know dead women don't sue. But the case was by no means a fore-gone conclusion, and surely she would have come out of it at least as badly as you. At worst, it would have given the book a lot of publicity.' Lindsay squeezed down on the seat beside Cordelia, who rested her head on Lindsay's shoulder.

She sighed and said, 'You're right. I suppose I'll have to face them. Sorry, I'm not normally such a wimp. Oh God, I really don't want to go through with this. I wish I could just climb into bed and pull the covers over my head. Just sleep long enough for it all to go away.'

'That's not really on though, is it?'

'No. Instead, I've got to go and tell all to some tedious plod who will doubtless trip me up and proceed to arrest me for murder on the spot. Will you come with me?'

Lindsay nodded. 'Of course. They'll not let me

stick around while they take your statement, though, particularly with me being the resident hack.'

Cordelia chuckled softly. 'Oh no, they wouldn't want witnesses when they start pulling out my fingernails to get a confession.' They both laughed, and the tension evaporated. Lindsay felt slightly hysterical with a mixture of jubilation that her doubts about Cordelia had vanished, and shock reaction to the events of the past few hours. She got to her feet and Cordelia followed her out of the room.

On the way upstairs, Lindsay asked Cordelia, 'Do you know if there's a darkroom in the school?'

'Yes. Some of the seniors do photography as a hobby. There's a little darkroom in the science block, over at the back of the tennis courts. Why?'

'I took a couple of candid camera shots of Lorna this morning when she was out walking. I was up the hill. I wanted to take a look at them to see if they were at all saleable. Mercenary to the last, you see.'

'No, just professional.'

'Not a professionalism to be proud of, particularly. However, it does keep the emotions at bay.'

By then they had reached the doors of the hall. Most of the girls had left, but there was still a handful of staff members and a few of the girls Lindsay recognised as ushers and programme sellers. When they entered, Chris Jackson looked up and beckoned them over. They sat down on either side of her, a little way off from the nearest schoolgirls.

'How is it progressing?' asked Lindsay.

'Quite quickly, considering. They've finished with the head and Paddy, but Margaret's still in there. A lesser copper is interviewing the others – a "preliminary chat", he says. They'll be back tomorrow for more, I gather. At least they've got the decency to see everyone here instead of dragging us all down to the nick. The young copper's got Caroline Barrington in there just now. I know who I feel sorry for, and it's not Caroline.' Chris's nervous chatter suddenly ground to a halt.

'I want to have a word with one of the boys in blue,' said Cordelia, trying to appear nonchalant but failing. 'How long is she likely to be?'

Just then, Caroline bounced into the hall, calling out, 'Next please for the Spanish Inquisition.'

'That girl is impossible,' said Chris, exasperated. 'Why don't you go in now? That way, you and Lindsay can get off back across to Longnor at the first opportunity. Paddy asked me to say she'd see you over there. She's gone back to try to get the girls into some sort of order. Most of them seem to be behaving remarkably well, but one or two are going right off their trolleys.' Cordelia nodded and went off, Lindsay calling, 'Good luck,' softly after her. Cordelia disappeared through the swing doors with a nervous smile.

'Quite an upset,' Lindsay remarked, realising as she did so the banality of her words.

'Horrific, Lindsay, absolutely horrific. As soon as word of this gets out, there will be a mass exodus of girls from the school. If James Cartwright doesn't close us down, this certainly will,' said Chris Jackson sadly.

'It certainly closed Lorna Smith-Couper down,' said Lindsay drily.

'Oh, don't think I'm being callous. But I never knew the woman, so it would be hypocritical of me to pretend I'm heartbroken about her death. What worries me is that no one seems to be able to work out quite how it was done. I mean, from what I can gather – though we probably shouldn't be gossiping about it – there's no question of it being an outsider. It had to be someone who knew the layout of the building. I hope to God they clear it up quickly. I mean, no responsible parent would leave their child at a school with a homicidal maniac on the loose, now would they?'

Lindsay changed the subject as diplomatically as possible and managed to get Chris chatting casually for a while about other topics. They were interrupted by Caroline, who breezed up to them, excusing herself perfunctorily. 'I was wondering, Miss Jackson, could we beetle off back to Longnor now? The coppers have seen all the girls from the Houses; it's only main building girls who are left. And Miss Callaghan said we shouldn't come back on our own. I suppose it's in case we get bumped off *en route*. So can you or Miss Gordon take us across?'

Chris looked a question at Lindsay, who nodded, 'Of course I'll go back with you. If you don't mind waiting a few minutes till Miss Brown is finished with the police, then we'll all go together.'

'Fine, that's that solved at least,' said Chris, 'Now if you'll excuse me, I'll just go and check there are no girls hanging about in the music department. Thanks, Lindsay.'

She strode off, leaving Lindsay once more with the effervescent Caroline. Nothing, not even murder, seemed to take the bounce out of her. 'How did you get on with the police?' Lindsay asked quickly, hoping to avoid diving deep into dialectical dialogue.

'Oh, they were okay. I was surprised. I expected them to be a lot heavier. They asked all the questions you'd expect. About who was where and when, and if I'd been down to Music 2. I told them I'd only been as far as the storeroom for more programmes and that I didn't see a sausage. Mind you, I told them they'd probably find no shortage of people with axes to grind about Lorna Smith-Couper, judging by the stories you hear. That woman left a trail of human wreckage in her wake. Not entirely surprising that someone finally did her in, really,' she said, barely pausing for breath.

'What makes you say that?' asked Lindsay, more to pass the time than from any strong curiosity. But before Caroline could elaborate any further, the double doors swung open and Cordelia appeared, looking drained but relieved. There was nothing in Lindsay's world at that moment except concern for Cordelia. She immediately rose and went to her. 'Okay?'

Cordelia nodded. 'Tell you later,' she said, as Caroline found her way to their sides.

'Can we go now,' she asked. 'Only, we're all dying for a coffee.'

Lindsay nodded and briefly explained the situation to Cordelia as Caroline shouted, 'Okay, anyone for Longnor, Axe, Goyt, Wildboarclough. Come now or face the psychopath alone.'

Half a dozen girls peeled off from the group and followed Lindsay and Cordelia out into the back drive and down the well-lit path through the woods to the houses. As they left the main building behind, Lindsay glanced back at the window of the room where Lorna had been killed. A light still burned at the window as the police scene-of-crimes officers worked on. Something was nagging at the back of her mind, but she dismissed at once any idea that the killer could have come through the window. Only a chimpanzee could have made that climb without being instantly visible from the hall or the music corridor. She turned back, and followed the file of chattering girls, headed by Cordelia and Caroline who were already deep in animated conversation.

7

Having seen their charges safely stowed, Lindsay and Cordelia escaped to Paddy's sitting-room. Lindsay headed straight for the gas fire and warmed her hands, while Cordelia made for the cocktail cabinet.

'I don't suppose Paddy would mind if we fixed ourselves a drink,' she said. 'I could certainly use one.' She tried the door. 'Damn! It's locked.'

Lindsay stood up. 'She keeps it locked when she's not here. I noticed her unlocking it last night. I suppose there's always the chance that it might get raided by some adolescent alcoholic. I've got an Islay malt upstairs in my bag if you fancy that.'

'If that's some kind of whisky, yes please, I feel the need for some calming alcohol. Say, a couple of bottles for starters!'

Lindsay smiled to herself as she went to collect the drink. When she returned, she found Cordelia crouched by the fire, shivering. She immediately went over to her and put an arm round her shoulders.

'Silly, really. I can't stop shivering. Must be reaction. Be an angel and fix me a drink, would you? Water in it, please, about the same amount as whisky.'

Lindsay went through to the kitchen and poured out the two drinks, mentally scoring another plus point to Cordelia for drinking her whisky properly – in other words, as Lindsay preferred it. Cordelia followed her and took her tumbler gratefully. She gulped down a large slug of whisky and water, shuddered convulsively as the fire in the peaty spirit hit her, then relaxed.

'Better?' asked Lindsay.

'Much. Let's go back into the warm.'

They sat on opposite sides of the fireplace. Lindsay offered her a cigarette and they both lit up. 'Thank you,' sighed Cordelia. 'Not just for the cigarettes and whisky. Thanks for making me pull myself together earlier on. You were right; it was foolish even to think of any other course of action. I was in a state of shock, I suppose. I couldn't believe I was off the hook about the libel suit, and I simply didn't want to involve myself in Lorna's death at all. I panicked.

'I felt sure I'd be the prime suspect – you know, one sees and reads so much that makes the police look both bent and stupid that one comes to believe that every encounter with them will inevitably end in disaster.

'But it wasn't too bad at all. I mean, they were actually quite reasonable, when you consider that I must be one of their suspects. The detective sergeant took my statement and asked me not to leave the school premises until the Inspector has had the chance to interview me in the morning.' She smiled wanly. 'He also told me, very politely, that there will be a police guard on the main gate. "To keep out undesirables," he said, though I suspect it's more to keep us in.'

Lindsay was about to question Cordelia more closely when Paddy came in. She greeted them with a brief, 'Hi', and headed for the drinks cupboard.

'Three minds with but a single cliché,' said Lindsay. 'If you're going to expose us to murder on a regular basis, Paddy, you'll have to give us a spare key to the booze cupboard.'

'Oh God, I'm sorry,' groaned Paddy. 'Have one now?'

'We're all right, thanks,' said Cordelia, 'Lindsay has come to the rescue for the second time this evening. She does a good impersonation of the US Cavalry. I'll have to make her a permanent feature at this rate.'

'Drinks, fags and a shoulder to cry on. All part of the service,' Lindsay replied, trying to cover her blushes.

Paddy sprawled out on the couch, clutching a large brandy. 'What a bloody day,' she complained and then fell silent.

'How did you get on with the local constabulary?' Cordelia asked, 'I found them remarkably pleasant, in spite of my having to confess to being on the spot during what seems to be the crucial period.'

'Were you? Well, if you were there after I left her, they've probably crossed you off their list already. I seem to be the odds-on favourite at the moment. If they knew I had the shred of a motive, I'd probably be under arrest by now,' Paddy replied, bitterness in her voice.

'Why is that?' asked Lindsay.

'Because nobody admits to seeing her, speaking to her or even hearing her warm up on her cello after I took her up there. I showed her up to the room and went in with her to make sure she had everything she needed. I took the opportunity to thank her for keeping her mouth shut about the circumstances of our previous acquaintance. She smiled like a fox and said she saw no reason so far to break her silence, but she'd have to consider the good of the school.'

Paddy sighed deeply and went on. 'I left it at that and took off. I was around the backstage area till right before the concert when Jessica Bennett came to fetch me because one of the fifth form in Longnor was sick and Jess didn't want the responsibility of dealing with it. By the time I got back, the first half was in full swing, so I went straight backstage again via the back stairs to avoid disturbing the audience.

'So I'm there. For all they know, I might have had a reason for murdering her, and I had a better chance than anyone else of getting to her. Because, you see, she locked the door behind me as I left. She said she wanted to be sure of getting some peace.'

'But if you're supposed to have done it, how do they think you got the key on the table through a locked door?'

'There's a spare key in Margaret Macdonald's room, which was unlocked all evening. The key for Music 2 wasn't where it should have been, either. Whoever put it back last put it on the wrong hook. But it could have been like that for weeks because those keys were hardly ever used. On the other hand, I or almost anyone else could have done it tonight. Everyone was milling around backstage. I doubt if anyone could positively say I didn't slip into Margaret's room.'

There was a moment's chill silence. Then Lindsay spoke with quiet excitement. 'But there would be no point in you killing Lorna while she was at the school. Not just to silence her. Her murder will surely mean the end of the school's chances of raising the money for the playing fields. It's bound to mean hard times or even closure for the school itself, so you won't have a job in any event.'

'Agreed. But the police wouldn't necessarily see it like that,' Paddy argued. 'After all, if I felt sufficiently threatened, I wouldn't necessarily think things through to their logical conclusion.'

That set the three of them off in a discussion about motive. Lindsay put forward her line of argument, but Cordelia countered that, in the heat of the moment, the murderer could well have panicked and seen no further than the immediate, short-term benefit.

There was a deep hush, broken by Cordelia's forced cheerfulness as she said, 'But there must be others besides you – and to a lesser degree, me – who were on the spot and have reasons for hating Lorna. Let's face it, she'd never have won a popularity contest, would she?'

'That's right,' said Lindsay, 'Caroline Barrington seems to have hated her guts – and seems to think there were others in the same boat.'

'I can imagine people hating, but I can't imagine anyone killing her,' said Paddy dubiously. 'Not killing her.'

'Well, what about this property developer?' asked Cordelia. 'It would definitely be in his interest to get rid of Lorna and discredit the school in the process.'

'He wasn't there tonight,' said Paddy. 'They're still going to find me firm favourite if they come up with a motive.'

'But we've come up with Caroline and the property developer guy in just a few minutes and we scarcely know the people involved,' Lindsay protested, alarmed by her friend's defeatism. 'There have got to be others. Listen, I heard someone having an argument with Lorna only this afternoon. I don't know who it was, but they were going at it hammer and tongs.'

'What about?' demanded Cordelia.

'I don't really know. He wanted her not to play at the concert or something and she wasn't having any.'

'You should tell the police about that,' Cordelia urged.

'Yeah, I'll get round to it when I see the Inspector tomorrow,' Lindsay replied. 'So that's another one to add to the list. And if we're talking about people who knew the terrain and had access to keys and cello strings, what about Margaret Macdonald? She's seemed really uptight all weekend.'

'She wouldn't hurt a fly,' said Paddy positively. 'I know the woman; God damn it, if anyone is incapable of murder, it's Margaret.'

'No one is incapable of murder,' said Lindsay vehemently. 'This particular murder may just have been the one that she was capable of.'

And they were off again. None of them seemed to be able to hang on for long to the idea that this was a real murder. None of them was willing to face the fact that, once the first horror had worn off, there would be fear, suspicion and isolation left. No one seemed keen to make the first move towards bed, afraid, perhaps, of sleeplessness and speculation in the early hours.

It was after two when they reluctantly decided to end their talk. Paddy went off to make her last checks of the House, having promised to wake Lindsay early and take her across to the dark-room so she could process her film.

Cordelia and Lindsay sat in a companionable quiet, broken only by the hiss of the gas fire. Finally, Cordelia got to her feet and stretched languidly. 'I'm off,' she said. 'You coming now or staying up a bit?'

'I'll be up in a little while. I'll have one last smoke before I get my head down.'

'Okay. See you in the morning. And thanks – again.'

'Don't mention it. It was little enough.'

'One day, when all this horrible business is over, I shall cook you a special banquet as a thank you. I'm famous among my friends for my cooking, I promise you.'

'I'll look forward to that.'

'Goodnight, then.' And she was gone, leaving Lindsay alone to stare into the fire and conjure her own dreams out of its flickering light. It was very late indeed when she finally climbed the long stairs to her bed.

Sunday dawned dull and misty on Axe Edge. Lindsay shivered as the raw cold bit through her jacket when she and Paddy emerged from the warmth of Longnor House at a quarter to eight. They were both silent on their walk through the trees, wrapped up in their own thoughts. Paddy unlocked the science block and led Lindsay to a compact but well-equipped darkroom on the first floor.

'There you are,' she announced. 'Hope you've got everything you need. I'll leave the keys so you can lock up after yourself. Sorry it's so cold in here; we always turn off the heating in this block at lunchtime on Saturday. How long will you be?'

'Half, three-quarters of an hour? No longer.'

'Okay. I'll see you in my rooms at around half-past eight, then.' Paddy left her curiously illuminated by the black-out lighting.

Lindsay quickly checked the light-proofing, then started work on her film. She pulled it from its cartridge and shoved it into the tray of developer she had laid out. She moved it round, then put it into the fixer, washed it, and snapped on a lamp to look at it more closely. Even in an unfamiliar darkroom she worked swiftly and efficiently, slotting the frames one by one into the enlarger, fumbling the photographic paper out of its light-proof envelope, and then exposed her prints. Half an hour later, she was looking at a dozen prints of Lorna Smith-Couper with her head thrown back in laughter.

It was not a bad picture, thought Lindsay. Though it was rather grainy, it would still reproduce quite well. It didn't look too much like an unauthorised snatch.

She had also printed a couple of copies of the full frame with Margaret Macdonald in profile looking remarkably upset – almost on the verge of tears, Lindsay thought. And, for her own amusement, she had printed up the shots she had taken of Cordelia. They were not particularly flattering, but they were good likenesses and very different from the other, posed photographs she had seen. There was a grittiness and determination in the face that casual acquaintance with Cordelia gave no hint of. Lindsay smiled to herself and cleared up. She let herself back out into the woods, carefully checking that all doors were locked behind her.

She slipped upstairs and sorted out the photographs. The ones of Lorna she put into a large envelope scrounged from Paddy, the others she put straight into her bag. Then she went downstairs to join Paddy.

'Mission accomplished,' she said.

'Good,' Paddy replied. 'Pamela Overton has just been on the phone. She's already had two calls from newspapers and has told them that you're the only journalist who will be given any co-operation by the school, also that you'll be supplying a story later today. She would like you to have breakfast with her, and after that she's arranged for you to speak to Inspector Dart – he's the one we all saw last night; he's running the show as far as I can see.'

That was the last minute of peace Lindsay had all day. Breakfast with Pamela Overton was sticky and uncomfortable for both of them, and

afterwards, Lindsay felt she had been profession-
ally stalled on every question apart from the
purely superficial. She did know for sure that the
fund-raising would go on and that Pamela
Overton was anxious to get across the message
that she was convinced it was the work of an
outsider and that none of the girls was in danger.
But that was all Lindsay had gathered in terms
of fresh information.

She walked slowly up to the hall where the
police had taken over a small classroom and asked
a uniformed constable if she could have a word
with the officer in charge. After a brief wait she
was ushered in. Over by the window, a young
plain-clothes officer was sitting at a desk with a
sheaf of paper around him. Behind the teacher's
desk stood a tall lean man whose face would have
been handsome were it not for a mass of old
pitted acne scars. He looked in his mid-forties,
with greying sandy hair and sleepy grey eyes at
variance with his sharp features and lined face.

Lindsay introduced herself and he looked
keenly at her over the bowl of a pipe he was
lighting. When he spoke, his voice was rich and
slow. 'I'm Inspector Roy Dart,' he said. 'I'm
running this investigation. What are you after?'

'Miss Overton has asked me to handle press
liaison for her. I'll be putting out copy to all the
dailies later on today, so I would appreciate
anything you're in a position to give me.'

'I'll not be saying anything to you that I won't

be saying to any reporter who picks up a phone and calls me. You get no special favours here, I'm afraid. And I expect information to be a two-way street, understood. Anything you dig up that I should know about, I want to hear from you, not read in the papers. Now, officially you can say we are treating Lorna Smith-Couper's death as murder. We are pursuing several promising avenues of inquiry.'

With an air of finality, he picked up some papers from the desk. Lindsay refused to accept dismissal and asked, 'Do you anticipate a quick arrest? Obviously, with a school full of young girls, there's a lot of anxiety about a murder like this . . .'

'We're doing everything in our power to bring this matter to a swift conclusion. There are policemen on the school premises at all times and I do not expect any further incidents,' he retorted forcefully. 'The girls are being looked after properly. Rest assured on that point. Now, if there's nothing else?'

This time the dismissal was explicit. Lindsay moved towards the door. Just as she was about to leave, she turned and tried again. 'Off the record, I take it you expect to mop it up soon?' She smiled warmly.

She might as well have saved her charm for Cordelia, where it could have done her some good. Dart looked up from under his eyebrows and said, 'You're wasting your time, Miss Gordon. Don't waste mine.'

Lindsay walked back down to Pamela Overton's study ruefully, thinking of all the reasons why she hated having to be polite to senior police officers. The headmistress had left the study free for Lindsay to work in, and she started putting together a holding story that she could send out early to the wire services for the radio news bulletins. She noticed with a wry smile that an ashtray had appeared since the night before. She made a couple of attempts to speak to Margaret Macdonald, to inject a bit of colour into her story, but the music mistress steadfastly refused to say anything, pleading pressure of work.

She phoned over a factual piece to several papers, promising more material later. Then she set about trying to sell the dramatic last pictures of Lorna. The first paper she rang didn't want to know because of the price she was asking, but the next tabloid she rang seemed keen.

'They're the last pix taken of her, and I'm offering them exclusive,' she explained.

The picture editor at the other end of the phone spoke with all the false enthusiasm of his breed. 'That's terrific. What do the pix show?'

'The murdered woman is standing in the garden of the school where she was killed. She's laughing in a couple of them, and there's one pic of her just straight-faced. The laughing ones are a good line to go for – carefree musician enjoying a joke unaware that within twelve hours she'll be dead; that sort of routine. I can let you have a deep caption to go with it, say five or six paras,' persuaded Lindsay.

'Who took these, then? What's the quality like?'

'I took them with a telephoto zoom. They're a bit grainy, but they'll reproduce all right.'

There was a pause. 'And you've got them to yourself? What sort of price are we looking at?'

'£250 seems reasonable to me.'

'Including syndication rights?'

'I suppose you've got to get your money back somehow.'

'It's a deal, then. Two-fifty. How are you getting them to us?'

'I'll put them on a train to Manchester. Your desk there can pick them up, can't they?'

'Sure thing. Phone them and let them know what train they're on. Thanks again, Lindsay.'

She called a taxi to take her down to the station. As soon as she put the phone down, it pealed. She picked it up to hear a crime reporter baying for details. Four months ago she would gladly have given him all she had. But her brief spell as a freelance had taught her the hard fact that staff reporters don't do favours to anyone except themselves. The only way she could be sure of making her information work for a living was to keep it to herself. As she put the phone down after a heavy exchange, she sighed. Another potential ally lost for a while. She was pleased when the taxi arrived for the small oasis of calm the trip to the station provided in the chaos of the day.

Back at the desk, she got to work again, Lunch and dinner were snatched meals eaten from a tray in the study. The desk had lost its formal tidiness. Now it was covered with scribbled sheets of paper as Lindsay drafted out the various versions of the story tailored to each paper. Used coffee cups and cigarette packs added to the general clutter. She had escaped from the smoke-filled room a couple of times to collect some quotes for her stories. But for the rest of the day she was confined to the study, with a phone jammed to her ear for most of the time. Paddy stuck her head round the door a couple of times to make sure she had everything she needed, but it was after nine before she could call a halt to her work on the 'mystery killer grips school with fear' stories for the next morning's papers.

She walked back alone through the woods to Paddy's room without giving a thought to the lurid prose she had despatched about the hand of terror that made schoolgirls go everywhere in groups. She found Cordelia watching the television news and sipping brandy. 'What's happening, then, ace reporter?' she demanded.

'Police have gone home for the night, leaving the statutory constable to repel boarders, journos and ghouls. No arrest has been made. No one has been held for questioning. They have been taking statements all day and as yet are not in a position to make any comment. Several parents are arriving tomorrow to remove offspring. James Cartwright is unavailable for comment. The body has been removed and the music room sealed. The funeral will be on Thursday in London, with a memorial service to be arranged. Cause of death thought to be asphyxiation. Or whatever it is when you are garrotted. End message,' Lindsay rattled off.

'Looks as though you've had a busy day.'

'You're not wrong. What about you?'

'I had a brief chat with the charming Inspector Dart who doesn't seem terribly interested in me except in so far as I seem to provide an end point in his timetable. He seems to think she was dead by then. Since which time, I have been sitting around reading Trollope and avoiding human contact like the plague, apart from dear Paddy who looks more harrassed with every hour that passes. She's at a staff meeting just now, they're all wondering what the hell to do next. I just wish the bloody police would get a move on and arrest the bloody murderer,' said Cordelia, trying unsuccessfully to force some lightness into her voice.

'Are you leaving tomorrow?'

'I should really. I'm supposed to have lunch with my agent, and I've already put her off once. I'm torn, I must admit, between hanging on to see if I can be of any help and wanting to put as much distance as possible between me and the school. I expect I'll go, though. Good agents are hard to find! What about you? Heading back tomorrow?'

Lindsay shrugged. 'I'm aiming to get a train about three at the latest, so I can be back in Glasgow at a decent time of night. Then I'm going to get well pissed in my local. Put all of this out of my mind.'

'You seem to be doing that rather well anyway,' Cordelia commented drily.

'What do you mean?' asked Lindsay indignantly.

'Well, I couldn't have sat on the end of a phone all day rattling off sensational stories about Lorna's murder. I don't know how you can be so cool about it.'

Lindsay shook her head, disappointed. 'It's the job I do. I've been trained to forget my feelings and do the business. And I do it very well. Don't think I've enjoyed today.'

'That's exactly what I do think. You came in here like you were coming off a high. Like you'd got a real buzz from doing the business, as you call it. I find that very strange, quite honestly.'

The remark stung Lindsay, who was not about to admit its truth. She took a deep breath and said angrily, 'Look, Cordelia, at the end of the day, I have to make a living. Lorna's murder cost me money, to be brutal about it. The feature I was supposed to write would have cleared me £150. Now, I've got to earn myself at least that this weekend otherwise things start happening in my life that don't appeal to me. Like the phone gets cut off. Like I can't afford to have the car

106

exhaust repaired so I can't work. I didn't know Lorna, so I'm not personally devastated by her death. By doing what I'm doing, I do myself the favour of earning a bit. I'm also doing the school a favour. Make no mistake about it, whether I supply the raw copy or not, all the papers are going to have their sensational stories. But at least this way, we know they're getting accurate copy to start with. And if they get it wrong, well, Pamela Overton knows who to blame and where to find me.

'It's easy to criticise the job I do, but most people never have to make the moral decisions I take as a way of life. And whatever they may think, few of them would make a better job of it than me. I could have a go at you about the anti-feminist slant of your telly scripts. But that's none of my business because I don't know the pressures on you. Until you understand the pressures on me, don't knock me.'

Cordelia looked stunned by the onslaught. 'I didn't realise you were so sensitive about it,' she said huffily. Conversation died there. They both pretended to watch television, each reluctant to bridge the gap and swallow her pride. Eventually Lindsay rose and poured a drink. 'I'm taking this up to bed with me,' she announced. 'I feel like flopping with a good book and trying to forget the day I've had.'

'Okay. Listen, Lindsay – I may not get much chance to talk to you tomorrow because I'll probably be off about nine. I haven't forgotten that meal I promised you. So when are you likely to be in London next?'

Lindsay shrugged. 'I don't know. I've no firm plans. It's hard for me to take a weekend off because Sundays especially are good days for me and I can't really afford to turn down work at the moment. But I'd like to come down soon and see some magazine editors – I give myself till the end of the month to get organised. That'll probably be in the middle of the week.'

'That's no problem for me. I can easily arrange my work schedule to fit round your visit. Do you have somewhere to stay?'

'I've got friends in Kentish Town I usually stay with.'

'Well, if you're stuck, you're welcome to stop over at my place. I've got plenty of room and it's good to have company.'

'Thanks,' Lindsay said shyly. 'I might take you up on that.' There was an awkward pause. 'Well. Goodnight, Cordelia.'

'Goodnight. Sleep well.'

In the morning, Lindsay again breakfasted with Pamela Overton. She was nervous about the encounter, having risen early and made a trip into Buxton in Paddy's Land Rover to pick up a full set of the morning papers. Most of the tabloids, being a little short on alternative tales of shocking horror, had gone to town on Death at Derbyshire House. But Lindsay was put at her ease at once by Pamela Overton's praise for her efficient and unobtrusive work.

'I can't pretend that I particularly enjoyed the sensational aspect given to the story by most of the newspapers,' she remarked, 'but I do realise how much more difficult things would have been for us if we had had to deal with a whole battery of reporters. As it is, we have managed to keep them all out of the school, thanks to the joint efforts of yourself and the police, and have retained some measure of control over the stories that have appeared. I am only sorry that you can't stay longer to defend us, but Miss Callaghan has explained the position to me, and I do realise that you have commitments you must stick to. I want to say again how grateful we are, and if ever I can be of any help to you, don't hesitate to let me know.'

Lindsay went on to ask about the future of the school and the playing fields fund. The head-mistress looked troubled for the first time since Saturday's horrors.

'I am very much afraid that we'll have to give up the idea of saving the playing fields – and concentrate instead on saving the school. Already, seventeen girls are being withdrawn, and I fully expect more to follow. One can scarcely blame the parents. I hope the police will deal swiftly with this business so we can reassure parents that their girls are in safe hands. I care about this school, Miss Gordon. I very much hope that we shall not be destroyed by what has happened.'

Lindsay felt the strength of the other woman's determination, and it stayed at the back of her mind as more than just an angle for the news story of the day while she went for a walk on the ridge that Monday morning. She looked down on the privileged panorama of Derbyshire House Girls' School and resented the fact that Pamela Overton had infected her with her determination. She knew that whether she liked it or not, she, too, was in some degree involved with the school. She realised that in spite of herself she cared what happened to it.

8

Few assignments appealed less to Lindsay than royal visits. To be stuck with the rest of the pack, trailing behind some lesser scion of a monarchy she despised, festooned with badges of different colours to tell the security guards where one could and couldn't go, was not her idea of a good day's work. And as a common freelance she could not even complain as bitterly as the rest of the press were doing, for she was glad of a day's work, tedious though it might be. And on that Tuesday, tedious it certainly was, particularly after the excitements of her weekend in Derbyshire. A children's hospital, an art exhibition and a new youth club on a housing estate had all been superficially visited and the correct rituals observed. The photographers had taken their pictures, the reporters had scrambled their words together, everyone had kept in their rightful places. So, as she stood watching the royal jet take off through the rain in the late afternoon, Lindsay felt an enormous sense of relief. Another day, another dollar.

She said goodbye to her photographer and found a phone. It was after five by the time she had finished dictating copy, but she was nevertheless surprised when the newsdesk told her not to bother coming into the office for the last couple of hours of her shift and to call it a day. 'See you tomorrow, then', she said, quickly putting down the phone before they could change their minds. There was a spring in her step as she walked over to the car park and climbed into her MG. Being in love made a difference, she thought wryly. Even with a possible murderer.

Twenty minutes later she was unlocking the front door of her top-floor tenement flat. She sighed with pleasure as she closed the door behind her. There was something on the answering machine, she noticed, but she ignored it, went through to the living-room and poured herself a generous whisky. She took her glass over to the window, sat down and lit a cigarette as she gazed over the trees to the distant university tower which stabbed the skyline to her left. She always relished returning to her eyrie, and loved the view that had nothing to do with the Glasgow of popular mythology; that hard, mean city composed of razor gangs and high-rise slums was not the city that most Glaswegians recognised as their home. Sure, there were bits of the city that were barely civilised. But for most people Glasgow now was a good place to live, a place with its own humour, its own pride.

After a while, she got to her feet with a sigh and went back through to the hall to listen to her messages. She switched the machine to play-back and rewound the tape. The voices came through. 'This is Bill Grenville at the *Sunday Tribune*. Can you do the eleven o'clock shift for me on Saturday? Ring and let me know as soon as possible.' Bleep. 'Lindsay, Mary here. Fancy a pint tonight to get the royal dust out of your throat? I'll be in the bar about nine.' Bleep. 'This is Cordelia Brown. I'm catching the six o'clock shuttle. Meet me at Glasgow Airport about quarter to seven. If you're not there, I'll wait in the bar.'

'Hellfire!' Lindsay exclaimed. 'It's five past six now. What the bloody hell is she up to?' There was no time to shower, but it took only five minutes to change from her working uniform of skirt, shirt and jacket into a pair of jeans, a thick cotton shirt and a clean sweatshirt, and to give her face a quick scrub. Then she was running down the three flights of stairs, shrugging into a sheepskin jacket and into her car again. She had deliberately not allowed herself to wonder what was bringing Cordelia to Glasgow for fear that hope would betray her. To keep her mind off the subject, she turned the car radio on to hear the tail-end of the news. She drove fast down the expressway and over the Kingston Bridge, trying to convince herself that the day's financial report was truly fascinating. Then, in the middle of the news headlines, she had her second shock of the hour, a shock so acute it caused her to take her foot clean off the accelerator momentarily, to the consternation of the driver behind her, who flashed his lights as he swerved convulsively into the outside lane.

Lindsay could hardly believe that she had heard correctly. But the newsreader's words were branded on her brain: 'Police investigating the brutal murder of cellist Lorna Smith-Couper at a girls' boarding school at the weekend have today made an arrest. Patricia Gregory Callaghan, aged 32, a housemistress at the school, has been charged with murder and will appear before High Peak magistrates tomorrow morning.' Now she understood why Cordelia had jumped on the first plane to Glasgow. Lindsay threw the car round the bend in the airport approach road and parked illegally outside the main entrance, grateful for the royal visit sticker which still adorned her windscreen.

The arrival of Cordelia's flight was being announced as she ran up the escalator. She resisted the temptation to slip into the bar for a quick drink and headed for the Domestic Arrivals gate. She could see the first passengers in the distance as they walked up the long approach to the main concourse. They were only about twenty yards away when she spotted Cordelia. Then Cordelia was through the gate; without pause for thought, the two fell into each other's arms and held on tight.

'You've heard, then?' asked Cordelia.

'Yes. Only just now, on the radio in the car.'

'I thought you would have heard at work.'

'No, I've been out on the road all day. Look, we can't talk here. Let's go back to my flat.'

Lindsay picked up the leather holdall which Cordelia had dropped when they met and led the way back to the car. Cordelia was silent till they were roaring back down the motorway. Then she said, 'I'm not just here off my own bat. I did want to come up to see you because I know you love Paddy as much as I do, but I wouldn't have had the nerve to do it without being prodded. Pamela Overton rang me not long after the police took Paddy away. She wanted to enlist your help, and mine, in trying to find out what really happened. Can you believe it? She put it perfectly, though – just enough flattery to pull it off. "With Miss Gordon's talent for investigative journalism and your novelist's understanding of human psychology, you might be able to ensure there is no miscarriage of justice." You see, she knows Paddy couldn't have done it.'

'She's got a way of making people do things, hasn't she? I can't imagine why she thinks we'll be able to succeed where the police have made an absolute cock-up,' said Lindsay. She was focusing on the road ahead and talking about Pamela Overton, but her thoughts were on

Cordelia and the nagging fear at the back of her mind.

'I suppose she thinks that our personal interest in Paddy will make us that bit sharper,' Cordelia replied. There was silence as they swung off the motorway on to the Dumbarton road. Lindsay pulled up alongside an Indian grocer's. The street was as busy as midday, with people shopping, gossiping and hurrying by to keep out the cold of the raw autumn weather.

'Won't be a tick,' she promised, hurrying into the shop. She returned a few minutes later, clutching a cooked chicken, some onions, mushrooms and natural yoghurt. 'Dinner,' she muttered as she drove off again.

Lindsay pulled up outside her flat. 'But this is beautiful,' Cordelia exclaimed. 'I didn't know Glasgow was like this!' She gestured in the sodium-lit darkness at the crescent of trees outside Lindsay's door, at the Botanic Gardens and the River Kelvin beyond, at the newly sandblasted yellow sandstone tenements elegant under their dramatic lighting.

'Most people don't,' Lindsay replied defensively as she led the way upstairs. 'We've also got eighteen parks, some of the finest art collections in the world, terrific architecture and Tennents lager. It's not all high-rise flats, gap sites and vandals. But don't get me started on my hobby horse. Come on in and have a drink and something to eat.'

Lindsay lit the gas fire in the living-room and poured them both a drink. She said, 'Now, come through to the kitchen with me while I get some dinner together and tell me exactly what you know.'

As Lindsay put together a quick chicken curry, Cordelia spoke, pacing up and down the kitchen floor. 'The first I knew about it was when the phone rang this afternoon. It was Paddy. She used her one permitted phone call to ring me because she knows I have a good solicitor and she wanted either her or someone local recommended by her. She wasn't able to tell me much except that she'd been arrested and charged, and that somehow the police had found out she had some sort of motive.

'So I called my solicitor who put me on to a firm in Manchester who got someone out there right away. It's a very bright-sounding young woman called Gillian Markham who specialises in criminal work. I'd just got all that organised, plus phoning Paddy's parents to break the bad news, when Pamela Overton rang.

'She told me they'd had Paddy in for questioning for most of last night. Obviously, she doesn't know all the details of why they've arrested Paddy, but she did tell me this much. You see, no one saw or heard anything of Lorna after Paddy had left her. And now they've got a couple of other bits of evidence which, as far as they're concerned, tie the murder to Paddy. They have statements from several people, saying Paddy was hanging around in the music department for ages for no apparent reason. And the toggle on the garrotte comes from Paddy's own duffel coat. It normally hangs in the cloakroom just outside her rooms.'

'How can they be sure?'

'It's got special horn toggles, not ordinary wooden ones.'

'Oh God, they've tied her up well and truly, haven't they? It's all circumstantial and I doubt if they'd get a conviction before a jury if that's all they've got. But it hangs together, especially since, from what you said about motive, they obviously know all about the drugs business,' said Lindsay, slicing onions savagely.

'What drugs business?' Cordelia interrupted, bewildered.

'Paddy's supposed motive. I thought from what you said that you knew all about it,' Lindsay replied, and proceeded to tell Cordelia the depressing tale. As she led the way back to the living room, she added, 'So what are we going to do? How do we go about making this mess any less chaotic?'

They sat down. Cordelia stretched out on the faded chintz sofa and looked appraisingly round her at the spacious, high-ceilinged room. Lindsay had painted the walls chocolate brown, with cream woodwork, picture rail and ceiling. The room was big enough, with its huge bay window, to stand it. On the walls were Lindsay's black and white photographs of buildings and street scenes in Edinburgh, Oxford, Glasgow and London. Book cases stretched the length of one wall; along another was a massive carved oak sideboard which Lindsay had inherited when she bought the flat and which she feared she would have to leave behind if she ever left as it was so enormous. There was a stereo which Lindsay had built into a series of cupboards under the bay window, with shelves for records and cassettes alongside. She said, 'I like this room. But it seems very heartless of me to be relaxing here while Paddy languishes in some spartan bloody cell. How could they be so stupid? Any fool can see that Paddy couldn't hurt a fly. She might demolish people verbally, but violence is something she'd simply find beneath that dignity of hers. Not her style at all.'

'So what are we going to do about it?'

'Will you come back to Derbyshire with me? When we were talking on Sunday night, you seemed to have one or two ideas about other people with motives. We can see Paddy and find out if there's anything she can tell us. If we can get people to talk to us, maybe we can find out things the police have missed. I know it all sounds a bit *School Friend* and *Girl's Crystal* stuff, but perhaps we can just pull something off. After all, we're starting from a different premise. We know Paddy didn't do it.'

Lindsay thought for a moment. 'I can't go

anywhere till tomorrow night. I've got to work tomorrow. I can cancel Thursday and Friday, but I can't afford to let the *Clarion* down tomorrow. We could go down then.'

'Fine. A few hours can't make that much difference. Besides, I've no idea how to go about this. What should our plan of campaign be?'

Lindsay shrugged. 'I've no experience of these things. Usually on investigative stories, you have a source who tells you where to look for your information. Or at least you have an idea where to find some background. This is a very different set-up. It always seems so easy for the Hercule Poirots and Lord Peter Wimseys of this world. Everyone talks their head off to them. But why should anyone want to talk to us?'

'Because people love being interviewed. It makes them feel important, and besides, no one who knows Paddy would want her to go to prison.'

'No one except the murderer. And I hope whoever it is can sleep easy tonight. Because he or she won't have many easy nights once I get after them, that's for sure.'

9

An hour later, after food, more whisky and wrangling, they had produced a sheet of A4 paper covered in the following:

1. James Cartwright. Motive: wants the playing fields to turn into expensive development. Opportunity: poor – not at concert. Where was he? Access to weapon: presumably knew Longnor House since daughter is there. Anyone could get hold of a cello string. Find out about financial position.
2. Margaret Macdonald. Motive: unknown but seen in emotionally charged discussion with Lorna on Saturday morning. Opportunity: excellent. In all the bustle, could easily have slipped into the room after Paddy left. Access to keys and weapon: good – even though she lives in a different house; any member of staff could presumably wander in and out of Longnor without raising any suspicion.

3. Caroline Barrington. Motive: not clear, but makes no secret of her hatred for Lorna. Opportunity: took a long time getting programmes from music storeroom, only yards from murder room. Access to weapon: lives in Longnor, probably knew music-room stock, and likely to know where keys are kept.
4. Sarah Cartwright. Motive: love of father, deserted by friends over playing fields. Opportunity: unknown. Supposedly asleep in Longnor. Access to weapon: lives in Longnor. No known connection with music rooms.
5. Cordelia Brown. Motive: to avoid unsavoury and costly libel action. Opportunity: reasonable. She was away from her seat for a significantly long period around the crucial time. Hard to believe she could have done it without being spotted. Access to weapon: spent the night in Longnor and knew her way round the music rooms. Would have had difficulty concealing weapon as she was wearing close-fitting dress with no bag. If her, action must have been premeditated – weapon must have been secreted in music room earlier.
6. Paddy Callaghan. Motive: to avoid exposure of drug dealing in the past. Opportunity: best by far. Was in the music room alone with Lorna. Last person known to have seen her alive and speak with her. Access to weapon: excellent.
7. Who was the man quarrelling with Lorna?

'Of course,' said Lindsay, 'I only include you and Paddy for the sake of seeming objective.'

Cordelia smiled wanly. 'Thanks for your confidence. Don't think I don't feel the cold wind at my neck. If Paddy weren't such a convenient choice, they'd be looking very hard at me. So are you suggesting that these are the people we should concentrate on?'

'They're our only starters so far. But enough of this, we're going round in circles. We can't actually get any further till we've spoken to the people concerned. And one thing I've learned from newspapers is that when you can't get any further, you go for a drink. We could nip down to my local and have one or two before closing time. It's only five minutes' walk. There's usually a couple of my mates in there. Fancy doing that?'

Cordelia looked doubtful. 'I'd be just as happy staying here with you. I'm not one for pubbing it, normally. But if you really want to . . .'

Lindsay looked at her suspiciously. 'You're doing the "English fear of the Scots drinking" number, aren't you? What you're really saying is that if this was some bijou wine bar with a rather nice house Muscadet, that would be okay, but some wild Glasgow spit and sawdust bar is really not what you have in mind – am I right?' She grinned to take the sting out of her mockery.

Cordelia had the grace to look sheepish. 'All right, all right. I'll come to the pub. But I'm warning you now, the first drunk that accosts me with, "See you, Jimmy" and I'm off.'

When they walked into the Earl of Moray Tavern, Cordelia felt all her worst fears had been realised. The floor was bare vinyl, the furnishings in the vast barn of a room were rickety in the extreme and had clearly never been much better. There was not another woman in sight, apart from the calendar girl on the wall. But Lindsay walked confidently through the bar, greeting several of the men at the counter, leaving Cordelia with no option but to follow. Let this be her baptism of fire, thought Lindsay grimly. At the far end of the bar, they went through a glass-panelled door into another world. The lounge bar was cosy, carpeted and comfortable. Lindsay piloted Cordelia to a table where a blonde woman in her early thirties was staring glumly at the last inch of a pint of lager. She looked up and smiled at Lindsay. 'I'd given up hope of seeing you tonight,' she greeted her. 'Everybody's either out of town or washing their hair or on the wagon.'

'Would I let you down?' Lindsay retorted.

'Not if there was drink involved. Who's your friend, then?'

Lindsay sat down and, hesitantly, Cordelia followed suit. 'This is Cordelia Brown. Cordelia, this is Mary Hutcheson, the best careers officer in Glasgow, an occupation rather like being lead trombone in the dance band of the Titanic.'

Mary smiled. 'Hello. What brings you to

Glasgow? Surely not the company of a reprobate like Lindsay?'

Before Cordelia could reply, the barmaid, a gentle-faced woman in her forties, came across to them. 'What'll it be Lindsay? The usual?'

'Please, Chrissie. And one for Mary. What'll you have, Cordelia? Glass of the house Muscadet?'

Cordelia looked bewildered, not certain if she was the butt of Lindsay's humour. Seeing her confusion, Chrissie said, 'We've got some Liebfraumilch too, or a nice Italian red if you like that better.'

Lindsay, struggling to keep a straight face, said, 'I think she'd maybe just like a whisky and water, Chrissie, that's what we've been on. Okay, Cordelia?'

She nodded. As Chrissie returned to the bar, Mary astutely demanded, 'Lindsay, have you been winding this woman up?'

Lindsay smiled broadly. 'Afraid so. Sorry, Cordelia, I couldn't resist. I've seen so many people come up from London and patronise this city of mine so thoroughly you wouldn't believe. So now we tend to get our blows in first.'

Cordelia lit a cigarette and looked at Lindsay, considering her. 'All right, I probably would have got round to deserving it. But just remember – one day you'll be on my patch and these games can cut both ways.'

It was two hours and several drinks later when they staggered giggling up the three flights of stairs to Lindsay's flat. 'Sorry about the stairs,' she panted. 'Top flats are always the cheapest, you see.'

Lindsay shut the door behind them and fastened the bolts and chain, then turned to Cordelia with a diffidence far removed from the brash assertiveness she'd been displaying all evening and said, 'I don't know what you want to do about sleeping arrangements. There's a spare bed in my study if you want it. It's up to you. I . . . I don't want you to feel anything's expected . . .' She leaned against the door, shoulders slightly raised against the rebuff she felt sure was coming.

Cordelia stood, hands in pockets, looking far more casual than she felt. 'I'd rather like to sleep with you,' she said softly.

Lindsay's uncertainty made her scowl. 'You're sure? You don't just feel you've got to?'

Cordelia moved to her and hugged her close. 'Of course not. But if you're going to make an issue of it, I'll begin to think you don't want me.'

Lindsay held her tight and laughed nervously. 'Oh, I want you all right. Even if you do turn out to be the big bad murderer.'

She felt Cordelia stiffen. 'You still think I might have done it?' she demanded, pulling away.

Lindsay held on to her hand, refusing to allow her to escape, 'I hardly know you. The fact that I turn to jelly every time you come near me doesn't cancel out what I know with my head.

You were there. You had a motive. I don't believe you did it. But I'm still clear-headed enough about you to know that at least half the reason I don't believe it is because I don't want to believe it.'

'You really know how to kill desire stone dead, don't you?'

Lindsay shook her head. 'I don't want to do that. I've sat in that pub for the last two hours wanting you so badly it hurt,' she said passionately. 'The only reason I wanted to get out of the flat was that I didn't think I could sit all evening in a room alone with you and not make a bloody big fool of myself. Of course I want to go to bed with you. But it's going to mean something to me, you'd better be aware of that. And if it's going to mean something to me, then I'm not going to bed with you under false pretences. So let's spell it out. Yes, I still think you might have done it. With my head, I think that. But all my instincts tell me you're innocent.'

They stood bristling at each other. Cordelia shook her head, wonderingly. 'My God, you're honest. You don't spare anyone, do you?'

'If you start with lies, nothing you build can be honest. It's true in every area of your life. And I tell you now, honesty's the point at which my previous relationships have come unstuck. So if we're going to be lovers, let's do it with our cards on the table.'

'All right, honest journalist.' Cordelia moved

back towards Lindsay. 'Cards on the table. I didn't kill Lorna. I don't go to bed with people just for kicks. It'll mean something to me too. I'm not committed to anyone else. I have all my own teeth. I love Italy in the spring. I hate tinned soup, and I want you right now.' She kissed her suddenly and hard. Lindsay tasted cigarettes and whisky and smelled shampoo. And was lost.

Glued to each other, they performed a complicated sideways shuffle into Lindsay's bedroom. Because it was the first time, the clumsy fumbling to undress each other lost its ludicrous edge in mutual desire.

They tumbled on to the duvet, both bodies burning to the other's touch. Lips and hands explored new terrain, hungry to commit the maps of each other's bodies to memory. Later, as they lay exhausted among the ruins of the bedding, Cordelia ran her hand gently over the planes of Lindsay's body where she lay face down, head buried between her new lover's small, neat breasts. Lindsay propped herself up on one elbow and licked her dry lips. She smiled and said, 'I taste of you. You taste like the sea. That's what I miss, living in the city. I grew up by the sea. My father earned his living with what he could pull out of the sea. I've always associated the best times in my life with the smell and taste of the sea.'

Cordelia smiled. 'You saying I'm like a piece of seaweed?'

'Not exactly. Not everyone tastes like the sea.

Everyone tastes different. Everyone smells different.'

'Maybe you just bring out the best in me.' They chuckled softly, and because it was the first time, they didn't move apart, but simply fell asleep where they lay, somewhere in the middle of their conversation.

Lindsay was wakened at eight the next morning with a cup of coffee. Cordelia stood by the bed, looking better in Lindsay's dressing gown than its owner ever did, and said, 'I woke early. I always do. So I just made myself at home in a corner of your kitchen and did some work. I thought you might like a coffee.'

Lindsay could tell at once that everything was all right between them. There was no constraint, no trace of regret for either of them. It had been the right thing after all, thought Lindsay with relief. She pushed herself upright and took the coffee. Cordelia sat down on the bed as if it was something she had been doing all her life.

'Anything in the papers about Paddy?' asked Lindsay.

'Just the bare fact that she has been arrested and will appear in court this morning. I wish I could be there to give her some moral support. I wish she knew where I am and why.'

Lindsay smiled wryly. 'No doubt she won't be in the least surprised to hear how things are between us. I suppose I should be feeling guilty that we've been enjoying ourselves while she's locked up.'

'Paddy would be furious if she heard you say that,' said Cordelia with a grin, getting up. She took a track suit and training shoes out of her bag and put them on, adding, 'She knows that we'll be doing everything we can as quickly as possible, and if on the way we've found time for ourselves, well, that's nothing to be guilty about. Now, I'm going out for a run. What's the best way to go for a bit of scenery?' She jogged gently on the spot.

'Go down to the Botanic Gardens across the road, and down the steps to the river. There's a good long walkway by the banks of the Kelvin, whether you turn left or right.'

'Terrific. Who'd have thought it in Glasgow, she says, sounding like every patronising Southerner who ever arrived here. Now, what time do you finish work?'

'I'll be through about quarter to seven. Can you meet me at the office to save time? All the taxi drivers know it – just ask for the back door of the *Clarion* building. I'll check the office library today for anything about Lorna that might help us. What are your plans?'

Cordelia carried on jogging and said effortlessly, 'I'll make some phone calls to old girls, friends in the music business, anyone I can think of who might have some background gen. Have you some spare keys so I can get in and out – I presume you'll be gone by the time I get back?'

Lindsay yawned and stretched. 'Unfortunately,

yes. There are keys on the hook by the phone. I'll have to be off as soon as I've had a shower. Help yourself to food, drink, phone, whatever. There's eggs, cheese, bacon and beer in the fridge.'

Cordelia shuddered. 'What a disgustingly unhealthy diet. What about the fibre and vitamins?' She stopped running and leaned over Lindsay. 'Have a good day. I'll miss you.' They kissed fiercely, then Cordelia rose to go.

'By the way,' said Lindsay, 'I have a couple of pictures you might be interested in. The full frame of the snatch I sent out to the papers. I'll leave them on the kitchen table. See if they mean anything to you. Enjoy your run.'

Lindsay lay back and luxuriated in thoughts of Cordelia as she listened to the front door closing behind her. Then she shook herself and jumped out of bed for her shower.

Half an hour later she pulled into the *Daily Clarion*'s car park and headed straight for the office library, pausing only to drop by the newsdesk and tell them where she was going. Their file on Lorna was not extensive but fairly comprehensive. Critical notices and a couple of profiles fleshed out what Lindsay already knew. She had jotted down one or two names without much hope that they might be worth talking to before she came across two clippings that seemed to provide more fertile ground. One consisted of a couple of paragraphs from the *Daily Nation*'s Sam Pepys' Diary linking her name with Anthony

Barrington of the Barrington Beer brewing empire. The other was a few paragraphs long and reported that Lorna had been cited in the Barrington divorce a few months later. 'Caroline!' Lindsay breathed.

She went back to the counter and asked if they had anything on file on Anthony Barrington. The librarian vanished among the high metal banks of the computerised retrieval system that still hadn't managed to render obsolete the thick envelopes of yellowing cuttings. He returned with a thin file and a current edition of *Who's Who*. Lindsay started with the reference book:

Barrington, Anthony Giles, m.1960 Marjory Maurice, m.diss.1982. 1 son 2 daughters. Educ. Marlborough, New Coll., Oxford. Managing Director and Chief executive Barrington Beers. Publ: *Solo Climbs in the Pyrenees, The Long Way Home – an Eiger Route.* Interests: mountaineering, sailing. Clubs: Alpinists, White's. Address: Barrington House, Victoria Embankment, London.

'Interesting,' she mused. The file cuttings comprised the two she had already seen and a story about a climbing team he'd led reaching the Eiger summit by a new route. By no means a run of the mill businessman. Lindsay could see why Caroline might have good reason to hate Lorna if she had caused the break-up of the girl's family.

Lindsay had no time for further thought, because the tannoy announced at that moment that she was wanted at the newsdesk.

Duncan Morrison, the news editor of the *Clarion*, was the typical Glasgow newspaper hard man with the marshmallow centre. Although he spent a lot of time winding Lindsay up about her views, she knew that he thought she was good at her job. He didn't seem to mind that she argued with him in a way that none of his staff reporters would dare. As she approached the newsdesk, he threw a memo to her and said, 'Get busy on that. A real tear-jerker there. Just the job for you. What it needs is a woman's touch.'

Lindsay flicked quickly through the memo. It had come from a staff reporter who had spotted the story in a local paper and noted the bare bones on a memo to the newsdesk, suggesting it be followed up. The story was about a woman who had given birth to twins after surgeons had told her she would never have a child.

'Wait a minute, Duncan,' Lindsay moaned. 'I'm not here to do this sort of crappy feature. Woman's touch, my arse. What this needs is a dollop of heavy handed sentimentality and you bloody well know that's not my line.'

'Don't come the crap with me, lassie,' he returned. 'It's a real human interest story, that. I thought you'd be over the moon. The story of a woman who's fulfilled her destiny in spite of the setbacks. It's all there. Blocked fallopian tubes,

133

thirteen miscarriages, doctors say she'll die if she gives birth – Christ, this woman's a heroine!'

'This woman's a head-case, more like.'

'A head-case? Lindsay, you've got a heart like a stone. Can you not see how this woman's triumphed against all the odds?'

'By putting her life at risk? You'd think after thirteen miscarriages she'd have realised there's more to life than babies. There are plenty of kids up for adoption who need love and affection, you know.'

'It's a good story, Lindsay.' There was finality in Duncan's tone.

'Sure. Look, Duncan, I've been busy being a real reporter for the last three days, in case you hadn't noticed. You know, murder, heavy-duty stuff. I'm good at the serious stories. You should take advantage of that and use me on them. If you've got to run this sexist garbage, get someone who'll make a better job of it. What about James? He's a big softie.'

Duncan put his head in his hands in mock sorrow. 'Why do I employ the only reporter in Glasgow who thinks she knows better than me how to do my job? I give the girl the chance to be a superstar with her name in lights and what do I get? She wants me to go and set fire to an orphanage so she can be a real reporter. All right, Lindsay, you win. Away down to the Sheriff Court. There's a fatal accident inquiry on that guy that came off the crane at the shipyard. You cover that. After all, I don't really want a feature about how male doctors conspire with husbands to convince women that motherhood is their finest achievement. Sometimes I wonder why I give you shifts.'

They exchanged smiles and Lindsay set off. By five she was back in the office, writing her copy. Just before she left, at seven, Duncan called her over to the newsdesk. 'Right then, kid,' he said. 'Now, you've got the rest of this week off as far as I'm concerned. Not that I'm paying you, mind. But one favour deserves another. You come up with anything good on the murder and I want first bite of the cherry. A cracking good exclusive, right? I know we're not usually interested in anything highbrow and south of the border, but she was at least born in Scotland and the scandals of the upper classes always sell papers. Is that a deal?' He fixed his bloodshot blue eyes on her and scowled.

'It's a deal,' said Lindsay resignedly, 'I don't mind cutting my financial throat for you, Duncan; you're such a charming bastard to work for.'

'I'll make it worth your while, Lindsay. Don't worry about that. Now on your bike and get working. You've had a nice restful day to set yourself up. The next time I hear your voice, I want it to be saying, "It's a belter, Duncan."'

Lindsay chuckled to herself as she ran down the three flights of stairs to the back door. Cordelia was waiting for her there, and she again experienced that tight feeling in the chest on seeing her. She was glad to feel it, because it meant that this was more than just simple lust. Their eyes met and Lindsay could see that Cordelia was just as pleased to see her. They walked to the car arm in arm, Lindsay for once not giving a damn who might see and what they might think. It gave her immense satisfaction to stow Cordelia's bag in the boot beside her own.

'What kind of day have you had?' asked Cordelia.

'Busy,' Lindsay replied, revving up the powerful engine. 'I've only just had time to read the evening paper report of the remand hearing. Did you see it?'

'No, but I heard something on the radio at your place,' Cordelia answered. 'After that flat recital of Paddy's remand in custody without bail, I need something to lift my mood. Did you make any progress? For God's sake, say yes!'

'Well, I'm a bit further forward than I was this morning,' said Lindsay, pulling out on to the urban motorway that cuts a broad concrete swathe through the heart of Glasgow. Cordelia scribbled down notes of what Lindsay told her she'd learned.

'I have a lousy memory,' she explained. 'I bought a notebook this morning, just for this business, and copied out what we jotted down last night. And now, do you want to know what I unearthed?' Cordelia continued without waiting for Lindsay's nod. 'I picked up a fair bit of gossip, most of it general rather than specific to Lorna's death. The more we discover, the less I like her. There was one little gem I picked up, however.

'A lesbian friend of mine, Fran, plays the violin for the Manchester Philharmonic. She told me Lorna once said something to her that might just be relevant. She says she particularly remembered it because, for once, Lorna wasn't trying to score points or stage a put-down but was actually sounding human. It was along the lines of, "I tried it your way once and I must say I found it all indescribably sordid. But then I was still at school and didn't know any better. Though the other person involved certainly should have known better." That's all. Fran tried to get more out of her, but she clammed up. As if she regretted saying what she had and was determined to say no more. But I thought . . .'

'That a teacher might just fit the frame?' asked Lindsay. Cordelia nodded. 'And the strong possibility for that would be Margaret Macdonald, wouldn't it? It would certainly explain that scene between them in the garden on Saturday morning.' Lindsay went on. 'They presumably had a lot of close contact, given Lorna's talent. I don't know who else is still at the school who was teaching when Lorna was a pupil, but her music teacher's got to have been close to her. We'll have to see what Margaret Macdonald has to say about this. I hope to goodness we can rule that piece of information out as irrelevant. Now, did your researches produce any other results?'

'Lorna's current lover. He's a television producer for Capital TV, Andrew Christie. But they've only been together for a couple of months, so I don't know how much use he'd be to us. Still, I think we ought to see him anyway. If he can fit us in tomorrow night, we can shoot up to London and stay over at my place.'

Lindsay agreed to this, and they both fell silent. As the car sped on through the night to Derbyshire, Lindsay put a cassette of *Cosi fan tutte* on the stereo and Cordelia sank back in the seat. It was shortly after eleven when they pulled into the forecourt of a small hotel where Cordelia had booked them a room. As they collected their bags, Cordelia said, 'I thought it might be better for everyone if we didn't actually stay at the school. Pamela Overton is insisting on paying our bill, much to my humiliation, but who can argue with a woman like that? We can phone her from here and tell her we've arrived and that everything is under control.'

'You really think you can make her believe that?' said Lindsay with a grin. 'Tell her we'll be up in the morning. I want to see the music room again. I didn't really take it in on Saturday night. Lorna's body distracted me.'

They took their luggage up to a large, rather spartan room at the top of the three-storey Victorian building, then went out in search of food. Eventually they found a fish and chip shop on the market place that was still open and returned to the car with fish and chips, Cordelia muttering all the while about cholesterol and calories. By midnight, they were in bed together, staving off their misgivings about what lay ahead.

10

Lindsay woke on Thursday morning to the sound of Cordelia pulling the curtains open. 'Look at this view!' she exclaimed. All Lindsay could see was a square of grey sky.

'Do I have to?' she groaned crossly. 'What time is it?'

'Half-past seven. I'm going for a run.' Already she was dressed in the familiar training shoes and track suit. It occurred to Lindsay in her jaundiced frame of mind that Cordelia was certainly fit enough to have sprinted to the music department, garrotted Lorna and sprinted back again without even being out of breath, Cordelia added, 'I'll be about half an hour. You can have a lie-in if you want.'

Lindsay groaned again. 'Some lie-in! I may as well get up. I'm awake now. I'll take a walk and see if I can pick up the papers.'

'See you later.' And she was off, running down the wide staircase.

Lindsay struggled out of bed, wondering if she could stand the pace and promising herself once again that the fitness programme should start soon. She walked over to the window to see the view and was impressed in spite of her drowsiness. The room looked out over a couple of football pitches to a broad sweep of mature woodland, and beyond that to distant hills folding into each other. Even in the grey morning light it was spectacular. She dressed hurriedly and went off in search of a newsagent, planning the interview with Margaret Macdonald as she walked.

It was shortly after nine when they arrived at Derbyshire House, and they went straight to Pamela Overton's study. The headmistress was dictating letters to her secretary but as soon as she saw them, she stopped and dismissed her. In the four days since Lorna Smith-Couper had died, Pamela Overton had aged visibly. Her face was grey and pale, and there were dark circles beneath her eyes. But her manner was as decisive as ever.

She greeted them in her usual formal manner, and faced them across her desk. 'No one here can believe in Miss Callaghan's guilt. Her arrest is frankly incredible. And it hasn't stopped the rot, I'm afraid. Already we have lost twenty-one girls and I feel sure others will follow.' She sighed deeply. 'But I should not burden you with my problems. That will get us nowhere. How can I help you?'

Lindsay spoke first. 'I think Cordelia mentioned that we would like to see the room where it happened. I want to get the scene completely clear in my mind, and it might suggest some possibilities. I take it the police have finished with it now?'

'There will be no problem there,' said Miss Overton. 'Their forensic people finished their work there on Monday. The room has, of course, been cleaned and put in order now that they have done with it, but we are not yet using it as a classroom. It's been locked up to avoid any ghoulishness, but I have the key here. You also want to question some people, don't you?'

'Yes, we do,' Cordelia replied. 'But we'd like to keep it on an informal basis as far as possible, especially where the girls are concerned. It's mainly a matter of details at the moment. We'd also like to talk to Miss Macdonald, since no one knows the business of the music department better than her. Can you tell us when she's free today? Also, we'd like a letter from you that we can use as an introduction to people outside the school, saying that we're inquiring into matters on your behalf and asking for co-operation. And finally . . . we'd like to use Paddy Callaghan's rooms as our base within the school.'

Pamela Overton moved over to the wall where the timetables were displayed. She studied them for a moment, then told them Margaret Macdonald had one free period later in the morning and another in the afternoon. 'If she's not in her department, try her rooms in Grin Low House,' she explained. She returned to her desk, took a sheet of headed notepaper from a drawer and wrote a few lines. She handed it to Cordelia, who read,

> To whom it may concern; Cordelia Brown and Lindsay Gordon are making inquiries on my behalf regarding the death of Lorna Smith-Couper. I would be grateful if you would give them the fullest co-operation, Yours faithfully, Pamela Overton.

Then Miss Overton gave Lindsay a handful of keys taken from another drawer. 'The single key is for the music room, the bunch is Miss Callaghan's.'

Cordelia nodded. 'Thank you.'

'One more thing,' Lindsay chipped in. 'What can you tell us about James Cartwright? This isn't a large community; you must know a fair bit about him. We have virtually no background, I'm afraid,' she apologised.

The headmistress thought for a moment, a flicker of distaste appearing momentarily in her eyes. Finally, she said, 'He is a very successful builder. He started off in a small way, as a one-man business working locally. He did general work, but began to specialise in buying old properties, doing them up and converting them into flats and selling them at a handsome profit. In the property boom of the seventies, he made some very shrewd deals and amassed a considerable amount of money. He expanded to employ a fairly large workforce and now takes on work throughout the Peak area. He is generally thought of as having done very well.

'He still keeps a close contact with the day-to-day running of the business – it's not unusual to see him up some scaffolding with a hard hat and a bricklayer's trowel. He is well liked locally, though some find him ostentatious. However, I must say there have been fewer signs of that lately. His wife left him and Sarah about nine years ago. I believe she left him for an American civil engineer, though I know little about the circumstances. Mr Cartwright has done his best to give Sarah a decent life – and not simply by spending money. He tries to spend time with her, though the pressures of his business don't allow him much free time. She in her turn worships him. He is ruthless, but not, I think, insensitive. Will that do?'

Lindsay smiled and said, 'Admirably. Thank you. We won't take up any more of your time now.'

As they moved towards the door, Miss Overton spoke again. 'I will be here at all times to answer any questions. I know you may well be reluctant to discuss your progress with me, but I ask that if you think you have reached a solution you tell me before you communicate with the police.' It was a command rather than a request.

'Of course, if that is possible,' said Cordelia. Then they managed to leave. They walked down the corridor to the back stairs, Cordelia muttering, 'She terrifies me. If I didn't have the evidence of my own eyes that she didn't budge from the hall, I'd swear she was the only person cool enough to get away with murder under everyone's nose.'

Lindsay grinned, then said thoughtfully, 'Yet whoever it was must have done just that. There were so many people flitting around it must have been an extremely dodgy exercise. It's hard to believe anyone could have got away with it completely unseen. Oh, and by the way, you've just fallen into the oldest trap. You said you have the evidence of your eyes that she didn't budge from the hall. But don't forget that you were out of the hall yourself during the crucial period. All you can say is that she was there when you left and there when you returned. For all you know, she could have slipped out, just like you did.'

'Except that, by my own admission of where I was, we would have bumped smack into each other on the doorstep.'

'Unless one of you was actually in there committing murder.' Lindsay stopped on the stairs. 'Now what am I saying? Oh God, I'm sorry, Cordelia. It's just my love of perversity . . . Look,

I know it wasn't you. And I know it wasn't Pamela Overton, because I *do* have the evidence of my own eyes to go on there. Forgive my crassness.'

Cordelia stood a couple of steps above her, smiling 'Nothing to forgive. I don't expect two nights of passion to convince you that I'm above suspicion.'

They were suddenly grinning at each other like schoolkids who have just discovered that they are best friends. Together they ran up the few remaining stairs. Only the sight of the music room door sobered them into rather frightened adults again. Cordelia put the key in the lock, then paused. 'Ready?'

Lindsay nodded. Cordelia turned the key and opened the door. It swung open silently to reveal a completely ordinary music classroom. It smelled faintly of a mixture of polish, chalk and resin. In one corner was a neat stack of music stands. On open shelves along one wall were piles of sheet music. Glass-fronted cupboards beneath the shelves revealed boxes of strings, reeds, percussion instruments and piles of blank manuscript paper. There were about twenty chairs scattered around. At the far end of the room was a baby grand piano, the teacher's desk on a raised dais in front of the blackboard, and a walk-in cupboard whose open door revealed neatly ordered string instruments in racks; violins, violas, cellos, even a mandolin and two guitars.

The two women walked in and closed the door behind them. Cordelia wandered round slowly, uncertain of what she was looking for. After a moment, she joined Lindsay who was examining the windows. Below was a drop of about eighteen feet to the ground. There was no down-pipe within ten feet. The three windows were ordinary casements with pivotting catches. Lindsay took a Swiss Army knife from her handbag and selected the thinnest blade. She fiddled idly with one of the catches. It rose smoothly and fell back, allowing the window to swing open.

'Perfectly smooth. Not in the least stiff,' she remarked. 'Pity the murderer couldn't have got in that way. And a ladder's out of the question. It would have to be smack bang in the middle of the drive, which would have been more than slightly noticeable.' She turned back to the room. 'Lorna was sitting over there in front of the dais, facing the door, back to the windows. There was a music stand in front of her, overturned. Sheet music all over the floor. Her cello under her. Not a pretty sight.' She pushed the window shut smartly and the latch promptly fell back into place. 'Have you seen enough? It rather gives me the creeps, being here. I can still remember all too vividly how Lorna looked.'

Cordelia gave her hand a squeeze and nodded. 'Yes, I've seen quite enough. Let's go over to Paddy's room. We've got nearly an hour to kill before we can see Margaret Macdonald and we can use the phone in Paddy's room to see if we can set up a meeting with Andrew Christie.'

Paddy's sitting-room looked as if she had only slipped out to take a class. The Sunday papers were still strewn around. On the table was a half-drunk cup of coffee, and there was still a record sitting on the silent turntable. Lindsay went through to the kitchen to brew up while Cordelia struggled with the television company switchboard.

She was replacing the receiver and sighing with relief when Lindsay returned with the coffee. 'Will he see us, then?' Cordelia nodded. 'You smooth-talking bastard! I could use your gifts of persuasion on the doorstep next time I've got a sticky one,' Lindsay enthused. 'What time, and where?'

'It was touch and go, but he'll see us at eight at his place in Camden Town. For God's sake don't tell him you're a journalist! He was very twitchy about it all, and no wonder. He's had the police and half your lot in the last few days, and as far as he's concerned, it all ended with the arrest.'

'It might feel like that for him, but I'm bloody sure that's not how it feels for Paddy. I think we should try to go and see her this afternoon. Did the solicitor tell you what the score is on visiting arrangements?'

Cordelia shook her head. 'Why don't you give her a call? I don't suppose we'll be able to visit, anyway – I mean, don't you have to have a visiting order or something?'

Lindsay shook her head. 'Not when the prisoner is on remand. Paddy's legally entitled to a fifteen-minute daily visit from family or friends. Plus unlimited time with her legal advisor. Give me the number for this solicitor.'

She was quickly connected with Gillian Markham, who sounded brisk and competent. As they talked, Lindsay's face grew more puzzled and angry. She finally put the phone down and said, 'Well, there's no problem with the visit. We can see Paddy if we get there between three and half-past. Gillian thinks it will take us about an hour to drive to the remand centre. We can take food and cigarettes with us, and Paddy would apparently like some fresh clothes since she's opted to wear her own gear rather than prison uniform. Does that still give us time to get to London, assuming we get away about four?'

'Given the way you drive, I don't anticipate any problem with that,' Cordelia replied tartly. 'But what's the matter? You look as if you've just been kicked in the teeth.'

'From what Gillian's just told me, I think it's Paddy who's been kicked in the teeth, not me.'

'Meaning?'

'Gillian's just had a tip from a contact inside the force about a new piece of circumstantial evidence against Paddy. Remember all that carry-on with Sarah Cartwright on Saturday morning? Well, guess where Paddy took her to cool down?'

Cordelia looked dismayed. 'If I said Music 2, would I be wrong?'

'You'd be spot on. As if that wasn't bad enough in itself, Sarah has given the police a statement saying that Paddy passed a remark along the lines that the room had been nicely spruced up for its VIP guest. Sarah also maintains that Paddy was wandering around idly opening cupboards and picking things up while they talked.'

'Oh God, no! Surely the girl must be lying?'

'I suggest we check that out with Paddy before we confront the girl with anything. If she's telling the truth, it wouldn't in itself be damning. Those seem to me to be perfectly normal things to do and say, taken by themselves. But coupled with the other bits and bobs the police have against Paddy, it can only be seen as more evidence weighing the scales against her. If Paddy denies that those events took place, we're in a very different ball game. We'll have to look at the reasons why the girl might be lying.'

'Surely she'd only tell that kind of lie against Paddy if she had something to hide,' Cordelia protested.

'Not necessarily. It could be she's lying to protect herself. It could also be that she's lying to protect her father because she knows he was involved. Or it could simply be that she's made up this story because she only fears her father may be involved and she's trying to divert police attention well away from him. Either way, we need to talk to Paddy about this. And quite honestly, with the interview we've got next, I'd rather put Sarah and her motives right to the back of my mind.'

They drank their coffee in a tense silence. Neither was looking forward to the forthcoming interview. Cordelia cleared away the cups, taking Paddy's with her to the kitchen, and called through, 'Have you got the photo?'

'Yes, in my handbag. I did a couple of seven by fives of the heads. Let's hope I don't have to use it as a shock tactic.'

Cordelia re-emerged. 'I'm beginning to wish we'd never taken this on. I like Margaret Macdonald, for God's sake. She taught me to like music, to listen properly to it.'

Lindsay got up and hugged her. 'Just think of Paddy,' she whispered. 'It may be unpleasant but you're doing it for all the right reasons.'

They walked through pale autumn sunlight to Grin Low House and mounted the stairs in silence. Margaret Macdonald's rooms were at the end of the first-floor corridor. Lindsay knocked on the door and was rewarded with, 'Come in.' They entered to find the teacher sitting at a desk correcting some music in manuscript. When she saw who it was, she seemed startled. It would have been easy to read guilt into her look. Neither Lindsay nor Cordelia set much store by her reaction, since they already knew she was hiding something.

'I was rather expecting you two,' she said. 'Miss Overton told me she'd asked you to help sort out this terrible business.' She stood up and gestured towards the three armchairs that were ranged round her gas fire. 'Let's be comfortable. Now, I suppose you want me to tell you about the concert and the music department, that sort of thing?'

Cordelia took this as a cue to begin gently probing. 'When you were backstage on Saturday night, did you see anyone at all going down the corridor towards Music 2?'

'I don't really remember. I was rushing round so much organising the choirs and the orchestra. But I would have thought nothing of it even if I had, because the music storeroom is there too, and that's where the programmes were being kept.'

'Did you go to your own room?'

'Several times, but I didn't stay there for any length of time, as I've already told the police. I didn't pay any attention to the keys, and I didn't see anyone else go in or out of my room.'

'How many people knew that Lorna was going to be in Music 2 before her performance?'

Margaret thought for a moment. 'It was no particular secret,' she replied. 'Most of the girls involved in the concert could have worked it out for themselves, since that room had been left free.

I think I mentioned in the staffroom that I'd had the fifth form clearing it up on Friday so that it would be tidy for Lorna. I wanted to make sure that everything was just right, so there could be no criticism from her of my preparations. So the answer to your question is that anyone could have known. There's no way of narrowing it down.'

'I suppose in theory you yourself could have taken the key, gone to Music 2, done what you had to do and put the key back in the wrong place – deliberately?' Cordelia inquired.

Margaret Macdonald's hands worked in her lap. There was fear inadequately hidden in her eyes and Lindsay noticed a trace of sweat on her upper lip. 'I suppose I could have. But I didn't. Look, Lorna was the most distinguished pupil I've ever taught; she was about to give a concert in aid of the school. Why should I have wanted to kill her? This is nonsense!'

There was a pause. Lindsay could sense that when it came to questioning her former teacher, Cordelia had no killer instinct. But she was loath to take the hard line of questioning herself. For once she felt unhappy at subjecting someone to her professional probing. She didn't want to strip this woman's defences down because she was sure she was a sister of sorts. She should be offering her support, not giving her a hard time. Then she thought about Paddy, 'I know you taught Lorna, and obviously she owed a lot to you,' she said decisively. 'Did you remain close?'

Margaret studied the carpet as if inspecting it for some clue as to how she should respond. She said quietly, 'Not since she left school. We exchanged Christmas cards, that was all. She had a very hectic life.'

'I'm surprised you didn't stay more closely in touch.'

Again there was quiet in the room. It wasn't easy for Lindsay to become the interrogatory machine, but she stifled her feelings and continued remorselessly. 'You went for a walk with her on the morning of the day she died, didn't you?' she demanded.

Swiftly, Margaret's head came up. There was no mistaking the fear now. 'No!' she replied sharply. 'No, I didn't go for a walk with her.'

'You were with her in the gardens on Saturday morning and you were arguing.'

'That's not true.'

Lindsay slipped the photograph from her handbag and offered it to the music mistress who glanced at it then rose to her feet and walked to her desk where she collapsed in her chair.

Lindsay spoke gently. 'I was up on the hillside taking some photographs. The red sweater you were wearing caught my eye. I haven't shown these to the police yet. There seemed to me to be little reason to do so. But now Paddy has been arrested, I think I might have to go to the police with them. Unless I am convinced that they have nothing to do with the murder and would therefore serve no purpose in helping Paddy.'

Margaret Macdonald looked Lindsay straight in the eye. Her fear had been replaced by resignation. She shrugged, then said bitterly, 'After all, why not? If anyone can understand it, maybe you two can. They say it takes one to know one.'

Lindsay kept her eyes on the teacher, but on the edge of her vision she was aware of Cordelia turning away, whether from sympathy or embarrassment she could not tell. Margaret sighed deeply. 'I've never told anyone this, and I hoped I would never have to.

'Fifteen years ago, Lorna was a seventeen year old with a blinding and brilliant gift. The cello was my own instrument, and though I could never play like she did, I'm a good teacher. I had experience and so much enthusiasm to pass on. She wanted to absorb all she could from me, and I was happy to show her every secret.

'We spent hours together, practising, listening to music, or just talking. I had always known I was different from most of my friends. I only ever felt emotionally attracted to my own sex. It's ironic really – everyone assumes that it was my love of music and teaching that made me choose this life. But for me it seemed the only option because it was a life I could lose myself in.

'I had never acted on my desires in any way before Lorna – it was a different world when I was young. It wouldn't have been possible to have fulfilled my dreams and still have done the things I wanted to in my career. It would have set me too far apart, and I'd never have got a teaching job. I was never attracted to the idea of living a secret life, I never had that kind of nerve.

'When Lorna came along, I was thirty-five. Suddenly I felt that my life was slipping past me without meaning. I needed love. Lorna was half my age, but she worshipped me for what I could give her.

'And I worshipped her talent. I knew I could never play like that, but to have Lorna to listen to was the next best thing. We were each obsessed by what the other could give.' Margaret paused. 'It only lasted a matter of a few months. Then Lorna left to go to the Royal College. And that was the end. The week after she left here, she wrote saying that she didn't want to see me again. She took everything she could then simply discarded me. As you can imagine, it has haunted me ever since. I've never dared to get close to a pupil again, for fear I would fall into the same trap. I got what I deserved. I betrayed the trust of my position and she betrayed my love.'

Cordelia rose and held her hands up to the fire. It was warm in the room, but she felt cold as ice. Neither she nor Lindsay felt capable of further questioning. But Margaret Macdonald continued unasked.

'I didn't see her in all those years, apart from going to the occasional concert where she was playing. I never spoke to her. We did exchange Christmas cards and I bought all her records, but that was all. When Pamela Overton told me she had persuaded her to come here, I didn't know what to do or how to act. On Friday, I had no chance to be alone with her. But on Saturday, I saw her going for a walk and followed. God help me, I could still see in her the girl I had loved. I caught up with her when we were out of sight of the house. I didn't really know what I was going to say, but I didn't get much chance to speak.' She let her head drop into her hands but kept talking in a low monotone.

'She taunted me for being pathetic and afraid of the consequences of my actions. She said she supposed I'd come to plead and beg for her silence; she said. "If you'd said nothing, of course I would have kept quiet. But this sneaking out behind me, this cringing and crawling makes me despise you. It devalues a pretty worthless past. So why should I protect you?" I said that wasn't what I meant to do at all, but that yes, she could damage my present and future with a few words. Not to mention the damage she would do to both our memories of the past. She laughed in my face, then walked off. It was all disgustingly melodramatic. I found it sickening.

'You may think this gives me a reason for wanting her dead. But she was already dead to me. Her reaction that morning killed the last dreams I had about her. The school is a very important part of my life, and has been for many years. But not as important as my music. If I had been inclined to murder, I wouldn't have done it here, before the concert. I wanted to hear her play. I wanted to be sure that she could still play like an angel. And if she had told anyone of our past, well, so be it, I would have lost the school, but I could have made a new life for myself teaching privately. Lorna could only destroy a fragment of my life, I see that very clearly. I didn't kill her for that fragment. Besides, Paddy Callaghan is probably the closest friend I have. I couldn't sit back and watch her suffer if I had committed this crime. Whether you believe me or not, I didn't kill Lorna.'

'I believe you,' said Cordelia, turning back to the room, 'I don't think there's anything more we need to ask. I'm sorry we've caused you pain.'

'Thank you,' echoed Lindsay. 'You have helped us a great deal. I'm sorry I had to be so hard.'

The music mistress remained silent as they left. Then she subsided into heavy, silent sobbing.

Lindsay and Cordelia walked back over to Paddy's room without talking. Lindsay went straight to the drinks cupboard, unlocked it and poured two liberal whiskies. 'I'm glad I wasn't born twenty years earlier,' she said, furious. 'And I hope to God I never have to find the kind of courage she's needed all these years.'

'You did believe her, then?'

'My God, yes. I believed her all right. You don't lie like that. Not with so much obvious pain. She might well have felt like killing Lorna, but I don't believe she did it. She's had the guts to live like this for so long; she must have known inside herself that she could have dealt with any blow that bitch could hand out,' said Lindsay bitterly. 'She may not have chosen to deal with it, but she had the strength to. You know, suddenly, this has stopped being a game. I didn't really take it seriously till now.'

'I know what you mean,' said Cordelia, 'we've been fooling ourselves into thinking this would be some civilised exercise in detection like it is in the books, without understanding that there are real emotions involved. While the only thing we had to think about was Paddy, it wasn't difficult to imagine being detectives. The great righteous crusade. All that sort of rubbish. But I'm not at all certain that I can handle this kind of thing.'

Lindsay nodded. 'I know,' she said. 'But we're committed now. We can't back out. And if we don't do something for Paddy, who will? None of us can afford proper private detectives – and anyway, would we have any notion how to find a good one? We've still got the advantage of knowing Paddy and knowing something about all these people, especially Lorna, and I'm hopeful that Paddy can give us some ideas. We have to keep pressing on, no matter how much we hate it. Haven't we?'

For answer, Cordelia took out her notebook and started scribbling rapidly in it. 'You should be doing this,' she complained. 'You're the journalist; you should remember what people say. Who's next for the Lindsay Gordon Spanish Inquisition?'

In spite of herself, Lindsay smiled at the echo of Caroline's words on Saturday night. She said, 'James Cartwright. I feel like working off some of my spleen, and from the little I've heard of him, I reckon he's a prime candidate for that.'

'But we've really got nothing on him at all. What the hell are we going to ask him?' Cordelia demanded.

'We'll just have to try an elaborate con job, I suppose, and hope I can rattle him enough with my penetrating questions.'

'I'll leave it to you, then. After all, you've already displayed your professional interrogation skills today,' said Cordelia drily.

'I didn't get any pleasure from that success, if success you choose to call it,' said Lindsay. 'Usually when I monster people like that in the course of getting a story, I know they're villains. It's not too hard to get heavy and put on the pressure when you know your victim is no stranger to putting the screws on somebody else. There's no satisfaction in hammering somebody like Margaret Macdonald, believe me. At least Cartwright should be sufficiently tough for me not to have any qualms about turning nasty if I have to.'

'I feel sorry for the poor bloke,' Cordelia mocked. 'Almost as sorry as I feel for you, sweetheart. What a way to make a living!'

11

By any standards, James Cartwright's was an impressive house. Rather than choosing something he had built himself, he had opted to live in the dramatic flowering of another man's imagination. It was three storeys tall, built in extravagant Victorian Gothic in the local grey stone with twin turrets and superb views across open fields to the distant White Peak. In front, a Mercedes sports car and a Ford Sierra were parked. Even fortified by whisky and coffee, Lindsay felt daunted as she parked her car at the end of the semi-circular sweep of gravel. She switched off the engine and said, 'Suddenly I feel I'm driving a matchbox. Just look at that garden! He must employ a battalion of gardeners. Have you got the letter from God?'

'It's right here,' said Cordelia. 'Now, let me check . . . have I got the thumbscrews, or have you?'

Lindsay scowled. 'Very funny.'

'Only teasing,' Cordelia replied sweetly.

Lindsay opened the car door. 'Sometimes I wish I'd become a bloody fashion writer on a women's magazine,' she muttered.

They walked up the drive to the front door. Lindsay looked at Cordelia, pulled a face at her then pressed the doorbell. Its sharp peal was loud enough to make them both start. Cordelia stood almost to attention facing the door while Lindsay turned away, pulled up the collar of her leather jacket and tried to force a profoundly casual aspect on her appearance. As the door opened, she turned to face the young man who stood in the doorway. He was smartly dressed in a well-cut, pin-stripe suit and his hair was beautifully groomed. When he spoke it was with a strong Derbyshire accent.

'What can I do for you,' he demanded sharply.

Lindsay spoke. 'We'd like to see Mr James Cartwright.'

'Have you an appointment?'

'If we had, you'd be expecting us, wouldn't you?' she responded sweetly.

'I'm afraid Mr Cartwright is a very busy man. He doesn't see anyone without an appointment,' said the young man brusquely. 'Are you from the papers?'

'If you would take this letter to Mr Cartwright, perhaps he'll be able to fit us in,' Lindsay replied nonchalantly, handing over the envelope containing Pamela Overton's letter. 'We'll wait and see, shall we?'

163

The young man turned to enter and Lindsay nipped smartly into the porch behind him. Cordelia, surprised by this manoeuvre, took a moment to follow her. The inner door to the hallway was closed neatly in their faces by the young man, and Lindsay turned to Cordelia, saying, 'Easy when you know how, isn't it?'

Cordelia muttered, 'Brazen hussy!' They stood in an awkward silence till the young man reappeared a few moments later at the inner door. 'He can give you a quarter of an hour. He's got to leave after that for an important meeting in Matlock.'

'Talk about delusions of grandeur,' Lindsay muttered to Cordelia, who struggled to swallow a nervous giggle as their footsteps clattered on the polished parquet of the wide hall in the wake of the young man. Cordelia sized up the stained pine doors and skirting board, the Victorian-style wallpaper dotted with framed photographs of sailing ships and nineteenth-century harbours, and the stripped pine church pew and pine chests that were the only furniture in the hall. The cushion on the pew matched the wallpaper. 'Straight from the pages of a design catalogue,' she remarked. At the end of the hall, the young man waited by a door. As they reached him, he opened it and gestured them to enter.

The room was painted white. On the walls were two calendars and three year-planners. The floor was covered with carpet tiles and the furniture comprised equally functional office equipment. There were two metal desks, filing cabinets the length of one wall, a large computer terminal with printer attached and, in the bay window, a draughtsman's angled desk with a battery of spotlights above it.

At the larger of the two desks, a man was working. As her eyes swung round to him, Lindsay felt as though she'd been punched in the chest. She recognised the man she had last seen storming through the music department on the afternoon of the murder. She rapidly revised the outline of what she was going to ask him.

He had not looked up when they entered but continued to write notes on a large plan laid out on his desk top. It was Cordelia's first sight of Cartwright and she was impressed in spite of herself. He was in his middle forties, a big man, at least six feet tall. His torso looked solid without being flabby and his hands were the strong tools of a man used to strenuous physical work. His dark hair was thinning and greying at the temples, and his skin was weathered and lined. When he finally looked up his eyes were surprisingly dull and tired.

'Sit yourselves down, girls,' he said. Like his assistant, he had kept his local accent. 'Now you tell me just why I should extend you my fullest co-operation. Why should I care what happens to any of that lot up there, apart from my Sarah?'

There was silence for a moment, Cordelia flicked a glance at Lindsay, who calmly took out her cigarette pack and offered it to Cartwright. 'Smoke? No? Clever boy.' She passed one to Cordelia and lit both. Then she answered him. 'It strikes me that a businessman with your obvious acumen would not have kept his daughter on at Derbyshire House after the question of the playing fields came up unless there was some highly pressing reason. After all, it gave her an awkward conflict of loyalties, didn't it? I'd guess that you didn't remove her because the school has given her the security and friendship she never found anywhere else.'

Cartwright slammed his hands flat on the desk. 'You've got a hell of a nerve! My daughter was sent there for the best education, and she'll stay there till it's finished. Are you suggesting I don't treat her properly?'

Lindsay continued unflustered, 'Quite the opposite', she said calmly. 'I think you and Sarah are very close. I think you both care deeply about each other. But you're a very busy man. You must often be away from home, working late, whatever. Obviously, a growing daughter needs more than you can spare. If she's found something she needs at the school, it would be a very important reason for letting her stay there, in spite of the conflict of interests.'

'They must be better off up there than I thought if they can afford smart-arsed psychological private eyes to try and clear their homicidal staff,' sneered Cartwright, still angry but cooling fast.

'We're not private eyes, and we're not being paid,' Cordelia retorted, no longer able to hold back her irritation. 'We happen to be friends of Paddy Callaghan. And we're certain she didn't kill Lorna Smith-Couper. We intend to find out who did. Now, if you're prepared to help us, well and good. If not, also well and good. We'll simply have to get the answers we need by another route.'

Lindsay managed to hide her surprise at this display of iron in Cordelia's soul. Cartwright sat back in his chair, considered them both for a moment, then spoke slowly. 'All right,' he said. 'Bloody nosy women, that's what you are. I suppose you can ask me your damn questions. I don't promise to answer any of them, but I'll listen to what you have to say. Just remember one thing – I wasn't at that concert on Saturday night.'

'I didn't see you, certainly,' said Lindsay. 'But I imagine you know the school well enough both as a parent and as a builder to know how to find your way around without falling over the audience at a concert.'

'Point taken, young lady,' he replied. 'As it happens, I do know the school. I've done most of the building jobs there in the last fifteen years. Now, let's hear these questions.'

'I suppose the police have already asked you, so it shouldn't be a problem to remember where you were on Saturday night between, say, six and eight-thirty.'

'I was out walking on the moors late Saturday afternoon till about half-past six. I had a drink in a pub down near the Roaches, those rocks on the Leek road. The pub's called the Woolpack. Then I wandered over to the Stonemason's Arms near Wincle. I had a few pints there and something to eat. I left there about nine. You can check with the landlady; she'll probably remember – I'm a regular there.' He leaned forward again, looking smug. 'The police have already checked me out. Not that they were at all suspicious of me; they were just going through the motions. Roy Dart is a friend of mine. He told me it was just routine.'

'Did you see Sarah at all on Saturday?' asked Lindsay.

'No. Why should I have? I wasn't near the place all day.' He did not flinch at the lie. He kept his eyes fixed on Lindsay as she asked the next question.

'So you didn't know she had a set-to with her friends about your bid to get your hands on the playing fields?'

'No, I didn't. Not that it surprises me. Half those silly little girls at that school don't know what it means to live in the real world. They occupy some cloud-cuckoo land, where everything will be all right because someone will always make it all right for them. So, of course, they turn on my Sarah when the usual magic doesn't work.'

Cordelia leaned forward and asked, 'You're pretty sure about getting the land, aren't you?'

'I am now,' he answered readily. 'But don't go reading too much into that. I was anyway. This charade they're putting on about raising the cash is just that – a charade. It would never have happened, take my word for it.'

Lindsay gathered together her bag and fastened her jacket. 'Well,' she said, 'I think you've covered what we wanted to know, more or less. We won't keep you from Matlock any longer. Just one thing, though – you say you weren't near Derbyshire House on Saturday. Now that seems a little odd to me. Because I saw you there about five o'clock. Just when you were walking on the moors, according to what you've said.' She got to her feet, as did Cordelia, who felt a little bewildered. 'Funny that,' added Lindsay. 'You must have a double.'

They got as far as the door before he spoke. 'Wait a minute,' he said uncertainly.

Lindsay half turned towards him. 'Yes?'

'All right, dammit,' he said, 'all right. I did drop in at the school. I was looking for Sarah, if you must know. But I couldn't find her, so I just buzzed off again. I saw no point in mentioning it; it might have given the wrong impression.'

'It certainly gives me a strange impression, Mr Cartwright. And I'm sure your good friend Inspector Dart would think the same, especially if I told him that I'd also seen the person you were talking to – or should I say arguing with? And it wasn't your Sarah.'

If she had expected James Cartwright to collapse at her words, she was mistaken. His eyes suddenly came to life and there was venom in his voice. 'Don't you sodding well threaten me! I don't have to explain myself to two bloody girls. If you heard so much, what's the need for your bloody questions? Unless you heard nothing and you're trying to bluff me. Well, I've news for you. I always call bluffs.'

'Okay,' said Lindsay. 'Call mine, then. It won't take long to tell all this to Inspector Dart. It may not make him release Paddy Callaghan on the spot, but it will provoke some hard questions and give her solicitor enough fuel to make a pretty bonfire at the committal hearing, especially if she asks for the reporting restrictions to be lifted. What price your business then, Mr Cartwright?'

She had opened the door and had gone half-way down the hall with Cordelia at her side before Cartwright caught up with them. 'What did you hear?' he demanded.

Lindsay stopped. 'So you want to talk, then?' He nodded and they all walked back to his office. He threw himself petulantly into his chair. The women remained standing.

'What did you hear?' he repeated.

'Enough to know that you tried to bribe Lorna Smith-Couper into pulling out of the concert. You can't have been so sure about Derbyshire House failing to reach their target. I also heard Lorna sending you off with a flea in your ear, threatening to expose you. And I saw the expression on your face. Murderous, I'd call it. None of it very edifying, is it?'

'All right, so I did try to bribe her. But that's no crime, not compared with murder. And I didn't murder her. I've already cleared this up with the police. I was in one of those two pubs at the time. Look, I'll write their names down. You can check up.' He pulled a memo pad over, scribbled the names of the pubs with a thick, dark pencil and handed the paper over to Lindsay. 'There you are, take it. Murder's not my way, you know. I may have been underhand, but I'm not one of your bully boys that believes violence is the answer.'

'And you're sure you didn't see Sarah?'

'I didn't. I didn't go there to see her. I went to see Lorna Smith-Couper.'

'How did you know where to find her?' asked Cordelia.

'I rang her up before she came to the school and asked for an appointment because she refused to discuss business over the phone. She agreed, and rang me on Saturday morning to arrange a meeting in Music 2 at quarter to five. I knew exactly where that room was – in fact, when I was just a little two-man operation, I replaced all the windows on that floor. Like I said, I've done most of the building work there. The woman was there, sorting out some strings for her cello. I put my offer to her. She laughed in my face. When I left, she left too. I don't know where she went, but I went straight to my car and drove around for a while. When the pub opened, I went in for a drink. I didn't feel like going home to an empty house – I often don't – so I went to the Stonemason's. I wanted to put my thoughts about the matter out of my head for a while, so I had a meal and a few pints. That's that. There's no need to tell the police after all, now is there?'

For a shrewd businessman, he was a shade too eager, thought Lindsay. She shrugged. 'I make no promises,' she said. 'I don't see the need just at present. Thanks for your time, Mr Cartwright.' Again, she and Cordelia left the office. This time, they made it out of the front door and back to the car.

'Phew!' Cordelia sighed. 'So he's the man you saw arguing with Lorna. You sure as hell are good value for money. Nobody would guess you hadn't planned any of that. It must have been a hell of a shock when you recognised him. Do you normally eat villains for breakfast?'

'Come on, Cordelia. He told us hardly anything we didn't already know. He's only scared about more police inquiries and bad publicity. It's only a guess, but I think he might be in deep water financially. A lot of small and medium-sized builders are really strapped for cash now. And he didn't get that squash court contract. If that's the case, he would badly need the playing fields

172

project. He's a worried man, but I'm not sure that's because he's a murderer.'

'By the way,' said Cordelia, 'why were you so insistent about whether he'd seen Sarah?'

'Don't really know. It just seemed important. Journalist's nose, I guess.'

Cordelia giggled. 'That sounds like a particularly nasty complaint!'

'It leads to complications. Like broken legs. I'm told. Now . . . I want to check this so-called alibi of his. What time is it?'

'Just before two. We'd better get a move on if we're going to see Paddy.'

'I'll drop you back at the school and you can sort out some clothes for her, if you don't mind. Then I can go into town and buy some sandwiches for us and some goodies and cigarettes for Paddy. And I want a good, large-scale map of the area. We're going to have to do some checking out on Cartwright's tale. It all sounds a bit too convenient to me.'

Half an hour later, they set off. Cordelia navigated them across country for fifteen miles, then they shot up the motorway. They turned off in the depths of rural Cheshire and drove down country lanes for a few miles. Lindsay finally pulled into a car park beside a high wall. The two women got out and looked around them doubtfully.

They walked across to a high, forbidding gate and rang a bell. A small door opened and a prison officer appeared. Through the gap, Lindsay spotted an Alsatian guard dog chained to a security booth, Cordelia explained who they were and, after waiting for a couple of minutes while they were checked out, they were allowed in. Ahead lay twin inner rings of mesh fencing topped with ugly loops of barbed wire. Incongruously, this was succeeded by wide, beautifully trimmed lawns and flower beds, well stocked with mature rose bushes. Beyond that lay the red brick buildings, clean-cut functional, modern. They could have been offices, except for the barred windows and heavy double doors.

A woman prison officer walked them across the lawn to a square, three-storey building with a small plaque by the door reading. 'Female wing. Hospital Wing.' As soon as they entered the building they felt enclosed, almost claustrophobic, in spite of the bright colours of the paintwork and the occasional plant on the window sills. They were shown into a room that smelled of sweat and cigarette smoke. A listless man in his forties with a tired-looking teddy-boy haircut glanced at them without interest as they sat down at the opposite end of a long wooden bench. They sat in silence for more than ten minutes. Then another officer entered the room at the far end.

'Lindsay Gordon, Cordelia Brown,' she said. They stood up. The officer indicated the door she had come in by and the three of them trooped through. Lindsay noticed that the door was locked behind them. The officer took the clothes, cigarettes, books and food that they'd brought for Paddy and showed them to a table. They faced a glass screen with strips of wire mesh at each side. At every corner of the room there were more prison officers. Even Lindsay, whose job had taken her to most extreme circumstances, found the atmosphere oppressive and alienating. She could barely guess at the effect all this would have on someone like Paddy.

After a few minutes, a door at the opposite end of the room opened, and the officer returned with Paddy. Already life behind bars had left its mark on her. Her skin had an unhealthy sallowness. There were dark bags beneath her eyes. But what was most striking was that she seemed to have lost all her self-confidence. Fewer than three days of living behind bars had cut her down to less than life-size. She looked uncertainly across the room. When she saw Lindsay and Cordelia, relief flooded her face. But even the eagerness with which she approached them seemed tempered with uncertainty. It was as if she expected them to have changed as much as she had and couldn't quite believe that they were still completely normal.

Cordelia spoke first. 'My God, Paddy, this is dreadful. How are you managing to cope?'

Paddy shrugged and said, 'You just have to, Cordelia. Most of the time, I try to switch off and project myself back home. It's not easy. It's routine that's the killer. Up at half-past seven, wash, breakfast in the dining-room with Radio One blasting out, then cleaning and sewing till lunch, then back to the workshops, unless Gillian's managed to get here. Then it's tea, then it's telly, and then it's bed. It's so debilitating. All you hear is Radio One and the sound of keys. You're not expected to think for yourself at any time; it's amazing how quickly you lose the habit.'

Lindsay nodded sympathetically. 'You must feel really shut off from everything. But don't think you're forgotten. Pamela Overton's got us working overtime to try and find out what actually happened. I know it must seem pretty pointless, expecting a pair of wallies like us to get to the bottom of things, but we're doing the best we can.'

'Gillian told me. I appreciate it. It's not easy to feel optimistic in here, though. I feel condemned already. After all, what can you do against the combined forces of the police and the legal system?'

Lindsay pulled a wry face. 'Probably not a lot. But we've got an advantage over them – we *know* you're innocent.'

Paddy produced a tired smile. 'Thanks for that. But you can't really know that for sure. I'm beginning to wonder if I didn't have a brainstorm and I just can't remember it now. You never think that a miscarriage of justice is going to happen to you, do you? I've spent all my life in a world where the police are the ones you call when the house gets burgled, or some drunk is falling through your hedge at midnight. Even when I was dealing dope I never really believed they'd touch me. You never expect them to get it wrong for you.'

'You mustn't begin thinking like that,' pleaded Cordelia. 'Eventually they'll realise that they've made a terrible mistake. We're just trying to speed the process up a bit, that's all. You'll be out of here a free woman in no time at all.'

Paddy shook her head. 'I'll never be able to think of myself as a "free woman" again, Cordelia.'

Seeing that the conversation was moving into channels likely to depress Paddy even further, Lindsay interrupted.

'Look, Paddy, we're only allowed quarter of an hour. We need to pick your brains about the other people involved in this business. We've already talked to Margaret Macdonald about her relationship with Lorna – believe it or not, it turns out they were lovers years ago.'

'Margaret? And Lorna?' Paddy interrupted. 'That's incredible. I thought I knew Margaret well. But I'd no idea. My God, the skeletons are falling out of the cupboards now, aren't they?'

'You're not wrong there. But we think we'll have to rule her out and we don't want to have to drag her in as a red herring just to cast doubt on the evidence against you, not unless it's absolutely necessary. We've also got something on Sarah Cartwright's father that could be promising. But we need some other lines of attack. Who else might have wanted to see the back of Lorna?'

Cordelia butted in, 'For example, did Caroline Barrington think that Lorna was behind her parents' marriage break-up?'

Paddy lit a cigarette before she replied. 'Caroline blamed Lorna totally. I tried to talk her out of seeing it that way, but she wasn't having any. I don't know the full story, but apparently Lorna had an affair with Caroline's father which he was more wrapped up in than she was. The marriage broke up over it, but Lorna and he never really got it together. Caroline was very bitter at the time, and when she heard Lorna was coming to the school, she was furious. I was quite surprised when she volunteered for the programme selling at the concert.'

'What about the girl who came to fetch you from Longnor? The one with the amazing head of red hair. Is there anything she might be able to tell us that could help?' Lindsay asked. Paddy shrugged again. 'I doubt it. Though if there was, Jessica would certainly tell you. She's another one who hated Lorna's guts, you see. That's why she wasn't playing at the concert even though she's one of our best young musicians. You remember that row I had with Margaret in the staffroom, Lindsay? That was about Jessica. She'd come to me at the last minute and explained she couldn't go through with the concert with Lorna there.

'It was all to do with her brother, Dominic. He was a brilliant violinist, and Jessica worshipped the ground he walked on. There was some business between him and Lorna – she latched on to him and promised him the first vacancy in her string quartet. But things went wrong between them and she gave the post to someone else. Then there was some business about a reference she wouldn't give him for some other orchestral job, and he didn't get that either. The pressure of being rejected twice like that was too much for him – he killed himself. He clearly wasn't at all stable; in fact from what I've heard the blame was as much on his side as on Lorna's, but Jessica will never see it that way.'

'I don't see how you can be so bloody charitable about Lorna,' Cordelia burst out. 'She was nothing but trouble to us while she was alive; and now she's dead, she's carrying on the good work.'

'Leave it, Cordelia,' soothed Lindsay. 'What's the girl's full name, Paddy?'

'Jessica Bennett.'

'Thanks, we'll have a chat with her. Now, what about Sarah Cartwright? Gillian tells us that she's given the police a statement about Saturday morning.' Lindsay succinctly outlined what the lawyer had said on the phone. 'What have you got to say to that, Paddy? Did it happen like she says?'

Paddy looked bewildered. 'I don't know . . .

It's true that I took her to Music 2 because I knew that nobody else would be using it and I wanted to get her on her own in the hope that she might open up a bit. I don't remember the other things she says happened – but then, I was very abstracted. I was worried about her; I had the play on my mind; and I was still twitchy about Lorna. So they might have happened. I honestly can't say definitely that they didn't take place. After all, there's no reason why the girl should lie.'

'But of course there is,' argued Cordelia. 'She could be protecting either herself or her father.'

Paddy shook her head. 'I don't think she'd have deliberately done something that would cause me trouble. I'm closer to the girl than anyone else in the school. I can't believe she would calculatedly lie about me.'

Lindsay interrupted gently. 'I know it's hard to believe, Paddy, but try to think objectively. Don't you think that Sarah might just do anything for her father's sake? Even to the extent of killing?'

Paddy considered the question. 'She's cool enough under normal circumstances to pull it off, I suppose. And she feels passionately protective of her father. Perhaps she might not be too worried about putting me in a spot if she looked at it as a straight choice between him and me. But when it comes to murder – I can't believe that. For one thing, I don't think she knew the music department well enough to set it up. And besides she was so upset after her row on Saturday morning, I doubt if she'd have been able to compose herself sufficiently to get it all together. No, I can't see Sarah as the killer at all.'

Seeing that this line of conversation was upsetting Paddy, Lindsay decided on another approach. 'Is there anything you can think of that might give us a new line to work on? Anything at all? Some little detail you might have noticed but not bothered about – in the room or in the music department?'

Paddy slowly shook her head. 'Nothing springs to mind. Don't you think I've already been through it a million times in my head these last three days?' She rubbed her eyes with her fists. 'After all,' she sighed, 'there's not a lot else to fill my head.'

They all sat back in their chairs for a moment, Lindsay trying to hide her pity for her friend and her disappointment that nothing more substantial had emerged from the conversation. She leaned forward again and said reassuringly, 'I've managed to come up with the goods on investigative stories before with less to go on than we've got here. And with Cordelia to keep me right, I'm sure we're going to crack this one too. I'm not giving up on you, Paddy, I owe you one.'

For a moment, Paddy's face looked animated and she almost smiled, but at that moment the prison officer approached Paddy and said that their time was up. Immediately, Paddy's eyes became bleak again and she got to her feet. 'Come again when you can,' she implored before vanishing through the door once more.

When they emerged into the open space of the car park, Lindsay gulped air in as though that would somehow cleanse her. She leaned against the car, shoulders slumped and face full of dismay. Cordelia leaned against the wall, fighting back the tears. 'It's so bloody unfair,' she spat.

'I know,' Lindsay sighed. 'I feel completely inadequate. How the hell can we sort this mess out? I just don't know where to start.'

'At least she's given us a couple of leads. We've got reasonable excuses for talking to Caroline and Jessica now.'

Lindsay nodded wearily. 'I suppose so. I kept on thinking there was something important I should have asked Paddy, but I don't know what it was. There's something which has been nagging at the back of my mind since Sunday and it won't surface for long enough to grasp it. But I know it's somehow significant, whatever it is.'

Cordelia shrugged herself away from the wall. 'Come on, we'd better get on the road to London. Maybe Andrew Christie will hold the key that will unlock all of this.'

'I doubt it,' Lindsay muttered. 'But let's go anyway.'

12

Andrew Christie ushered the two of them into the living-room of an elegant and expensive flat. It occupied the basement and ground floor of a tall, narrow Victorian house, and the large living-room was exactly what Lindsay imagined a slightly pretentious television producer should inhabit. The furniture was Habitat – inevitably tasteful without exhibiting any taste – three two-seater settees and a plethora of low tables piled with magazines, newspapers, scripts and half-full ashtrays. But the room was dominated by the electronic media. There was a giant tele-vision screen and a normal-sized set, two video recorders, an expensive hi-fi system and yards of shelves containing records, cassettes, video tapes and reel-to-reel tapes. Lindsay found it the least relaxing room she'd ever been in. Christie was in his late thirties, with shaggy blond hair, slim and wiry and dressed in tight olive green jeans, an open-necked plaid shirt and a shapeless hairy sweater. He looked the part.

'Sit down, do,' he said in a voice like a radio announcer's. 'I don't quite know how I can help you. Lorna and I had only been seeing each other for about three months and I can't say I was aware of her having enemies of sufficient seriousness to . . . well – to do this.'

'We were hoping you'd be able to tell us a bit about her. Her personality, her lifestyle, her friends, that sort of thing,' Lindsay responded gently. She knew she wouldn't be able to press this man as she had done Cartwright. She understood his grief too well. 'The more we know about Lorna, the more chance we have of finding out why she was killed. And by whom. I know it's not easy to talk when it's only just happened and we do appreciate you giving us some time. I know we've got no official standing here, but it's important to us to establish who really did this. If you knew Paddy Callaghan like we do, you'd know that it would have been impossible for her to have committed such a cowardly crime.'

For the first time, emotion flickered across his face. 'I miss Lorna,' he said. 'I know a lot of people didn't care too much for her; she had a very cutting tongue at times. But to me she was always very tender. She used to make me laugh. She could be very funny at other people's expense. I don't think she especially meant to be cruel, but not everyone could see the humour behind what she said.'

There was a pause. 'How did you meet?' asked Cordelia. 'I'd known her slightly for quite a long time – we had some mutual acquaintances and found ourselves at the same parties. Then I was producing a drama-documentary about Elgar and I needed someone to play the cello concerto. She seemed the obvious choice. I was very impressed by her attitude as I worked with her. She was the complete professional. I know she put people's backs up by criticising their talent and motivation, but that was simply because she was such a perfectionist herself. But no one gets killed for that. It makes no sense to me at all. I keep thinking about all that beauty gone out of the world just because of some evil bastard's inability to cope with life.'

'Did she say anything about last weekend before she went? I mean, did she mention anyone in particular?' asked Lindsay.

He paused, then said, 'She was looking forward to it. She said it should be good for a laugh, at least. She said there were one or two people she'd take pleasure in showing that she'd arrived and was somebody. She didn't mention any names. She also said it would be good for publicity because of the controversy about the fund locally. She hated talking to the press; she thought they were scum. But she was too good a businesswoman to ignore the value of publicity. Sorry, that's not much help, is it?'

'More than you think,' said Lindsay. 'Now, I'm going to ask you if some names mean anything to you, if you'd ever heard of any of them before the weekend. For example, had she ever mentioned Cordelia here?'

'Yes. At first, she was terribly amused that some people seemed to think that a nasty character in your last novel was based on her. She said it wasn't terribly likely, since you hadn't spent any time together for years. Then a few weeks ago when your novel was nominated for the Booker, it all flared up again and she began to get cross with people for making the same remark over and over again. She decided that if she was going to get all this stick, she should get something in return. So she set the wheels in motion to sue. She was amused that you were going to be at the school. She said – sorry about this – it would be fun to watch you squirm.'

'Did she indeed!' said Cordelia through frozen lips.

'Had you ever heard her speak of Paddy Callaghan?'

'Never.'

'James Cartwright? Or his daughter Sarah?' The mechanical recital of names was helping Lindsay relax into her questioning.

'Definitely not.'

'Jessica Bennett, Dominic Bennett's sister?'

'She never mentioned a sister, but I know about•Dominic, yes. He was quite a gifted young musician, Lorna said, and she'd encouraged his talent. She told him that one day she might be able to use him in her string quartet. But he wasn't quite up to scratch when a vacancy came up, so of course she had to turn him down. He was more distressed than she realised, and he killed himself soon after. Where does his sister come into this?'

'She's a pupil at the school. Does the name Margaret Macdonald mean anything?'

He shook his head. 'Sorry.'

'Caroline Barrington?'

'Barrington? Any relation to Anthony Barrington? He had a relationship with Lorna. She told me about him. Apparently he couldn't accept it when she cooled off, and went to the extent of divorcing his wife to try to force Lorna to marry him. But she wouldn't have it. They split up about six months before we got together. I got the impression that he caused her a lot of grief. But she never tried to make one feel sorry for her, for what she'd suffered in the past. She always said you start relationships with a clean sheet. God, I'm going to miss her,' and he pressed the back of his hands against his eyes in a curiously vulnerable gesture. 'The worst thing is that I can't get peace simply to sit and grieve. The police, the press and now you. Not that I blame you. I like to think that I'd do the same for a friend of mine. But there will be no peace until after the court case. And probably not even then. It makes me so bloody sad. A complete waste.'

'And damage done to the living,' said Cordelia. 'There's been enough of that already and it's not finished yet. One last thing before we go – how many people knew she was going up to Derbyshire last weekend? Is there anyone else you can think of who might have had a motive for wanting to harm her – I mean in the widest sense?'

'Thousands of people knew where she was going. There were a few paragraphs about it in the *Daily Argus* diary column last week. As for motives – no, I don't know anyone who'd be crazy enough to want to harm her. It's all insane. All of it. It doesn't feel real. I've been working these last few days on the final stages of the Elgar documentary. It's going out in three weeks. It's very weird watching the film and hearing the soundtrack of her playing and knowing that's all that's left. I must have actually been working on that with the editor when she was being killed. It's hell.'

'I know,' said Lindsay. 'I lost someone I loved once. You feel like part of you has been amputated. And nothing anyone says makes the slightest difference.'

Cordelia cleared her throat. 'Well, thanks for your help. We'd better be off now. I'm sorry if we've upset you.'

He saw them to the door. His parting words as they climbed the shallow steps up from his basement entrance were, 'Thanks, I wish you could have known her as I did.'

They got back into the car. Lindsay had found the interview extremely painful. The man's grief had taken her back three years to the death of her lover. It was an experience she thought she had learned how to handle. But now she felt again the vivid pain that had filled her life for months after Frances' death had devastated her world.

'At least one person grieves for her,' said Cordelia. 'I can't decide whether she did a magnificent con job on him or whether he genuinely saw a side to Lorna that was hidden from the rest of us.'

'Who's to say?' Lindsay replied. 'Either way, it's not going to affect his memories. Unfortunately, however, I don't think our little chat has taken us any further forward. If anything, it only widens the field to the entire readership of the *Daily Argus*. Still, it was edifying to find out what Lorna apparently thought of Dominic Bennett and Anthony Barrington. Now, how do I get to your place?'

Under Cordelia's careful guidance, Lindsay drove them to a quiet cul-de-sac of tall Victorian terraced houses overlooking Highbury Fields. Feeling somewhat overawed by the fact that Cordelia's home was obviously one of the few three-storey houses that was not converted into flats, Lindsay followed Cordelia up the steps to the door. Cordelia caught sight of Lindsay's expression and grinned.

'Don't worry,' she said, 'it's not as grand as it looks. My accountant told me that property was the best investment, so I lashed out on this with the proceeds of my early successes in the mass media.'

They stepped into the narrow hall. Cordelia flicked on the subdued lighting that revealed watercolour sketches of Italian landscapes. 'In here,' she said, opening one of the doors leading off the hall. Lindsay stepped through into an L-shaped living-room that was twice the size of her own in Glasgow. Four wooden-shuttered windows stretched from ceiling to floor. There was an enormous grey leather Chesterfield on one side of the fireplace and two matching wing chairs on the other side. On the polished wooden floor a couple of good Oriental rugs provided the only splashes of colour. Round the corner was the dining area, furnished with an oval mahogany dining-table and six matching balloon-backed chairs.

'My God,' said Lindsay. 'It's like living in a page out of *House and Garden*.'

Mistaking her contempt for admiration. Cordelia laughed and said, 'As I spend an enormous amount of time in this place, I took a great deal of time and trouble to furnish it. I indulged myself completely. Do you really like it?'

Lindsay looked around her again in amazement. 'To be honest, I don't think I'd ever feel at home in these surroundings, Cordelia. You could buy my whole flat in Glasgow with what you've spent on this one room.'

'But what's wrong with being comfortable, for God's sake?'

'There's comfort and there's comfort. I feel comfortable in my flat with its tatty chairs that don't match and the threadbare carpet in the spare room. Put it down to my Scottish puritanism or my politics, but I find it a bit over the top.'

'I'm sorry if you find it oppressive – I'll just have to re-educate you to appreciate it,' Cordelia replied acidly.

'I'm sorry, I didn't mean to sound rude, I was just being honest. I get outraged about anyone spending so much money on a place to live. Though I suppose if I had the money I'd lash out a bit myself.'

'But your flat's lovely. All the rooms are so airy. Now take my study. It has practically no light at all; even in summer I have to have the desk lamp on most of the day. My mother keeps telling me it'll make me go blind. I tell her she's getting muddled and my eyesight is in no danger.' They laughed. 'Fancy a drink? I could do with one, and you must be exhausted after all that driving. There's whisky, sherry, gin, vodka, you name it . . .'

Lindsay settled for wine and together they went through to the kitchen. Cordelia said, 'We'll have something to eat. The freezer's full of food. I have a binge every three months – I cook like mad, fill the freezer and live out of it.'

The conspicuous consumerism of the kitchen took Lindsay's breath away. The units were oak, and the worktops bristled with gadgetry. 'I love kitchen machines,' said Cordelia as she tossed the chosen lasagne-for-two into the microwave.

'I never realised writing was so lucrative,' said Lindsay wryly, picturing her own kitchen whose sum total of gadgetry was a liquidiser, a coffee grinder and a cooker, and whose decor consisted of theatre posters begged from friends.

'Well, to be fair, it's not all the proceeds of my sweated labour. My grandmother died three years ago and left me rather a large legacy. That went on the deposit for this place. Most of the rest of the money has come from telly, radio and the film I scripted last year. Crazy, isn't it? The novels are what I really care about, but they wouldn't allow me to live in a bedsit in Hackney, let alone here.'

'You really are one of the obscenely privileged minority, aren't you?' remarked Lindsay. 'I don't know what I'm doing with you at all. In my job, I see so much poverty, so much deprivation, so much exploitation, I can't help feeling that luxury like this is obscene. Don't you want to change things?'

Cordelia laughed and replied lightly. 'But what would you have me do? Give all I've got to the poor?'

Lindsay saw the chasm yawning at her feet. She could leave the argument lying for a future day when there might be a strong enough relationship between them to stand the weight of disagreement. Or she could pursue the subject relentlessly and kill the magic stone dead. She turned away and deliberately picked up a cookery book.

That night, the love-making was more tentative, less urgent than before. The reverberations of their earlier differences had died down as they had explored each other's history during the evening. Cordelia was already in bed by the time Lindsay came through from the kitchen with a tumbler of water. She undressed quickly. As she slid beneath the duvet, Cordelia turned on her side and they embraced. 'All right?' she enquired.

'I feel a bit drained, to be honest. It's been quite a day. Margaret, Cartwright, Paddy in prison. And tonight. I haven't worked so hard for a long time.' She smiled ruefully. 'And then, boring you with my life story. Very exhausting.'

'I wasn't bored. But I know what you mean. I feel pretty done in too.'

'Not so tired that all you want is sleep?'

In reply, Cordelia leaned over and kissed her warmly.

More than the chaotic coupling of the previous nights it sealed them close. For the first time, neither was trying to prove anything. Lindsay lay awake as Cordelia slept. No matter how much she buried herself in the joyous sensation of making love with Cordelia, the uncomfortable thoughts wouldn't disappear without trace. And now that she'd actually seen for herself the way her new lover lived, those uncomfortable thoughts had a new element.

PART THREE:
FUGUE

13

It was noon before Cordelia and Lindsay pulled in beside Paddy Callaghan's Land Rover at Derbyshire House on Friday. Lindsay had felt an increasing sense of unreality as the morning had worn on. The conversation of the evening before had all but restored her to her normal frame of mind, by recalling her past and awakening her desires for the future. Somehow that all seemed very distant from what had been happening in the last few days. It seemed absurd to Lindsay that she and Cordelia should have any pretensions about being able to solve the problem of Lorna Smith-Couper's death. She could not shake the increasing conviction that she was taking part in some elaborate but ultimately silly game. Only the presence of Cordelia made her determined to finish what they had started.

She was not even able to pause and collect her thoughts before they came face to face with Jessica Bennett at the door of Longnor House. The girl started when she saw them and a momentary panic flashed across her eyes before she regained her composure.

'Hello, Jessica. We haven't actually met, but Cordelia and I wanted to have a chat with you.' Lindsay announced before the girl could escape. 'We saw Miss Callaghan yesterday. She thought you might be able to help us with a couple of details. Are you busy at the moment?'

'Well . . . I suppose not. I'm meant to be in the library for private study, but no one will check up on me if I'm not there. They'll just assume I'm doing something else,' the girl replied nervously.

The three of them went to Paddy's rooms. While Cordelia made some coffee, Jessica seemed apprehensive, so Lindsay tried to put her at her ease. 'What are you studying for now? Is it A levels?'

'Yes. I'm doing music, history and maths. I know it sounds a funny combination – at least everyone says it is – but maths and music are very closely related in some ways, so it helps. The history I'm doing because I like it.'

'That's a good enough reason. What comes next? After this place?'

'I'm not sure. I'd like to carry on with my music, but I don't know if I'll be good enough to get into one of the Royal Colleges. If not, I'll settle for reading music at university, I suppose. If my results are good enough. It's just a matter of working hard now, I guess.'

Lindsay reckoned that Jessica was being so forthcoming because she did not want to come round to the subject of Lorna's death. So while the girl was still talkative, Lindsay started to slip in the more awkward questions. She said casually, 'I shouldn't imagine anyone's getting much work done at the moment. The upheaval of the last few days must take a lot of getting used to.'

Jessica's air of nervousness instantly returned. 'It hasn't exactly been a help to anyone,' she replied.

'If you'd known Miss Callaghan as long as I have, you'd know for certain she just couldn't have been involved in this,' Lindsay said, throwing caution to the winds. 'What are the girls saying?'

'No one – at least, no one I've heard – can believe it. Miss Callaghan's a marvellous housemistress. She really does have an instinct about the way people's minds work, and she gets under your skin to know how you feel underneath. She's always so understanding, you know? She tries to be a friend to us without being patronising, or playing favourites, like some teachers do. She gets angry with people sometimes and lets them know it, but nobody could imagine her being so . . . so . . . you know? We like her, you see,' Jessica explained anxiously.

'And you didn't like Lorna Smith-Couper, did you?'

Jessica did not flinch. She did not respond at all. Lindsay continued slowly and quietly. 'We have a problem. We're trying to get Miss Callaghan freed from prison, not just because Miss Overton has asked us to. We're not necessarily setting out to prove that any particular person did it. What we are trying to show is that there are other people against whom there is as much or as little circumstantial evidence as that which exists against Miss Callaghan. That way her solicitor can show up the weakness of the case against her.'

Cordelia returned with the coffee and handed the mugs round. She took over from Lindsay, saying, 'It seems to us, from what Miss Callaghan told us, that you might have some information about her movements that might possibly help. Let me repeat, we're not trying to pin the blame on you or on anyone else. We're simply trying to prove that other people were as likely – or unlikely, if you like – to have done this thing as Paddy. Now I think it's possible you didn't tell the police every detail of what you saw and heard. Perhaps you thought they might take it the wrong way because they don't know the people concerned. But you can tell us everything. You know whose side we're on.'

For a moment there was stillness. Then Jessica nodded and said, 'I don't mind talking to you. You could probably find out anything I have to tell you by asking other people, anyway. And Miss Overton asked us at assembly to co-operate with you as well as with the police. But I'd rather you heard what I have to say from me and not in a garbled version from other people. What do you want to ask me?'

The girl was still clearly very tense. There was little colour in her face and her freckles stood out like a rash. But as Cordelia asked the first question, she flushed an ugly scarlet. 'How did you feel about Lorna?'

Jessica started to speak, but bit back her words. She struggled for control, then said venomously, 'I hope she rots in hell. I hated her. And I despised her. I'm not surprised that someone killed her. I only wish it could have happened before she ever came near us. Then Dominic would still be alive now. I wished her dead, and I'm glad now that she is. I wish I'd had the nerve to think of doing it myself. I'd have enjoyed watching her suffer with the realisation that she was paying for what she did to my brother.' She ran out of steam, seeming surprised and a little dismayed at her vehemence.

'What did she do to your brother, Jessica?' Lindsay pushed.

'They were going out with each other, and she promised him that she'd give him a job. She ran a string quartet and there was a vacancy for a violinist. He was really good, you know, more than good enough for her quartet. Anyway, they had a row and she ended up giving the job to someone else who wasn't anything like as good. So Dominic applied for a job with the Garden Chamber Orchestra as a second violin. And she was such a bitch that she gave him a reference that was so unenthusiastic it cost him that job too. After that, he found it really hard to get decent work. All he ever cared about was making the best possible music. But Lorna put a stop to that. And he killed himself.' Her voice faded out, shaking and tearful.

'Was this the first time you'd seen her since your brother's death?' asked Lindsay.

'I didn't really see her, only across the room at dinner. I couldn't face going to the concert. I couldn't bear to hear her playing music I love. It would have hurt too much; Miss Callaghan saw that. That's why she left me in charge of Longnor, so I wouldn't have to be at the concert. And she sorted it all out with Miss Macdonald. I was supposed to be in the choir, you see, with a small solo. They got Karina Holgate to do it instead.'

'But you did come across to the hall, didn't you? I thought I saw you talking to Caroline Barrington,' said Lindsay.

Jessica nodded and took a gulp of coffee. 'I thought the police would have asked me about that, but no one seems to have told them I was there. I told you I was left in charge of Longnor. Well, one of the fourth-formers was ill. She kept being sick, and I suspected she might have been drinking. I didn't want to be responsible for what might happen, so I thought it was best to come across to find Miss Callaghan.'

'Did you see anyone hanging around outside, or anything else suspicious?'

Jessica shook her head. 'There were quite a few people milling around outside the hall, but they all looked as if they were going to the concert. I recognised one or two of them because I've seen them in the town, and some of them because they're parents. I saw Caroline's father getting out of his car when I came across, but I don't think he can have stayed for the concert because his car had gone when I came back with Miss Callaghan. But you'd better ask Caroline about that.'

Lindsay and Cordelia exchanged a look. Yet another complication had emerged. 'What happened when you got to the hall?' Cordelia asked.

'I asked Caroline if she'd seen Miss Callaghan and she said she thought she was still backstage. I went through and asked one or two people if they'd seen her, but everyone was too busy to have noticed. I went down the side passage as far as the storeroom to see if she was there, but there was no sign of her. Then I went back to the main corridor and looked into the rest of the music rooms. I finally found her just outside Miss Macdonald's room, round the corner. I told her what had happened and she said I'd done the right thing and came straight back with me. She stayed in Longnor then for about half an hour.' She ground to a halt.

'Did it seem to you as if Miss Callaghan had just come out of Miss Macdonald's room?' asked Lindsay cautiously.

'I don't think so. There are a few steps that lead down to the room. She was about half-way down them, looking out of the window down the front drive.' She hesitated, then said in a rush, 'She seemed to be miles away. I had to speak to her twice before she heard me.'

Lindsay and Cordelia looked at each other, both filled with dread at the thought of how this new evidence could be made to sound by a good prosecuting counsel. Then Cordelia roused herself and said, 'Did she seem upset or agitated at all, Jessica?'

'No, she just seemed to be very thoughtful. Preoccupied. Usually she's very lively and chatty. It was as if she had something on her mind. Not as if she'd just killed someone, if that's what you mean – not like that at all. She couldn't have done that, could she? Not someone like Miss Callaghan?'

'We don't believe so, no,' said Lindsay. 'Are you sure you didn't go any further down the side passage than the storeroom? You said you checked all the other music rooms on the main corridor. Didn't you check Music 2?'

'No, I definitely didn't go all the way down the corridor.'

'Why not?'

'Because I knew that's where Lorna Smith-

Couper had to be. I knew who was supposed to be in which room. I'd been involved with everything up to the last minute. I thought I could face her, so I'd taken part in the preparations. I knew the only room she could be in was Music 2 and she was the last person I wanted to see. If Miss Callaghan had been with her, I would just have had to wait till she came out again, or tried to find Matron. Nothing would have induced me to go anywhere near that room.'

'Why didn't you get Matron in the first place? Why come to the music rooms for Miss Callaghan at all?' asked Lindsay.

'Because I thought the girl had been drinking. I thought Miss Callaghan would deal with it more sort of sensibly than Matron.'

'Okay. Now, when you went down to the storeroom, did you see anyone outside Music 2?'

'I couldn't see round the corner of the corridor. But I did hear someone running down the back stairs. It sounded like someone wearing high heels. Could that be important, do you think?'

Cordelia replied, 'I don't think that would tell the police anything they don't know already,' she said, trying to sound nonchalant. The last thing she wanted was for the girl to think she had any ulterior motive in keeping her from giving information to the police. Lindsay and Cordelia exchanged a worried look. Almost certainly it was Cordelia that Jessica had heard. But if they encouraged her to go to the police with that

205

corroboration, she might also tell them about Paddy's state outside Margaret Macdonald's room. The question of what to do for the best completely put out of their minds any other questions they might have wanted to ask Jessica.

'Is that all, then,' the red-head asked.

Lindsay nodded. 'Yes, thank you. You've been quite a help to us. You'd better get off to the library now in case anyone's looking for you.'

Jessica rose and went to the door. As she left, she turned and said shyly, 'I hope you manage to clear Miss Callaghan. We all miss her.' And she was gone.

'Not exactly a convenient witness,' said Lindsay. 'Prosecuting counsel would have a field day with her and Paddy's preoccupations. And your disappearing footsteps could get the police putting you in the frame as an accomplice. Let's hope we can clear Paddy without the police ever becoming aware of Miss Jessica Bennett's evidence.'

'We're still not much further forward, though are we?'

'I don't know about that. We've got some hard questions to ask Sarah Cartwright, and now it turns out the jilted divorcee was on the scene too. We've got a decent list of possible murderers to present to Paddy's solicitor. But as I've said, I would rather tie the whole thing up than leave loose ends and red herrings haunting the lives of a handful of people. Now, it's alibi-establishing time. We can incorporate finding food with our examination of James Cartwright's alleged alibi.'

Cordelia smiled and said, 'I can't help feeling that we are mixing rather too much pleasure with our business.'

'That's what you get for tying yourself up with a journalist. We're great believers in looking after the comforts of the flesh while we do the business.'

'Okay, okay. I have heard that the Stonemason's at Wincle does excellent food . . .'

Once in the car, to Cordelia's bewilderment, they drove straight to the offices of the local paper. Lindsay left her sitting there and reappeared ten minutes later clutching a photograph of Cartwright. She said, 'I managed to persuade one of the local lads to let me borrow this picture. We might need it to identify him. I promised the bloke I'd tip him off if there's any change in the situation that might lead to fresh arrests. Which of course I probably won't have the chance to do, but he's not to know that.'

They drove back to the school gates, where Lindsay turned the car round in a spray of gravel. 'Show-off,' muttered Cordelia.

'Thank you. Now, I want to check some timings. Bear in mind that that Mercedes of his is faster than my MG, and that he knows these roads like the back of his hand. I want to see if this alibi can be cracked. We'll have to check timings as far as possible with the pubs, to see if he could have squeezed in enough time for the killing. I'm

207

not convinced by his injured innocence routine. Done any rally driving, Cordelia?'

Cordelia looked aghast. 'Certainly not,' she replied.

'Well, you'll have to try and navigate for me. I've marked what looks like the best routes on the map. You study that and the terrain and tell me what's coming next. Okay?'

'I'll try. Have you done much rally driving?'

'Not a bit,' said Lindsay blithely. 'But I know the theory.'

They set off back towards Buxton in an atmosphere of intense concentration, then turned down the Macclesfield road. Lindsay tore round the tight ascending bends in third, and as soon as they hit the straight stretch where they turned down the Congleton road, she flipped the switch that took the engine into overdrive. They turned off into a succession of country lanes and, after a hair-raising hurtle, they roared to a halt outside the Stonemason's Arms.

'Can I open my eyes now?' asked Cordelia mockingly. 'Fourteen minutes and about five seconds.'

The Stonemason's Arms was a long low stone building with a roof of heavy slate slabs. They found themselves in a clean, neat public bar, with matching wooden chairs, olde worlde wooden tables and chintz curtains at the windows. But the beer was real ale on hand pumps, so they perched on bar stools with a pint of best bitter for Lindsay and a dry white wine for Cordelia, having ordered two ploughman's special lunches. Lindsay wasted no time in eliciting information from the barmaid, a faded woman around forty who turned out to be the landlord's wife.

'I suppose you don't get much time off,' she said sympathetically.

'Oh, we always take Tuesdays off,' said the woman. 'You have to get away from the place sometimes or else you'd go mad. It was always my husband's dream to retire to a country pub. When he was made redundant a couple of years ago, it seemed the obvious thing. Myself, I think it's a lot of hard work and not as much fun as people seem to think.'

'Well, you certainly know how to please your customers. This is one of the nicest pints I've had in a long time. Actually, a friend of mine recommended this place to us. James Cartwright, I suppose you know him?'

'Oh yes, he's a regular in here. He often pops in for his evening meal. Living alone, with his daughter boarding at that school, I think he enjoys the company and not having to cook for himself. You'd think he'd have a housekeeper, really, but he seems to prefer looking after himself.'

'Yes, he was just saying to me yesterday that it's just as well he's a familiar face in here. He was telling me the police had some daft idea he might have had something to do with the murder on Saturday night, but that since he'd been here at the time he was completely in the clear. He said it was a real blessing you knew him.'

The landlady nodded vigorously. 'That's right. We had the police here on Sunday asking about him. He came in about five to eight, I remember, because I'd been watching *Go for Gold* on the telly. I told the police, don't be silly, Mr Cartwright couldn't have anything to do with a murder! He was just the same as usual, chatty and cheery. He had something to eat – I think it was the grilled local trout – and two or three pints of his usual and then went off about ten.'

'Lucky for him, really,' said Lindsay. She was spared any further conversation by the arrival of their generous lunches, and the two of them retired to a distant table. As they ate, Cordelia talked between mouthfuls of cheese and bread.

'Let me see . . . now if he got here about five to eight . . . it would have taken him about quarter of an hour from the school. Say ten minutes to do what he had to do, give five to get there and get out again, and I'd give about ten to fifteen back to the Woolpack. So if he left the Woolpack before . . . say, about ten past seven, he's got no alibi and he could just have done it.'

'Precisely. It all depends on what happened at the Woolpack. So eat, don't talk and we can buzz over there as soon as possible and suss them out.'

Half an hour later they were in the bar at the Woolpack. In contrast with the suburban charm of the Stonemason's, the Woolpack was spartan and cheap. The plastic-covered benches and the chipped laminated table tops fitted well with the smell of stale beer and old tobacco smoke. A couple of farm labourers leaned against a corner of the bar. They fell silent when Cordelia and Lindsay entered and stared blankly at them. Behind the bar was a bleached blonde in her twenties with too much eye make-up. 'Really know how to make you feel welcome, don't they,' Lindsay muttered to Cordelia as they approached the bar. This time Lindsay decided to drop the subtle approach and went straight to the point after she'd ordered her half pint of indifferent keg beer and a glass of white wine for Cordelia.

'Have one yourself,' she insisted to the barmaid. 'I wonder if you can help me? I'm a private investigator and I've been hired to look into this murder down the road at Derbyshire House School. I've been making inquiries into the movements of everyone connected with the case, and I want you to tell me if this man was in here on Saturday night.' She took the photograph of Cartwright from her bag and handed it over.

'You're not the first, love,' came the sullen reply. 'Police've been here before you. But I may as well tell you what I told them. This bloke comes in here occasionally, and he was in on Saturday. We don't open while seven of a Saturday teatime, and he came in on the dot – same as a couple of hikers. I served him first and he went through the side parlour with a pint. I don't know

211

how long he stopped; there's a door in there leads to the toilets and you can get out the back door that way. All I know is he was gone half an hour later when I went in to clear off the glasses. Now, if that's all, I'll get on with my work.'

Without waiting for a reply, she disappeared through the door beside the bar. 'A real charmer,' said Cordelia. 'Now do I have to finish this disgusting drink or can we push off?'

They left the pub and returned to the car for the second piece of timed driving. Lindsay drove the car to its limits and they shot into the drive a bare seven minutes later.

'I have the beginnings of a theory, thanks to you working out the times,' Lindsay mused, cutting the engine. 'Cartwright saw her sorting out strings, he says. Now, suppose she left them lying around in the room. He could fairly assume she'd be back there before she went on stage.

'He could have had a quick one in the Woolpack, raced back to the school, left his car in the trees beyond the houses, got the toggle from Longnor – after all, no one would have thought anything of seeing him there with Sarah doing her Greta Garbo routine. A quick dash through the trees to the main building. In by the side door, up the back stairs and into Music 2. He'd have had to go back home in the afternoon to pick up the school keys, by the way – I imagine he's got a set. Then he picks up a string – he's good with his hands, and strong. Then it's into the walk-in cupboard till Lorna arrives. As soon as Paddy goes, he's out and strangling her with one of the strings she's so conveniently left lying around. Then he's off, down the back stairs, drives like a madman and is back in the Stonemason's by five to eight. It could be done.'

Cordelia looked doubtful. 'It has its points. But you're assuming he has a set of keys. You're also assuming he could figure out her movements. I mean, it could have happened that Lorna didn't come into the room until just before she went on – he could have been stuck in the cupboard for over an hour, and where would his alibi have been then? And how the hell do we prove any of it?'

'You forget, we don't actually have to prove anything. We're not policemen, having to stand everything up in court. All we really have to do for Paddy's purposes is to demonstrate that she's far from being the only person with motive, means and opportunity.'

'I suppose so. I rather like the thought of Cartwright as First Murderer. He could have given himself a bit more time by making his preparations in the afternoon – making the garrotte and all that. He couldn't be sure he'd get there ahead of Lorna, but it was a reasonable assumption. And the confusion over Margaret Macdonald's keys could simply be a fortuitous red herring.'

'I don't know about you, but the more we find out, the more confused I get. We need to sit down and work out the permutations of what we know. What I need is a day off, to put all this to the back of my mind and do something completely different. But I know I can't walk away from this until we've at least got Paddy out of the mess she's in,' Lindsay replied in a very tired voice.

'I know just what you mean,' sighed Cordelia.

Back at the school, they drew up another of Cordelia's lists of essential information they'd picked up on their inquiries. As they suspected, the evidence still pointed in too many directions. Nothing had emerged that proved conclusively that Paddy could not have murdered Lorna Smith-Couper. Lindsay phoned Pamela Overton and asked her if Cartwright had a set of keys to the school. She promised to check up and let them know. Lindsay paced up and down Paddy's sitting-room, a worried frown on her face.

'There's something at the back of my mind that's got some bearing on the case. It's something I saw or heard. I can't even remember which. But some tiny thing has impressed itself on my mind and I've a feeling that it's the key to the whole damn business. Oh God, I wish I could remember! What a fool I am!' she exclaimed angrily.

'Relax,' soothed Cordelia. 'Try not to think about it and perhaps it will spring into your mind when you're doing something else.'

'I've tried that. It hasn't worked so far. Do you know any good hypnotists?' asked Lindsay with a wry smile. 'Now, we've still got things to do, you know. Shall we try to get hold of Caroline Barrington or Sarah Cartwright? It's almost four now, classes must be nearly finished.'

'I suppose Caroline's the next person we should see,' Cordelia sighed. 'She might just know something that will help us put more pressure on Sarah Cartwright.'

'Not until I've had another large injection of caffeine,' Lindsay groaned. 'Her heart seems to be in the right place, but she talks like a blue streak. I need to be fortified before we grill her or Caroline will end up grilling us.'

She rose to go through to the kitchen, but before she could get there, Paddy's phone rang. Cordelia reached across the desk and picked it up. 'Hello, Miss Callaghan's room . . . yes, that's right . . . Well, slowly at present, though I think we're making some . . . no, not as yet. No, we haven't been in contact with the police at all . . . well, I couldn't actually say. If you insist, we'll certainly do our best. Yes, four-thirty is fine. Yes, Lindsay knows that. Till then.'

Cordelia put the phone down and muttered, 'Damn and blast. That was Gillian. She wants to see us on Monday for a progress report. It looks as if the police are pressing for an early committal hearing and if she can demolish their case in the magistrates' court, she wants to have a go. So now we're battling against time, too.'

Lindsay groaned. 'That's all we need. We'd

better cancel the coffee and find the garrulous Miss Barrington. Who knows, she might have the answers to the whole sorry business.'

'If you were Hercule Poirot, she certainly would.'

'Ah yes, but if I was Hercule Poirot, you wouldn't fancy me, would you?'

14

Longnor House seemed eerily silent as the two women climbed the stairs to Caroline's room on the top floor. Cordelia knocked. There was no reply, so they opened the door and entered. They had already agreed that if Caroline was not there they would wait for her. Lindsay walked over to the window and perched on the radiator beneath the wide sill. Cordelia sat on an upright chair by the desk, her legs propped against the waste-paper bin. They both studied the room as if seeing it for the first time, Lindsay checking off its features as she had not done when she was actually using it as a bedroom.

The basic furniture was institutional: a bed, table, chair, wardrobe, cupboard and chest of drawers. But Caroline's personality was every-where. On the walls were a poster of Lenin, a large photograph of Virginia Woolf and a poster for a rally of peace women at Greenham Common. On the bookshelves were several textbooks. The rest of the space was taken up by dozens of books on politics, sociology and feminism. The table was untidy, but three things stood out. One was a desk calendar with photographs of sailing ships. But, as if by arrangement, both women's eyes reached out at the the same moment to the two framed photographs which were also on the desk. Cordelia picked them up. One was a family group, presumably consisting of Anthony Barrington, his ex-wife and their children. Caroline was between her parents, her brother and sister sitting on a sofa in front of them. The other was a photograph of the same man alone on top of a snow covered peak grinning into the camera. He was wearing climbing gear – old, stained clothes, heavy boots, ropes, a small rucksack. His face was lean and tanned, well-lined around the eyes. His eyebrows turned up slightly in the middle of his face, giving it a humorous cast. The rest of his face was unremarkable. But the eyes and their brows spoke of someone who might well be good fun to have around the place. No doubt Caroline thought so.

While Cordelia was studying the pictures more closely, the door opened and Caroline burst in, shouting over her shoulder, 'Not tonight, I've got too much work to do.' Cordelia started and almost dropped the pictures. Lindsay got to her feet as Caroline stopped in her tracks.

'Good Lord!' the girl exclaimed. 'Murderers and burglars in the same week. Altogether too much for me.'

In spite of herself, Lindsay smiled broadly. 'Not exactly, no,' she said. 'We wanted to be sure of seeing you and your door was open. I promise we haven't been reading your letters and sifting through your worldly goods.'

'Didn't for a minute think you had. Not that you'd find anything of interest if you did. I was just rather taken aback to find the super sleuths waiting to give me the third degree,' Caroline replied, throwing herself down on the bed.

Cordelia remarked to no one in particular. 'Good to see the old school grapevine is as efficient as it was in my day.'

'Oh, everyone knows what it is you're here for. Her Majesty anounced it at assembly. I suppose you want to ask me about that bloody woman. I must say she caused enough trouble when she was alive without turning the world upside-down now she's dead. Really and truly, I think whoever put a stop to her should be congratulated, not punished. Still, that's a pretty antediluvian view, isn't it? I must say, though, that I think it's very dim of the police to have arrested The Boss. I mean, there are some pretty primitive people around who might think that killing people is some sort of answer, but really, she's not that sort at all. Not at all, truly.' Caroline ground to a halt.

'The Boss?' queried Cordelia.

'Ooops! I mean Miss Callaghan,' Caroline replied, blushing furiously.

'Why The Boss?' Lindsay asked.

'Because she lets you know who's in charge, I suppose. Hey, I hope you don't imagine I might have had anything to do with the murder? I mean, everyone's always telling me how hopelessly indiscreet I am, and I suppose I have rather been shooting the old mouth off about the ghastly woman's death being rather a blessing in extremely thin disguise. But honestly, do I look like a murderer to you?'

Lindsay found herself laughing out loud at the idea. Caroline sprawled on her counterpane, the picture of injured innocence. 'Caroline,' said Lindsay, 'I can't honestly say that I think you're incapable of murder. But from what I've seen of you over the past week, I really have to say that if you had killed Lorna, you would have told the entire population of Derbyshire by now. If you're ever going to commit murder, you really must get laryngitis first.'

Caroline grinned enormously, and suddenly Lindsay was struck by her resemblance to her father. It was her attitude – a sense of joy in risk-taking, a devil-may-care attitude – and at that moment, Lindsay saw that Caroline might indeed have killed Lorna and have managed to keep her mouth firmly shut. What better disguise for discretion than a reputation for logorrhoea?

'Okay, so if you know I didn't do it, what do you want me to tell you? Shall I start with what I told the police?' asked Caroline eagerly. It was hard not to see her as some enormously good-natured but clumsy young bear-cub.

'Tell us first of anything that struck you as at all unusual at any time all day Saturday,' said Cordelia. Both women were conscious of the need not to waste the opportunity of a witness who seemed both talkative and observant.

'Well, the whole day was a bit funny, really. Miss Callaghan seemed a bit edgy, but I put that down to the general upheaval, plus she was responsible for both of you. Having a journalist on the loose about the place must have been a bit unnerving for everybody on the official side. I mean, only you know what you were going to say about us. You see, places like this are terribly insular, and being under constant attack from the forces of reason and equality make them even more on the defensive, you know? And then there was the business of Sarah Cartwright throwing a wobbler which upset more or less everybody – it threw Jacko into a perfect tail-spin and didn't exactly fill Miss Callaghan with good cheer.

'You were around, so I suppose you saw that carry-on. It was rather grisly, really. Sarah's a bit of a loner; I always get the feeling that she hasn't actually got much more to her life than this place, her father being so busy. I mean, my father is always up to his eyes in work, or climbing expeditions or whatever, but he always makes time to be with his children. It seems to me that Sarah's father puts work first – you know, if he's planned

221

to take her off somewhere and work interferes, it's, "Tough luck, old girl, we'll make it another time." So although she doesn't really have close friends here, I suppose this place is more or less home to her. At least people are pretty impressed by her sporting ability.

'So of course, when those half-wits started to have a go at her it must have been pretty hellish. And, since Miss Callaghan is always frighteningly perceptive about what goes on inside our tiny heads, it's my guess that she must have been a bit upset on Sarah's account. All that would make her a bit iffy, wouldn't it?'

'Possibly,' Cordelia replied. 'Was she okay by the afternoon?'

'I don't know much about what went on then, because I was out with my father. I suppose you know all about him and that bloody woman by now?'

Cordelia said quickly. 'We know a bit. Suppose you tell us what really happened.'

'It's been the main event in our family over the last couple of years,' said Caroline, her normal machine-gun delivery slowing down. 'I'm not entirely clear how they met, but once my father got to know Lorna, he fell for her like the proverbial ton. He didn't say anything, but I think Mummy knew something was happening. Anyway, he decided that he didn't just want an affair, so he told Mummy he wanted a divorce. It was all extremely messy – and very painful for everyone because deep down, he loved us all really.

'When the whole sordid business of the divorce was over, he went to Lorna and asked her to marry him. He hadn't seen her for about a month because she'd been off touring in the Far East. She laughed in his face and told him not to be a fool, that she had no intention of marrying him. She didn't have the sense to see she was turning down the best man she'd ever meet. And he was devastated. Who wouldn't have been? I mean, he'd thrown his marriage away, torn up his own life and our lives too, and all for nothing.' She paused.

'I can forgive him,' she went on, 'because everyone has the right to make at least one almighty blunder in their lives, and after all, he's still a part of my world. But I could never forgive her because, if she hadn't fooled him into thinking she wanted him, he'd have just let it be a stupid affair and that would have been the end of it. But no. She had to destroy his life. So I'm not sorry that someone killed her. Not a bit sorry.' Lindsay detected a trembling in Caroline's voice as she finished her story.

'Was there any special reason why he came to see you on Saturday?' She asked, trying hard to avoid sounding eager.

'He was doing a bit of rock-climbing on Sunday down at Ilam,' she explained. 'That's a limestone gorge about twenty miles from here. He said he'd come up early and take me out on Saturday afternoon. He often does that. I'm sure that's half the reason he sent me to Derbyshire House. The school he chose for my brother is in Perthshire, so he can get up in the mountains when he goes to see him. I sometimes think he loves the mountains and rocks more than anything else. Mountains, music, his family and his job. In that order, I suspect. But he gives so much to all of us, he's never made me feel that a moment spent with me is a moment he'd rather spend doing something else. I'm very, very fond of my father,' she added unnecessarily.

'How long did you spend with him on Saturday?' asked Cordelia.

'He picked me up at half-past two and we went for a walk in Chee Dale and Wye Dale. Then we went to have tea and he dropped me back here about a quarter to six. I told him about the concert, but he wouldn't come because she was here. I didn't expect him to. He said he'd send a cheque for the fund. He went off back to his hotel then, I suppose. He usually does. He has dinner, then sits in his room doing paperwork and listening to his Walkman.'

'Do you know where he was staying?' Lindsay chimed in.

'I think he was at the Anglers' Retreat, in Thorpe Dale. That's where he usually stays. Anyway, I came back here, had dinner, and then it was time for the concert.'

'And you didn't see him again on Saturday night?'

'No, how could I have?'

'Have you told the police any of this?' asked Cordelia cautiously.

'They didn't ask about anything except the concert. I suppose I was a bit nervy about them thinking my father might perhaps have had something to do with it. They don't know him like I do, after all. Should I have told them do you think? Could it help Miss Callaghan?'

'I doubt it would have meant anything to them, Caroline. Don't worry on that account. Can you tell us what you remember about the rest of the evening?'

'Well, after dinner I went straight to the hall and collected a load of programmes from the music storeroom. I didn't see anyone around who shouldn't have been there, I'm afraid. I went back later for some more programmes, and went to the loo as well. But I wasn't paying too much attention; it was pretty chaotic except for the actual corridor down to Music 2, because the only people going down there were the people selling programmes. Jess Bennett turned up in the hall at one point looking for Miss Callaghan and I sent her backstage because I'd noticed Miss Callaghan there when I came out of the loo, ticking off one of the choir for the state of her hair. That's about all I remember.

'It's pretty frightening, really, isn't it? I mean,

it's got to have been someone who knew the place well, hasn't it? And that more or less means someone we all, or at least some of us, know.' Caroline dried up finally. She suddenly looked very young.

'I'm inclined to think so,' said Lindsay. 'Tell me, did you see Sarah Cartwright or her father at all on Saturday after the business at the craft fair?'

Caroline thought for a moment. 'I didn't see him,' she said positively. 'He certainly wasn't at the concert. As for Sarah – I plodded along to her room when I got back from tea, just to see if she felt like coming in for dinner and wanted a bit of moral support. I knocked at her door, but there was no reply. I tried the handle, but the door was locked. I just assumed she was either asleep or not in the mood for company, so I buzzed off again.'

Lindsay reckoned there wasn't much more they could hope to find out from Caroline, so she flicked a glance at Cordelia, got to her feet and said, 'Thanks for being so honest with us. If you fancy a chat about anything. I expect we'll be sticking around for a few days. Okay?'

Cordelia's mouth twisted into a sardonic smile as she followed her friend on to the landing and she said drily, 'The working-class hero never gives up the struggle, does she?'

By now Lindsay was beginning to take Cordelia's mockery in her stride. It forced her to keep her wits about her. So she replied mildly, 'This place is so well defended that you can't expect me to ignore a chink in the armour. Now: do you want a conference, or shall we go straight on to see Sarah Cartwright? We should get her out of the way, I suppose.'

Cordelia shrugged. 'I haven't anything to say that won't keep. No flash of genius that will vanish for ever if I don't give it shape and form immediately. Let's see her and have done for today. Then we can go and have dinner somewhere and sort out what we've got so far.'

'That should see us through the aperitifs,' said Lindsay wryly. 'Now, where do we find her?'

'It's just down the corridor here. I checked with Paddy's list.' Cordelia led the way to Sarah's room and knocked. After a short pause a low voice invited them in.

Sarah Cartwright's room was furnished exactly as Caroline's, and had a splendid view of the trees that cut Longnor House off from the bleak moorland behind. But there were few of the personal touches that made Caroline's room so individual. The walls were bare except for a large black and white framed photograph of a gymnast on the beam who Cordelia identified as Nelli Kim, the Russian Olympic medallist. The books were all school textbooks except for several on gymnastics, and the desk was almost pathologically neat. On it there was one small framed wedding photo. The man was clearly a younger version of James

Cartwright. Lindsay assumed the dark-haired, vivacious-looking woman by his side was Sarah's mother.

The girl was sitting cross-legged on her bed reading a newspaper. As they entered, she folded it carefully and put it down. She had dark brown hair cut short and neat with a straight, heavy fringe, contrasting with pale skin untouched by the ravages of adolescence. She had an air of extreme self-possession, but her dark eyes were watchful. Unlike her father, she seemed prepared to let other people make the running. She looked inquiringly at them.

Lindsay felt instantly uncomfortable, as if she were an unwelcome intruder on someone else's private territory. 'I'm sorry to butt in on you,' she said, 'but I wondered if perhaps you could help us.' Sarah said nothing. Lindsay glanced at Cordelia in a mute appeal for help.

Cordelia took up the hard job of communication. 'Miss Overton has asked us to see if we can uncover anything that might establish Miss Callaghan's innocence. We've been talking to a lot of people in the hope that they might be able to come up with something to help and, basically, you're next on the list.'

'I know all about you,' said Sarah. Not surprisingly, there was nothing of the local accent in her tones. She might never have been north of Ascot. 'You've been to see my father. How absurd of you to think he could have anything to do with this.

I don't know what you think I could tell you either. I was here all the time on Saturday. I saw no one apart from Miss Callaghan. She came over at tea-time with some sandwiches and fruit for me. Anyone else who knocked I just ignored. There was no one I wanted to see. Except possibly my father, but he wasn't here.'

'You must have been very upset by what happened in the morning,' Cordelia probed.

The girl acknowledged this sally with raised eyebrows. 'Of course I was. It's not terribly thrilling to have people attacking you because of something your father is quite properly doing in the course of his business. Especially when you're supposedly among friends. All the same, it was quite a useful experience in one sense. It's helpful to know who your real friends are.'

'Like Caroline Barrington?' asked Lindsay quickly.

'Why her in particular?'

'Well, she did call round to see if you felt like going to dinner.'

'Did she? I don't remember. One or two people came by. As I said, there was no one I wanted to see. I locked the door and only let Miss Callaghan in because I felt it might be rather more trouble not to.' The girl's hostility was now becoming palpable.

'So you neither saw nor heard anything that might have any bearing on Lorna Smith-Couper's murder?'

'Correct. Now, if that's all, I have things to do. I was about to go down to the gym to run through some floor work before you arrived. Do you mind if I get on with that now?'

'If you don't mind, there are a couple more questions I'd like to ask,' said Lindsay pleasantly.

The girl's eyebrows flickered and she threw a look of contempt at Lindsay. 'If you've time to waste, go ahead and ask.'

'You told the police that Miss Callaghan took you to Music 2 on Saturday morning?'

'Correct. I told them that because that's exactly what she did.'

'Any idea why she took you there?'

'She was trying to be helpful. I was very upset, as I'm sure you understand. Miss Callaghan had the sense to see that the best thing for me was to be somewhere quiet till I felt all right again. She said, "Let's go to Music 2 because I'm sure it will be empty. It's been spruced up for our celebrity guest, so no one will be using it today."'

Lindsay's eyes bored into the girl. 'Are you sure she said that the room had been set aside for Lorna?'

'Yes, I'm sure.'

'Miss Callaghan doesn't remember anything of the sort.'

'I'm sorry about that. But it doesn't alter the fact that she said it.'

'You also told the police that Miss Callaghan had been opening cupboards in the room and picking stuff up. You're still sticking to that, are you? Because Miss Callaghan has no recollection of that happening either.'

Sarah's eyes flashed as she replied angrily, 'Yes, I'm still sticking to the truth. Why should I lie, for God's sake? I like Miss Callaghan.'

'I can think of several reasons why you might be telling less than the truth.' Lindsay paused, but Sarah refused to take up the challenge. Lindsay shook her head sorrowfully and said, 'Sorry we've been such a nuisance, I hope we haven't put you off your exercises.' Then she turned and walked out, followed by Cordelia. She marched down the stairs in a state of frustrated fury then suddenly saw the funny side and whirled round on Cordelia with a grin, saying, 'There is something about me that seems to get right up the Cartwrights' noses. I can't have gone to the right school.'

Cordelia dissolved into a violent fit of giggles, much to the amazement of a couple of sixth-formers who passed by as the two women staggered into Paddy's room.

15

Cordelia sat at Paddy's desk scribbling furiously in her notebook, while Lindsay wandered round the room, smoking and fiddling with the assortment of objects on the mantelpiece. Eventually she headed for the drinks cupboard and poured herself a small whisky. 'You want one?' she asked.

'That depends. Are we going out for a meal? And if so, when?'

'Must we go out? I'm just not in the mood tonight for all the palaver of menus and waiters and posing about the wine list. I thought I'd go off in search of an Indian takeaway. Buxton may not be the cosmopolitan centre of the universe, but it must have some kind of fast food apart from fish and chips. Unless you have any other ideas?'

'I was rather hoping we could find a nice little restaurant and splash out a bit.'

'Every day I spend down here is a day when I'm earning precisely zilch. I don't feel much like splashing out. Especially since I've got Paddy on my Presbyterian conscience.'

'My treat, Lindsay. I've got it, we might as well spend it.'

Lindsay looked outraged. 'No way,' she retorted. 'We have to know each other a lot better before I let you pay for me. If you feel the need to go out and spoil yourself, fine. But I'll settle for what fits in with my lifestyle, if it's all the same to you.'

Cordelia looked thunderstruck. 'My God,' she complained, 'you're so bloody self-righteous sometimes. Why the hell don't you just relax? There's no need for all this puritanical shit.'

'What do you mean, puritanical shit? Just because I've always paid my own way and I'm not about to stop now. I've worked hard to keep my independence and I'm not about to throw it away.'

Cordelia shook her head in bewilderment. 'Look, I only offered to buy you dinner, not become your sugar momma. You can let someone buy you a meal without becoming a kept woman, you know.'

Lindsay scowled. 'In my business, you learn quickly that there's no such thing as a free lunch.'

'God, you're impossible. All right, go and get a bloody curry if it makes you feel better. We'll split the cost to salve your conscience.'

Lindsay stormed out, slamming the door behind her. By the time she returned with an assortment of Indian food, she was regretting the scene. She found Cordelia lying on the sofa with a glass of wine, reading one of Sunday's papers, ignoring her return. Lindsay began unpacking the tinfoil containers of chicken, lamb and vegetable curries and rice, and said gruffly, 'I'm sorry. I was out of order.'

Cordelia didn't put the paper down. 'How much do I owe you,' she remarked coldly.

'Look, I said I'm sorry. Let's forget it, eh? Come and eat. Then we can talk about the information we've dug up.'

Cordelia folded the paper and got up. 'Okay,' she said quietly. 'We'll forget it. But don't push your luck, Lindsay. You should have the sense to know I'm not trying to buy my way into your life. You going to behave now?'

Lindsay nodded. She launched straight into her analysis of their current position, eager to re-establish their previous closeness. 'If we look at our original list,' she expounded, 'we can cross off Paddy, of course. And you.'

Cordelia smiled. 'That's very generous of you. But you haven't been able to prove I didn't do it. You're simply reacting on instinct. And that goes for Paddy too.'

'Not entirely,' said Lindsay. 'This crime has to have been premeditated to some extent. The fact that Paddy's duffel-coat toggle came from Longnor proves that. It means that the murderer had decided in advance what the murder method would be. It wasn't just a spontaneous reaction of anger in the music room. Now, Paddy didn't know until dinner was nearly over that she would have any opportunity to be alone with Lorna. After that, she had no chance to go back to Longnor to fetch the toggle.

'Paddy is not a member of the music staff and wasn't directly involved in the plans for the concert. Indeed, if she hadn't been asked by Pamela Overton to look after Lorna, she could reasonably have expected to spend the entire evening sitting with you and me. And there would have been no opportunity for her to go sailing off and commit murder. Also, I think we can rule out any conspiracy theory between Paddy and Pamela Overton. No, if Paddy had been planning to have a go at Lorna, she would have picked a different time and place. She'd have made sure she had some kind of alibi. But this way, she'd have had to go ahead with it knowing she'd be the prime suspect. And Paddy's not daft enough for that.' Cordelia slowly nodded agreement.

Lindsay went on. 'The same argument really applies to you. There is no reason why you should have imagined that any opportunity would arise that evening to kill Lorna. So it's highly unlikely that you'd be wandering around with a garrotte stuffed down your cleavage on the off-chance. Now, I know you're very fit, but I don't think you'd have had time to run to Longnor House and back and still get to the music

235

room in time to kill Lorna. Anyway, in both your case and Paddy's, why go all the way back to Longnor when there were dozens of coats in the cloakrooms in this building, amongst which there must have been the odd duffel coat?'

Lindsay broke off and loaded dahl into her mouth with a chunk of nan bread. Cordelia tasted the lamb curry suspiciously and said grudgingly, 'Not bad, this. Okay, then, Sherlock. Let's have the rest of your reasoning.'

Between mouthfuls, Lindsay continued. 'Up to now, we've rather been looking at this crime as if it had been a completely opportunist exercise. In reality, I think quite a bit of foreknowledge and forward planning was involved. On that basis alone, I'm prepared to exclude you and Paddy. Of the others, I feel strongly that Margaret Macdonald is out of the running. It would have been a completely unnecessary crime for her. As she said to us, her life wouldn't have been destroyed by any revelation Lorna could have made.

'Also, look at the actual nature of this murder. It was a very nasty way to kill someone. There was a lot of hatred in whoever did this. It wasn't done in a simple moment of anger or fear. The crime was vindictive; it had real unpleasantness in it, and a pretty gruesome irony in garrotting her with a cello string. Talk about hoist with your own petard! If Margaret Macdonald was going to kill Lorna, she wouldn't have murdered her like this. Their affair was dead, all passion spent far in the past. Margaret has lived for ages with the risk that Lorna might tell someone what had happened, and she made very sure that she lived a life whereby she could cope with the knowledge of that risk.'

Cordelia frowned and said, 'But look at it this way. Probably the only thing that kept Lorna silent in the past was fear for her own reputation. But now it's become rather fashionable to have had a bijou gay fling, so there was less need for her reticence. Surely the risk must have increased recently, and Margaret Macdonald must have realised that?'

'Not necessarily. I don't think Margaret moves in that kind of world. And besides, why would she take a duffel-coat toggle from Longnor? She wouldn't implicate Paddy, who's supposed to be her best friend here.'

'Ah,' said Cordelia with satisfaction, 'but at that stage she wouldn't have specifically been incriminating Paddy, would she? She would just have been diverting suspicion away from herself in a general sort of way. We've probably got enough of a case against her to cast sufficient doubt on Paddy's guilt to get the charges dropped, don't you think?'

'But if we clear Paddy and don't prove who really did it, people will always assume that it was Paddy. And I don't really think Margaret, if she were the guilty party, would allow that state of affairs to continue.'

Cordelia thought for a moment and gnawed a chicken leg. Then she said, 'You're presuming too much on friendship. I don't think I'd speak out to save a friend if my own freedom were at stake.'

'That's very candid of you. And you're probably right. Okay, leave Margaret in the running, but only as a rank outsider. Now, there's James Cartwright. We're cutting it rather fine as regards time, as well as assuming that he had access to a key to the music room. Not that that's a very big assumption, given the amount of work he's done there in the past. From their meeting in the afternoon he could have picked up that she'd be there again later. If we could only place him on the scene, we'd have a damn good case.'

'It would certainly be an excellent choice from the school's point of view.' Cordelia remarked.

'That's the least of my worries, to be perfectly blunt,' Lindsay replied with asperity.

'Fair enough, but it would be nice for Paddy to have a job to go back to if we ever manage to get her out of this,' said Cordelia. 'So how do we place him on the scene?'

'I don't know. If I could answer that we'd have a case to put to the police. Cartwright is certainly my favourite on balance. To be honest, I can't really see any of the girls having done it.'

'Even though any one of them might have had motive, means and probably foreknowledge of the opportunity? Be fair, you're being sentimental again. Don't forget that a growing-up process

238

which includes incarceration in a place like this gives a certain hard edge to one's character that most people don't acquire till much later in life. I wouldn't mind betting that young Caroline Barrington has enough guts to have carried out that murder if she had had a mind to,' Cordelia speculated.

'No, no, wrong timing again,' Lindsay parried. 'Caroline might have done it before her parents' divorce, while there was still a chance of salvaging her family. But I can't see her as the vindictive avenger of her father's lost face and her mother's lost pride.'

'Come on, Lindsay, you can't use that as a valid argument against Caroline as a suspect,' complained Cordelia.

'Why not? Look, I believe that we all have the capability to commit at least one murder. Fortunately, the precise set of circumstances never actually come together for the overwhelming majority of us. And since I believe that, I find the only way I can deal with the problems of a crime like this is to look at the psychological probabilities. I simply don't think that Caroline's psychology – in so far as I've seen it at work – matches the facts of this crime. I rule out Caroline, just as I rule out Margaret.'

Cordelia pulled a face. 'I'm still not utterly convinced,' she said.

Lindsay leaned back in her seat, lit a cigarette and continued her lecture. 'I can't say I feel so definite about the other two girls we've seen because I know even less about them than Caroline. But since you've told me not to be sentimental, let's look at them. Of the two, I'd say that Jessica was less likely, but with Sarah only marginally more so. Jessica might have killed out of immediate anguish for her brother, but I don't see her having the nerve for this crime. And I don't believe she really had time to do it. Remember – she'd have had to get the spare key to Music 2 and return it to Margaret Macdonald's room. The first part of the exercise wouldn't necessarily have been awkward, because she probably would have been able to do it in the afternoon. But if Paddy was a few steps away from Margaret Macdonald's room, where Jessica said she was when she found her – and it would have been too risky for Jessica to lie about that – then I don't see how such an obtrusive girl, with that mane of red hair, could have got it back unnoticed.

'As far as Sarah is concerned, from what we've seen of her so far, I'd say she might – just might – be capable of this killing. But we've no evidence at all to link her with the crime. Really, the only reason why she should be a suspect – apart from my nasty mind – is that we believe she's lied to the police in her statement about Paddy. But even that isn't certain, since Paddy seems to be suffering from amnesia on the subject.'

'And what about the latest addition to the list?' Cordelia demanded.

'Anthony Barrington. Well, he's in the locality. He comes fairly often, so he knows the layout of the school pretty well. Must do by now. He had a very large axe to grind with Lorna. He's a man of action, too, not the sort who'd sit back calmly and shrug off being crossed. However, there's the difficulty he'd have with the keys and remaining unseen. I suspect we're going to have to engineer a talk with him. Which I don't especially relish.'

Cordelia went through to the kitchen and made coffee. Lindsay followed her and said shamefacedly, 'There's one major problem. I'm committed to working next week in Glasgow. Wednesday to Friday. To be quite blunt, I can't afford not to.'

'I'm sure we can work something out with Pamela Overton if you're losing out by being here,' Cordelia said sympathetically.

'It's not just the money, though obviously that's a major consideration. It's the goodwill. The *Clarion*'s my major source of income right now, and if I don't keep up my availability for shifts, they'll find someone else. There are plenty of hungry freelancers around ready to snap up the holes in the *Clarion* shift rota. Also, I think I've got a strong chance of getting the next full-time staff job that comes along, and I can't pretend that I wouldn't jump at the chance. So far as this business is concerned, after Tuesday night I'm back on part-time only. Which makes me feel a bit of a shit.'

'That gives us four whole days. We'll see how we get on, and maybe the *Clarion* will give you more time if you need it. Don't despair yet. I'm sure we can do it. We've got to.'

Later, back at their hotel, Lindsay lay awake, listening to the deep breathing that signalled Cordelia's quick drift into sleep. The endless searchings of her restless mind would not let her drop off. She knew that somewhere there was a key that would unlock the closed book of Lorna's death. But the more she wrestled to find it, the more frustrated she became. After an hour's fitful turning and tossing, she slipped out of bed.

Moving softly, she dressed in jeans and a warm sweater. She searched in her bag till she found Paddy's bunch of keys. Then, by the moonlight, she wrote a note for Cordelia:

If I'm not here when you wake up, I'll be up at the school, probably in Paddy's rooms. Come up and get me in the car. Keys inside the boot. Love you dearly. Lindsay.

She propped the note up against Cordelia's alarm clock and quietly closed the door behind her. She crept downstairs and out into the car park. At the car, she unlocked the boot and took out the heavy walking boots and windproof jacket that she always kept there. She slipped the jacket on, then swapped her trainers for the boots. Finally, she

242

pocketed the Ordnance Survey map, dropped the keys into the boot, closed it and set off.

In the moonlight, she climbed steadily through the wood above the town till she emerged on high moorland at the foot of the Victorian folly Paddy had pointed out to her nearly a week before. She climbed the squat stone tower, blessing the almost full moon that made it possible, and gazed over the landscape. The site had been well chosen. In the moonlight, she could see for miles in all directions. Lindsay unfolded her map and gazed out over the terrain. She soon located her target and set off with regular, easy strides across the darkened landscape. The going was not difficult for it had been a fairly dry autumn and the ground was soft, but not as boggy as she expected moorland to be at this time of year. The only sounds were the occasional owl, the sudden quiet whispering of small animals in the tussocks of rough grass and the distant rumble of the odd car engine.

Forty minutes later, she was striding up the drive of Derbyshire House. It was after two by then, and the only lights visible were the dull glow of corridor night-lights. When she reached the main house, she walked all the way round, pausing several times to study the building. Finally, she let herself in by the door near the kitchens, using Paddy's master key. Once inside, she slipped off her boots and moved silently through the corridors. She climbed the back staircase to the music department, using the tiny pencil torch she always carried in her walking jacket, along with her compass, whistle and Swiss Army knife. She unlocked the door to the music room and closed it behind her.

Slowly she walked all round the room, not focusing on any one detail but letting her eyes and mind absorb everything around her. At the end of her circuit of the room, she sat down on the teacher's chair. She closed her eyes and forced herself to recall the scene she had witnessed when she had arrived in answer to Pamela Overton's ominous summons. Again she conjured up details of the room she had seen then and compared it with what she could see now. Nothing came to mind of any significance at all. She sighed, cursed herself for her incompetence, and got to her feet.

Lindsay locked up the music room behind her and prowled round the rest of the music department. But nothing struck her. She even probed around the recesses of the stage area, but still there was no echo in her mind. In despair, she wandered back down the corridor to the hall.

Then, as she had done on the night of the murder, she paused to stare out of the window to collect her thoughts. Not far away, she could see the lights of the squash courts building site. But everything else was in darkness. Below her was the roof of the kitchen area, with its sturdy iron railings and its tubs of miniature trees. And suddenly, Lindsay knew what her mind had been stubbornly hiding from her for the past six days.

16

There were two of them sharing the cell. At least being on remand meant they had certain privileges. For a start, Paddy had books to read and her own clothes to wear. Either Gillian Markham or her clerk visited daily, on Cordelia's instructions, bringing fresh reading supplies, tempting food and the half bottle of wine that Home Office regulations allow remand prisoners. But although these small luxuries made life a little more tolerable, it was just as hard for Paddy to submit to the indignities of prison life as it was for every other woman on the wing. Her plight had not really sunk in while she had been in police custody. The remand hearing in the magistrates' court had seemed unreal. But when she had arrived at the remand centre, she had started to feel like a condemned animal arriving at the abbatoir. Nevertheless, the strip search, degrading in its intimacy, had humiliated but not broken her. What prison food she had eaten had only disgusted her.

What was pushing her perilously close to breaking point was the isolation. Her cell-mate, who was on remand for receiving stolen goods, was pleasant enough to her. But there was no real point of contact between them. Marion was understandably obsessed by the problems facing her three young children and her unemployed live-in boyfriend. Despite that, she still found it impossible to understand how Paddy could exist happily without a steady man and a family. That inability undermined Paddy even further, making her question why she had never been able to settle for any of the men who had been part of her life for varying lengths of time. But at least Marion was not hostile, unlike many of the other women on the wing, who seemed to take positive pleasure in seeing a middle-class woman facing the same degradation they endured.

At the same time as Paddy was awakened by the bang on her cell door that heralded Saturday morning, Cordelia was wakened by the buzz of her alarm clock. She rolled over and switched it off in one movement, then turned over to where Lindsay should have been. At once she shot upright, taken aback by the sight of a rumpled, empty space. She had known Lindsay for long enough by now to realise just how slim were the chances of her rising early for the hell of it. It took her a moment to become aware that she was clutching a piece of paper in the hand that had switched off the alarm.

Cordelia read the note and instantly leapt out of bed. She dressed quickly, raced downstairs and out into the freezing morning air. She found the car keys where Lindsay had left them and climbed into the driving seat. She turned the keys in the ignition and nothing happened. Cursing, she tried again. Nothing. Then she remembered Lindsay telling her about the engine immobiliser she had installed. 'Bloody stupid gadgets,' she swore, fumbling under the dashboard for the switch. She tried the ignition again, and the engine started at once. It took her only six minutes to reach Longnor House. She burst into Paddy's living-room and began to panic when she saw no sign of Lindsay. Then she remembered the bedroom.

Lindsay's clothes were strewn on the floor by the bed, where she was sleeping deeply. Cordelia stopped to let her heartbeat return to normal. In sleep, Lindsay lost half her years. Her face was gently flushed, her hair tousled, her features completely relaxed. Then her instincts told her she was no longer alone, and she began to wake up.

'Morning,' Lindsay muttered sleepily. 'What time is it?'

'Twenty past seven.'

'Oh God, is that all? I thought you'd at least have your run before you arrived. I didn't imagine anything could come between you and your early morning exercise.'

'You leave me a note like that and expect me

calmly to go for a run and have breakfast too, I suppose, before I do anything about it?' demanded Cordelia incredulously.

Lindsay propped herself up on one elbow and nodded. 'Why not?' she asked. 'I didn't say anything about it being urgent.'

'But what are you doing here?'

'Oh, I didn't think Paddy would mind. I simply didn't feel like walking back at three o'clock in the morning. Exhaustion came over me in a wave, so I thought I'd kip down here. Very comfortable I was, too,' she smiled.

'God, you're exasperating,' said Cordelia. 'I meant, what possessed you to get up in the middle of the night and walk up here? I presume you did walk?'

'Yes, I walked. It's not far – only a couple of miles across the moors. I couldn't sleep, so I thought that if I came up here and wandered round on my own in the silence of night I might get some answers.'

'And did you, you tantalising pig?' Cordelia appealed.

Lindsay leaned back on the pillows and smirked. 'You really want to know?'

Cordelia jumped on the bed and grabbed her shoulders in affectionate annoyance. 'Of course I want to know!'

'I've remembered what it was I had forgotten.'

There was a pause. When Cordelia spoke it was almost a whisper, as if she did not want to tempt fate. 'And it's important? As important as you thought it might be?'

'I think so. If I'm right, it shows how the murderer committed the crime without being spotted in the music department. And it also narrows the field down considerably. But we'll have to talk to Chris Jackson this morning to see if my theory will hold water.'

'Well then, tell me; don't keep me guessing!'

'Okay. But only after you've made me a cup of coffee.'

'Oh, Lindsay Gordon, I could strangle you,' yelled Cordelia as they tussled on the bed. Finally she sat back and declared, 'All right. If coffee is your price, I'll pay. Besides, I could do with a cup myself.' She slipped through to the kitchen and set the percolator going. Then she returned to the bedroom.

'I've done my bit,' she reported. 'Now, while we're waiting, you can tell me what it is you've remembered. Who did you see or hear doing or saying what? If you see what I mean.'

'Nobody. It's not quite that simple. On Saturday afternoon, after the play and before the book auction, I sat at the very front of the hall, at the side, and stared out of the window in between jotting down some notes. Those windows look down on the kitchen roof and the woods. The curtains were drawn in the evening by the time the concert began. But at that time, it wasn't quite dusk, so no one had got round to shutting out the view. I could see the flat roof of the kitchen. I noticed the pots of conifers. And I noticed that strong iron railing going all round the roof.

'Later, after Lorna had been murdered, I was going back from the music room to the hall. The two windows in the corridor didn't have curtains at them, so again I could look out and see the kitchen roof, though at an angle because it doesn't come along as far as the music department. I was thinking about what Pamela Overton had said, and about what I'd just seen, so I was looking without really noticing anything.'

'I subconsciously registered that there was something different about the roof, but I didn't really focus on what it was because it was too far from the room where Lorna died to have anything to do with the murder, I thought at the time. Last night, however, I stood at the same window and I remembered what I'd seen. It hadn't been there on Saturday afternoon, and it wasn't there when I looked out again on Tuesday. But it was on Saturday night.'

The percolator burped loudly as Lindsay paused for dramatic effect. She grinned and went on. 'Four scaffolding poles and a pile of clamps. And I thought, what if someone put them together and clamped them to the railings? They could clamber along the frame, wait till Lorna was making enough noise to cover small sounds, slide up the window catch almost silently, as I did the other day with my knife, get into the room, creep up on her and kill her. All the setting up could have been done while everyone else was having dinner. The garrotte could have been made at any time during that afternoon, or even at dinner time. I also had a wander round the building site for the squash courts. There's lots of scaffolding poles there that look just the same as the bits on the roof.'

There was a pause as Cordelia considered these new possibilities. 'I think we both need that coffee now,' she said softly. She left the room and returned with two steaming mugs.

'That certainly answers one or two questions,' she sighed.

'All of them except the crucial one,' Lindsay replied. 'It explains why no one saw the murderer entering or leaving the room. It also explains the problem of the locked door. All the murderer had to do beforehand was to arrange the chair and music stand so that Lorna had her back to the window, to check out the window catches and to collect a cello string – a gruesome little touch. And if I'm right, it also cuts the suspects down considerably.'

'I suppose so,' said Cordelia meditatively. 'I haven't had long enough to assimilate the idea yet. Surely, though, it lets out Paddy and Margaret for a start?'

'I reckon it eliminates everyone who was visible or alibied at dinner and during the first half of the concert. That does mean Paddy and Margaret – and also Caroline and Jessica. And of course, you. There's no way you could have been shinning up scaffolding in that outfit! And much to my irritation I think we may have to exclude James Cartwright. It's got to be someone who had motive, means and opportunity, but also the skill and nerve to contemplate that particular murder method. Right now I can think of only one person who fits the bill.'

'The one man we haven't seen yet.'

'Well, who else really? Anthony Barrington is known for his climbing feats. He's got nerve and skill. He's a successful businessman, which means he must have a streak of ruthlessness in his make-up. Lorna had cost him a great deal in personal terms, and I'd guess from the way Caroline has spoken about him that his family was pretty important to him. Losing that would rankle deeply with such a man. We've got to see him, Cordelia, and soon.'

Cordelia thought for a moment. Then she said, 'I imagine the school secretary will have an address and telephone number for him. If we're lucky, we may track him down today without having to ask Caroline.'

'That would be all to the good. If we ask her, there's every chance that she'll tip him off and I'd like to hit him unprepared. So you try the school office and see what you can come up with. We'll also have to have a word with Chris Jackson to see if we can run a little experiment quietly. What normally happens on a Saturday morning?'

'Hockey and lacrosse matches for the games players. The rest are supposed to be involved in their hobbies – photography, woodwork, orienteering, you name it.'

'Are there many people drifting around?'

'There shouldn't be any, but there's always the odd one or two. It's probably quietest around half-past ten. Most people are busy by then. But don't forget Chris will almost certainly be refereeing some games match. It would be best to go into school breakfast and try to catch her there. Maybe she can get someone to stand in for her.'

Lindsay agreed to this, and while she showered and dressed, Cordelia sat scribbling in her notebook. When Lindsay reappeared, the other woman mused, 'I don't think you've thought it through completely *vis-à-vis* James Cartwright. He would have had to take something of a risk, but I think he's still in the frame. He wasn't at the Woolpack till seven, don't forget. He could have made the preparations while everyone was at dinner – in the same way as Caroline's father could have done. There's hardly any leeway in terms of time. But I think Cartwright's still a possibility if we have to give Barrington a clean bill of health.'

She waved her notes at Lindsay. 'Look. I've worked it out. Six o'clock he comes back to the school. He collects the scaffolding – don't forget, he was bound to know it was there, which Barrington may not have done. Then it's up the fire escape to the kitchen roof, where he assembles the frame. He would also know what he was doing, he's been a builder for years. If anyone knew how to erect that frame, it was him. He's still a strong-looking bloke. And he installed those windows. He'd know exactly what he was about, breaking in through them without making a noise.

'So he bolts the scaffolding to the railings. Then he nips into the music department and makes his preparations. I'm not sure why he took the toggle from Longnor – maybe he'd parked his car near there and it was only on his way back that he realised he'd need something to protect his hands. Anyway, he drives to the Woolpack, has a very quick pint and shoots back here. Along the scaffolding he goes, flicks open the window catch, pulls himself over the sill, and bingo! Even if Lorna had heard him and there had been a struggle, he's strong enough to have overpowered her easily. Then it's off into the night, pausing only to dismantle the scaffolding. He could have come back and taken it away at any time. What do you think?'

Lindsay grimaced wryly at Cordelia and lit a cigarette. 'Listen, sunshine,' she said, trying but failing to keep her voice light and jokey, 'I'm supposed to be the Sherlock Holmes around here. You're supposed to be the dumb Dr Watson who stands back in amazement when the great investigator propounds her extravagant but impeccable theories. Your role is to provide an appreciative audience for my little grey cells, not to steal my thunder. Nevertheless . . . you're absolutely right. I was too hasty in ruling him out. It's just as well one of us is cautious.'

Cordelia made a mocking bow at Lindsay. 'Your humble servant acknowledges her menial role. But I must be allowed at least one good idea per case. Is that what I'm supposed to say?' She looked hard at Lindsay. 'I don't care what you think you've got to prove, Lindsay. Don't try to do your proving on me. It's not necessary.'

Lindsay flushed. 'I was only joking,' she muttered defensively.

Cordelia winked broadly at her. 'Better luck next time,' she said, gently.

Together they walked across to breakfast and were lucky enough to find Chris Jackson sitting alone at a table ploughing her way through a mound of toast and bacon. They sat down beside her after collecting boiled eggs and rolls.

The Scottish gym mistress scarcely looked up from her morning paper and gave them a mono-syllabic greeting. A moment later, she took in who was sharing her table, for she put down the sports pages and focused sharply on the two women.

'How's it going, then?' she asked. 'I'm surprised you're still around. I thought you'd dropped poor old Paddy down the plughole since I hadn't seen you around for a couple of days.'

'No chance,' Lindsay replied. 'We've been chasing around like blue-arsed flies. There's no way I'm giving up till I've got somebody in the cells in place of Paddy Callaghan.'

'And have you got anybody in mind?' Chris asked, trying to appear nonchalant but failing dismally.

'Let's just say we've eliminated certain possibilities and we've considerably narrowed down the field. I could even go so far as to say that we reckon we'll soon be able to prove that Paddy Callaghan could not have killed Lorna. We'd like your help to do that. It's a matter of assistance with a little experiment we've got in mind,' said Lindsay.

Chris thought for a few seconds before she replied. 'Provided I'm not top of your list of suspects I'll do anything I can to help,' she said, a nervous undertone in her voice.

Lindsay grinned widely, and Cordelia declared quickly, 'Not at all, Chris. It's just that we need a bit of help and you were the only person we could think of with the necessary skills. Are you busy this morning?'

'Well, I'm supposed to be umpiring the First XI's match against Grafton Manor. I don't see how I can get out of it because I can't think of anyone else who's available to do it.'

'That is something of a problem. I was afraid you might be tied up,' said Cordelia with regret.

'No problem at all,' Lindsay interjected brightly.

'I know just the person. She's fighting fit for all that running around – and she knows the rules. Don't you Cordelia?'

Cordelia's mouth dropped open as she struggled for something to say.

Lindsay grinned. 'I know you don't want to miss out on our experiment, but after all, you did suggest that this morning was the best time. Now, I've done a spot of climbing in the past and Chris is a gymnast. We should be able to manage it. So if you don't mind relieving her, we might be able to wrap this whole thing up nice and quickly. Besides, you missed your run this morning,' said Lindsay in a rush.

'You rotten sod,' Cordelia muttered. 'You've got the cheek of the devil.'

'Ah well, where we come from, the sparrows fly backwards to keep the dust out of their eyes, don't they, Chris? Seriously, now, is that okay with you both?'

'It's fine by me. At least it's a home match, so you won't have to travel with the girls,' Chris replied. She quickly filled Cordelia in on her duties at the hockey match and turned to Lindsay. 'What exactly are we going to do?'

'I'll tell you when we meet,' said Lindsay. 'It's vital that you keep this to yourself. The murderer mustn't know what we're up to. I'll see you at about quarter past ten in Paddy's rooms.'

Chris agreed to this arrangement, so Lindsay and Cordelia left her alone as they went off to obtain information from the school secretary. As they walked down the corridor, Cordelia spluttered with good-natured grumbles.

'That was some bloody stroke you pulled on me,' she complained. 'Umpiring a bloody hockey match while you have all the fun. I could kill you, Gordon. You just better cover all the angles, that's all I can say.'

In the secretary's office they were lucky again. The files produced a weekday and weekend address for Anthony Barrington, complete with phone numbers. They were about to leave when the other door to the office opened and they found themselves confronted by Pamela Overton who ushered them into her office and asked them to sit down. Like mesmerised first-formers, they sat.

'It has been almost a week now since the murder, and Miss Callaghan is still unjustly imprisoned. Have your inquiries borne fruit so far?'

Cordelia shifted uncomfortably in her seat and gazed at Lindsay with mute appeal. Lindsay pulled herself together, trying desperately to feel like a mature adult instead of a naughty schoolgirl caught doing unspeakable things behind the bike sheds.

'We've made a certain amount of progress,' she said. 'We drew up an initial list of people we felt might have some possible motive for killing Lorna. We've managed to eliminate several people on that list. Right now we're taking some steps which we hope will produce results within the next forty-eight hours. We believe we'll be able to establish Paddy's innocence beyond question. I'm bound to say that the way things look at the moment, the criminal is neither a pupil nor a member of staff. We'll do our very best to let you know the results before the police are informed, if that's possible.'

There was a silence while Miss Overton digested this information. At last, she said, 'I hope you'll be able to bring this affair to a speedy end, and one that is satisfactory to the school. Now, some time ago you asked me a question about keys, and this I can now answer. As far as the Bursar is concerned, when Mr Cartwright does any work in the school, he is issued with the keys he needs and he returns them when the job is completed. We have no reason to suppose there are any of the school keys permanently in his possession. I hope this information will help. I won't keep you any longer, but I do hope to hear from you soon.'

Thus dismissed, they left hastily. 'She reduces me so,' complained Cordelia. 'I simply can't respond to her. You amaze me, you stay so composed.'

'All a front, I assure you. Inside, I feel fourteen and guilty as hell. I feel she can read my mind; she knows exactly what I want to do with you!'

Slowly they walked back to Longnor, discussing their plans for Anthony Barrington. They decided that Lindsay should phone his weekend cottage to try to find out if and when he would be there. Back in Paddy's rooms, she dialled the number. On the third ring, the phone was answered by a woman who sounded middle-aged.

'Llanagar 263,' she said with a strong Welsh accent.

'Hello,' said Lindsay, 'is Mr Barrington there?'

'I'm sorry,' said the voice, 'he's gone out on the hills.'

'Oh, that's a pity,' said Lindsay. 'I had hoped to catch him. Do you know what time he'll be back?'

'He's usually back about four this time of year. Who shall I say called please?'

'Oh, it doesn't matter. I'll call again later,' Lindsay replied, hanging up before she could be questioned further. 'I think I got the cleaning woman,' she said to Cordelia. 'He'll be back around four. Shall we shoot over there this evening? I'd like to see Paddy again this afternoon. How long do you reckon it will take to get to his place?'

'I suppose between two and three hours driving. I'm game if you are.'

They smiled at each other and began to prepare for their various morning activities.

PART FOUR:
FINALE

17

Cordelia left just after nine-thirty to drive the hockey team in the school minibus to the pavilion on the threatened playing fields. As she drove, she mused on the irony of a conservation policy that meant the town had nowhere to expand, being surrounded by Country Park and National Park. The result was that any piece of land inside the boundaries immediately shot up in value so fast that soon there would be no green left inside the town at all except pocket-handkerchief gardens.

Left to herself, Lindsay put a Charlie Mingus album on Paddy's stereo and settled back for a solitary think. She reviewed all she knew about the case, from its beginning to the present, to make certain she had not missed some glaringly obvious piece of evidence. But eventually she was satisfied that no other vital fragment of information was lurking in the corners of her mind. All the evidence seemed to point inexorably to

Anthony Barrington. She was forced to accept Cordelia's hypothesis that Cartwright was still a possibility, but she had reservations about him. She made a mental note to see if she could find out anything firm about the financial status of his business. If he turned out to be sufficiently solvent, his motive would be virtually demolished.

She thought for some minutes about how she could easily discover the relevant information, but there seemed no obvious answer. She would ask Paddy that afternoon, she thought. Paddy always seemed to have her finger on the pulse of life around her.

She shrugged and reminded herself that, in any event, Cartwright was only second favourite. Anthony Barrington was the horse she fancied. As the phrase formed in her mind, she brought herself up with a jolt. This was no horse race, no game. It was a sick and serious business that had already cost one life and would damage others before it was over. All she could hope to do was to limit the damage by helping to clear the woman she knew in her bones to be innocent.

'And,' she thought wryly, 'if I can't manage this, there's no hope on God's earth for Cordelia and me. We'll never be able to build any relationship with the shadow of Paddy perpetually before us. And I do want this one so very much.'

She was interrupted by a knock at the door. Chris's curiosity had fired her to arrive ten minutes early. She clearly had difficulty in holding back questions as Lindsay deliberately took her time in making coffee for them both. As she came through with two mugs, Chris could hold back no longer. 'What's all this about?' she demanded.

'I have an idea as to how the murderer got into Music 2,' Lindsay replied. 'And I need your help to try out my theory.'

'But I thought it was obvious how it was done. Surely whoever did it just pinched the key and put it back afterwards,' said Chris, frowning.

'I don't think so. Something's been puzzling me all week. There were dozens of people milling around backstage. But not a soul admits to seeing the key being taken or put back. Not a soul admits to seeing anyone in that corridor except Paddy. It seems impossible that anyone could have got in that way unseen. Now, I noticed some scaffolding poles on the kitchen roof. They hadn't been there earlier in the day and they were gone a couple of days later. I believe they were used to enter the murder room. Via the window. I want to check that it can be done.'

Chris looked stunned. 'You've got to be joking!'

Lindsay shook her head.

'Have you told the police about this?' Chris asked.

Lindsay sighed. 'They'd never believe me. You see, I knew there was something I couldn't remember and it only came back to me last night. They know I've been trying to find out what happened. They'd be bound to think I was making it up to put Paddy in the clear. Besides Cordelia and I believe it's not enough just to clear Paddy. We've got to find the real culprit if we really want to help her. I think we're very close to the truth now. So, can I count on your help?'

Chris looked worried. She said, 'I still think you should tell the police, but if you're dead set on doing it this way I'll help all I can. What do we do?'

Fortunately, both of them were properly dressed for their task, Lindsay in jeans, sweater and training shoes, Chris in the track suit and trainers she'd been wearing in preparation for the match. As they left Longnor, Lindsay picked up a selection of spanners and an adjustable wrench from her car tool box. They walked across to the squash court building site as Lindsay explained her theory more fully to Chris, carefully skirting round the subject of possible suspects. At the site, the gates were padlocked together, but it took Lindsay and Chris only a few moments to climb them. Then Lindsay selected the four poles she wanted and the clamps that would fasten the frame together. Back at the gate, they puzzled for a moment about how to get the equipment out, till Chris pointed out gaps between the fencing and the ground that would allow them to be pushed through.

They quickly clambered back over the gates, Chris complaining, 'I hope to God none of my bright sparks is watching this carry-on.'

Lindsay laughed, saying, 'There's worse to come. Let's go.' She insisted on carrying all four poles, though it was an awkward struggle. She was determined to do it herself, to prove that one person could do it alone. When they reached the main building, she nearly came to grief several times on the fire escape, that led up to the kitchen roof. Chris attempted to help, but when Lindsay explained the need for struggling on alone, she subsided. To Chris's surprise, she finally managed it, and the two women ended up on the roof in a confused heap of poles, joints, spanners, arms and legs.

The journalist lay breathing heavily and sweating. 'Bloody hell,' she moaned. 'That was a lot tougher than I anticipated.'

'That's because you did it all wrong,' said Chris. 'You should have roped the poles together, then they would have been a lot easier to carry. Then you could have fastened another rope to them and hauled them up to the roof. Much simpler.'

Lindsay looked at her with new respect. 'Thank you, Chris,' she panted. 'You have just resurrected my theory. Thank God for the practical mind. Now, onwards and upwards.'

After a few failures, they managed to bolt the poles together in a rectangular frame. Then Lindsay realised that the frame was too heavy and unwieldy for one person to place in position and bolt to the railings.

So painstakingly they took it apart again, and

Lindsay prepared to clamber over the railings on to the narrow ledge to fit the poles together one by one to form the frame. Before she could go ahead, however, Chris stopped her.

'Wait there,' she commanded, all the authority of her position in her voice for the first time since the two had met. 'Don't you dare do anything till I tell you.' And she rushed off down the fire escape. Lindsay kicked her heels crossly for about five minutes till Chris returned, carrying two sets of yachting harness. 'There,' she said, handing one of them to Lindsay. 'You put that on and clip the hook to the railings. I'm not having you splattered on our drive if I can help it.'

Strapped in, Lindsay gingerly climbed over the railings and bolted one short strut to them vertically. Then, after a struggle with the heavy and unwieldy equipment, she added a long horizontal pole, to which Chris had previously bolted the other upright. That turned out to have been another mistake, since the extra weight was almost too much for Lindsay. Finally, with muscles that were beginning to tremble in protest, she managed to bolt on a second horizontal pole at a height that came just below the window sill of the music room windows.

'Jesus,' Lindsay gasped, 'I'm even less fit than I thought I was. This is where you do your stuff. I don't think I'm agile enough for this bit. You go along the scaffolding till you get to the end window. Then you use a knife blade to slip the catch and climb into the room through the window. Be careful not to damage the paintwork. Do you think you can do that?'

Chris grinned. 'No bother at all. I'm a gymnast, you know, not just a lump of brawn. You'd need to be pretty sure-footed to do this by the way and pretty strong, given the fetching and carrying involved.'

At first she inched her way gingerly along, but soon she was moving with assurance along the lower bar. As she reached the window she pulled herself up and on to the upper bar. There she crouched, leaning against the window frame as she slipped out the knife Lindsay had given her. It took heart-stopping moments fiddling around with the blade before the catch slipped open, but once she had managed it, she unclipped her harness and was inside the music room in seconds.

A few moments later, she re-emerged on the window ledge. She leaned over and hooked her gear back on to the pole as a precaution. Then she slammed the window shut with surprisingly little noise and tested it to make sure the catch had dropped back into place.

Next she swung back on to the lower pole. She called to Lindsay, 'I may as well dismantle as I go,' and came back crabwise for the necessary tools. It was only a matter of a few minutes before they were both staggering back through the grounds to the building site to replace the bits and pieces. It was still not long after eleven.

They returned to Paddy's rooms to wait for Cordelia, and collapsed into armchairs. 'There's one thing,' she said. 'Whoever did that was definitely on the strong side, and very fit. I feel quite tired and I didn't even carry the scaffolding over. Unless whoever did it took more than one trip to get the stuff there.'

Lindsay agreed whole-heartedly. She knew just how heavy and how awkward the poles were. These were problems, however, that could be overcome by Chris's suggestions of more than one trip, and of using rope to get them on to the roof. Not wanting to discuss the details further, Lindsay steered the conversation into other channels, and when Cordelia returned just after twelve, they were deep in discussion about the relative merits of Lindsay's MG and other sports cars.

Chris broke off immediately to ask the score. 'They won three-two,' Cordelia reported. 'Sarah Cartwright played a fine game. She scored twice and laid on the third. Very impressive.'

'So she should be. She's playing for the county again this season and she should get a trial for the England schoolgirl side, though I doubt if she'll make it. She's not really a team player. Anyhow, who else played well?'

'The left half – is it Julia, Juliet? – had a good game. Caroline Barrington plays hockey like she does everything else – masses of energy, tearing off in all directions at once, unstoppable. I imagine she played her usual game – a little short on strategy but with endless goodwill. And you've got a bloody good goalie there. She only let the second one in because she slipped in the mud. They're not a bad side at all,' Cordelia replied.

'Good, good,' said Chris vigorously. 'Thanks again for standing in.'

'I don't think I made too many blunders.'

'I'm sure you didn't – but if you did I'm sure Caroline will let me know!' Chris said with a grin. 'Well, if you'll excuse me, I'll be on my way. I have to see the team captains about their matches and I'm sure you two have got plenty to talk over. Be seeing you. Thanks for the coffee.' She got to her feet.

'Don't thank me, thank Paddy,' said Lindsay. 'She'll have a fit when she gets back and sees the state of her coffee jar and drinks cupboard.'

'Listen, if you two get her out, that'll be the least of her worries,' said Chris as she left.

Cordelia slumped into the vacant armchair and immediately demanded information. 'Are you going to tell me how the intrepid mountain goats got on while I was tearing up and down the sidelines risking my reputation? Can it be done?'

'It can be done, yes. It would need a certain amount of strength and skill. Cartwright would certainly have known where the stuff was kept and would have had the skill to erect the scaffolding, while Anthony Barrington would undoubtedly have had the strength and skill to perform the actual feat. But I'm not at all sure that Cartwright would have had the agility to get from the scaffolding into the room. And we don't know how much Barrington would have known about the availability of materials on the building site. Certainly while we were up there I had a good look at the masonry and there were no signs of anyone having driven pitons into the pointing or stonework so Barrington couldn't have done it that way – which would have been the natural method for him to have used.'

'Well, we'd better get ourselves down to Wales tonight and see what Barrington's got to say for himself,' said Cordelia, reluctantly dragging herself to her feet. 'It must have been one of those two. I've never believed that a woman could kill another woman as Lorna was killed. The murder's got a man's psychology written all over it; your evidence with the scaffolding just proves what I've felt in my heart all along.'

It was just before three when they pulled up in the car park at the remand centre. It was busier than when they'd been before and there were a dozen other visitors by the gate when they arrived. Everyone looked depressed by their surroundings; Lindsay thought again how appalling it must be for those locked up inside. Any politician who made cheap gibes about luxury prison conditions only proved that a brick wall had more sensitivity, she thought bitterly. After a short delay at the gate, they were allowed in with a group of other visitors and escorted to the room they'd sat in before. This time, they had to wait longer for Paddy – there appeared to be too few officers to deal with a busy visiting period.

Paddy seemed to have retreated further inside herself. She forced a smile when she saw them, but it stopped at her lips. Lindsay felt anger rising in her when she saw the damage done to her friend. If she'd had any doubts about carrying on, they died then. Sod the *Clarion*, she thought, if there was still work to be done for Paddy, she wouldn't be travelling north on Tuesday night.

'How are you?' Cordelia asked.

Paddy shrugged eloquently. 'Anything becomes bearable after a while. Having something to read helps. And I've been doing some work in the laundry, which passes the time. My cell-mate is a pleasant enough soul; she keeps me entertained with tales of family life. Somehow she manages to stay cheerful in spite of being in here. God knows how she does it.'

'I don't want to build your hopes too high,' said Lindsay, 'but we're beginning to make some progress. We think we've worked out how the murder was committed, and if we're right it lets you right off the hook. We'll give Gillian a ring first thing on Monday morning and see what can be done.'

A slow smile spread across Paddy's face and this time it reached her eyes. 'Tell me about it,' she demanded.

Lindsay and Cordelia swiftly outlined the scaffolding theory, and when they came to the part about the experiment on the roof Paddy laughed out loud. 'I wish I'd been there to see you and Chris leaping around like a pair of moorland sheep. You must have given the girls fuel for weeks of jokes. Poor old Chris. They won't let her forget that in a hurry.'

'Fortunately, I don't think there were any girls around to see what we were doing,' said Lindsay.

'Don't you believe it. In a rumour factory like Derbyshire House you only need one person for a story to be all over the school in a matter of hours,' Paddy replied.

'We're still not sure who did it, however,' sighed Cordelia. 'The more information we get, the harder it seems to be to prove anything.'

'Which reminds me,' said Lindsay, 'do you happen to know anything about James Cartwright's financial position, Paddy?'

Paddy's eyebrows shot up. 'Not a lot,' she replied. 'The word is, he's not as flush as he used to be. Not getting the squash court contract was a bad blow. And he hasn't changed his car this year. I have heard this playing fields development is make or break for him, but I do find that hard to believe.'

After a moment's thought, she went on. 'Speaking of the Cartwrights, I've been thinking about what you were asking me the other day. About Sarah's statement. I think she's got it wrong, you know. In fact, it was the other way round. When I took her to Music 2, I stopped at the storeroom to have a quick word with a couple of juniors who shouldn't have been there at the time, and Sarah went on ahead. As I entered the room Sarah was standing by the cupboards looking through some sheet music. Which is slightly odd because the girl has no interest in music except as an accompaniment to gymnastics. I told her to be sure she put it back in the right place because the room had been tidied up for Lorna. I don't think one can read anything into all that but, just for the record, that's what happened.'

'I see,' said Lindsay thoughtfully. 'I think we're going to have to have another little chat with Miss Cartwright. I don't like people lying to me. Not when it's a question of murder. It makes me start asking myself what they're trying to hide.'

'Don't be heavy, Lindsay,' Paddy warned. 'She's not a very happy kid and I feel responsible for her.'

'She'll have to be spoken to, Paddy. There are more important things at stake here than Sarah Cartwright's finer feelings.'

'I know that, but take it gently. You'll get a pretty hostile reaction if you bully her.'

'You've got to be joking,' Cordelia said scornfully. 'The last time we saw her, the only monstering that was going on was her giving Lindsay a hard time. She's the only person, apart from Pamela Overton, who has succeeded in squashing your favourite journalist.'

Paddy laughed again and a little colour crept back into her cheeks. But before Lindsay and Cordelia could capitalise on this, the officer was there to take Paddy back to her cell. 'We'll soon have you out of here, don't forget that,' called Cordelia, as Paddy vanished through the door again.

They walked back to the car, arguing. Cordelia was all for heading straight down to Wales to talk to Anthony Barrington, but Lindsay had changed her mind and was determined to get her own way. 'I want to talk to Sarah right away,' she argued. 'Barrington's still going to be there later on tonight. Or we could go down tomorrow early. But I want to straighten out Sarah Cartwright as soon as possible. She's lying and I want to know why.'

'We can talk to her any time. Now we know she's lying, we only have to get at the reasons why. But we should get to Barrington as soon as we can. He's the only person who could have had a hand in this that we haven't talked to so far. And you seem to think he's the likeliest candidate. A little while ago you were desperate to get down to Wales to see him.'

'But don't you see? Sarah's answers could change everything. It may be that after we've talked to her again there will be no reason for us to talk to Barrington at all. We may manage to wrap the whole thing up. We lose nothing by seeing Sarah first – and we could gain a lot. I just *know* it's important.'

Cordelia sighed. 'You're like a bloody steam-roller. You flatten the opposition. You just don't listen, do you?'

'I know I'm right,' said Lindsay stubbornly.

'Well, I still think you're wrong.' Cordelia argued.

'We'll see,' said Lindsay. 'Now, is there a phone around here anywhere?'

'I think we passed one about a mile down the road towards the motorway. Who do you want to call?'

'I just want to leave a message for Sarah. To let her know we're coming. That should make her sweat a little. I want her nice and worried about what we may or may not know.' She got in the car.

'My God, you really can be a bully, can't you,' said Cordelia crossly to the empty air.

18

They parked the car outside Longnor House and marched straight up the stairs to Sarah's room. On the door a 'Do Not Disturb' notice was hanging. Cordelia said curtly, 'These notices are supposed to be sacrosanct, but for once we'll break the rules. After all, she should be expecting us.' She rapped on the door. There was no reply. She looked questioningly at Lindsay, who nodded encouragement. Cordelia turned the handle, opened the door and stepped inside.

What she saw made her gasp and turn away, her hand to her mouth. Lindsay caught hold of her and held her tightly. She looked over Cordelia's shoulder and took in a vision of absolute horror. She said harshly. 'We mustn't touch anything.' Lindsay gently released Cordelia and steered her on to the landing before forcing herself across the threshold. She quickly glanced around, feeling her chest tighten, then spoke commandingly to Cordelia. 'Go down to Paddy's room. Get

Pamela Overton here and call the police.' Cordelia stood numbly, seeming not to have heard. 'Do it now,' Lindsay cried. Cordelia shook herself and stumbled down the corridor.

Left alone, Lindsay somehow steeled herself to look at the appalling scene inside the room. She desperately wanted to see if there was anything obvious to explain the significance of what had happened there.

Sarah Cartwright – or what remained of her – sprawled half on the floor and half on the bed. Her left arm was slashed almost to the bone at wrist and elbow; her right arm had a matching cut, though far less deep, at the wrist. A sheath knife lay on the floor. She had obviously cut herself leaning over the washbasin for it was filled with a grisly mixture of blood and water. As consciousness had slipped away, she had fallen back and her blood had splashed the walls and soaked the carpet and bed. Lindsay badly wanted to be sick, but from somewhere came the strength to carry on her examination. She moved across to the desk, careful to avoid the blood.

On the top of the desk was a single sheet of foolscap paper, covered in neat handwriting. It was what she had half-expected to find. Across the top was written in block capitals, 'To anyone who has an interest in the death of Lorna Smith-Couper.'

The message continued,

I want to say first of all that I am sorry for all the trouble that I have caused, especially to my father, Miss Callaghan and the school. At the time, I thought I was doing the best possible thing and I did not think anything could be proved. I did not mean to incriminate Miss Callaghan.

I killed Lorna Smith-Couper. I fetched scaffolding from the squash courts and used it to climb from the kitchen roof to the music room. I climbed in the window and strangled her while she was playing. I knew she would be there because Miss Callaghan told me that morning when we were there together. I did it for my father. I wanted him to get the school playing fields to save his business, especially now I know what people at the school really think of me.

I thought Miss Callaghan would get off and I'd get away with it. But Lindsay Gordon and Cordelia Brown are coming to see me and I know they were messing about with scaffolding this morning. They must know I lied to Miss Callaghan, and it's all bound to come out now because I'm the only person who could have climbed up the scaffolding like that. And I couldn't face prison. I'm sorry for the pain I've caused my father. I did it because I love you, Daddy. Sarah Cartwright.

The tragic waste outlined on the paper angered

Lindsay. She turned to look coldly at the body of the young woman. She had not liked Sarah Cartwright, had been irritated by her condescension, but no one deserved to die like this. There was no dignity in this death, only fear and degradation. Lindsay could stomach no more of it. She walked out of the room, feeling appallingly guilty for having been so slow to the truth.

When she emerged into the corridor she saw Pamela Overton coming up the stairs towards her. The headmistress looked shaken and walked tentatively like an elderly woman as she approached Lindsay, who took a deep breath, feeling suddenly exhausted. 'I'm sorry,' she sighed. 'I was too slow. Sarah has killed herself.'

'Cordelia told me,' Miss Overton said bleakly. 'It's to do with Lorna's death?'

Lindsay nodded wearily. 'I'm afraid so.'

'But surely not Sarah? Not one of my girls?' It was an extraordinary plea, thought Lindsay.

'She has left a confession,' Lindsay replied. 'I can't imagine a worse way to clear Paddy's name.'

The headmistress said nothing. She looked coldly at Lindsay and walked a few steps down the corridor so she could stare out of a window. Lindsay leaned against the wall and closed her eyes. She could not have said how long it was before she heard heavy feet on the stairs and a murmur of voices as Inspector Dart arrived with a group of policemen, some in uniform and some in plain clothes.

'Miss Overton,' he said gently, 'I'm very sorry about this. I wonder if you'd be good enough to wait downstairs while we do what's necessary? And Miss Gordon – I'll want to talk to you and Miss Brown when I'm through. Will you wait downstairs with her?'

'Shouldn't someone inform Mr Cartwright?' asked Miss Overton.

'That is being taken care of,' Dart replied. 'Now, ladies if you'll just go downstairs.'

The two women made their way in silence to Paddy's room. When they entered, Cordelia looked up from an armchair and said shakily, 'You shouldn't have phoned, Lindsay.' She burst into tears.

Lindsay hurried to her and crouched beside the chair, putting an arm round her shaking shoulders. 'How could I know?' she asked desperately. 'I thought she was lying to protect him. I didn't know if she was doing it because she knew he was guilty or because she only suspected he might be. I really didn't think she had killed Lorna.'

Cordelia's head came up. 'She killed Lorna?'

'She left a confession. I think we'd better prepare ourselves for a sticky session with the police.'

Pamela Overton moved over to them. 'Do you mean to say that you may have had something to do with Sarah's suicide?'

'We uncovered some new information today. We also discovered that Sarah had lied in her statement to the police. I rang and left a message about an hour ago to say that we wanted to talk to her again. That's all.'

The headmistress stared hard at Lindsay. 'I had thought you were a reasonably sensitive and civilised human being,' she said. 'Please tell Inspector Dart that I will be in my study in the main building when he wants to see me.' She turned on her heel and left.

Cordelia wiped her eyes and blew her nose noisily. 'We really screwed up, didn't we?'

'I suppose so,' said Lindsay angrily. 'And since I'm now credited with being uncivilised and insensitive as well as just stupid, I'll put the finishing touches to everyone's low opinion of me.' So saying, she went to the phone and dialled through to the *Daily Clarion*'s sister Sunday paper's copy room.

'Hello? Lindsay Gordon here. I've got a belter for you. Ready? Murder squad detectives were called in today after a pupil at a top girls' boarding school was found dead. The detectives were already investigating the murder of internationally famous cellist Lorna Smith-Couper at Derbyshire House Girls' School a week ago. A teacher at the school, Miss Patricia Callaghan, has been charged with the murder, but sources close to the police investigation revealed today that there was some doubt as to whether the killer was still at large. The dead girl was Sarah Cartwright, eighteen, whose father James

Cartwright is a builder in the nearby town of Buxton. He is currently locked in a dispute with the school over his proposal to turn the school's playing fields into a luxury timeshare development.

'Sarah was found dead in her study bedroom at the school where she was a sixth-former. She had knife wounds to both arms. A keen gymnast and hockey player, Sarah hoped to become a PE teacher. Police said last night there were no suspicious circumstances. No one is being sought in connection with her death. End copy. Note to newsdesk; the girl left a note confessing to the Smith-Couper murder.'

Lindsay repeated the process to three other papers, then put the phone down. 'Bet you think I'm a real shit, don't you?'

Cordelia looked at her. 'I couldn't have done what you've just done.'

Lindsay shrugged, her face a mask. 'It's a way of dealing with what's happened. A way of hiding, a way of postponing.'

'It's your job, Lindsay. You chose it. I certainly couldn't have. However you cut it, what it comes down to is you doing your job. If you didn't go about it in a cold-blooded way, I suppose you'd be no use to your bosses.' There was no approval in Cordelia's voice, only coldness.

Before Lindsay could reply, the door opened and Inspector Dart came in, followed by the young detective Lindsay had seen with him before. He looked grim, his lean face set in hard lines. He walked over to Paddy's desk and sat down behind it. The young detective sat down on a straight-backed chair near the door and took out his note-book. Dart said nothing, but continued to glance from Lindsay to Cordelia and back again. Lindsay felt extremely exposed.

Finally he broke the silence. He spoke slowly and his deep voice had become a growl. 'I hate bloody waste,' he said. 'And I hate bloody pillocks who fall for the line spun by the media: that the police are not only woodentops but also corrupt and vicious. You know why I hate them? Because they think they know better than we do how to catch criminals. Usually, they never get the chance to put their crass little theories into practice. Just as well, wouldn't you say, on the evidence of today?'

Lindsay said nothing. She felt she deserved most of what was coming, and she resolved to bite on the bullet and not let this man see how upset she actually was.

'I've got what seems to be a confession here. A confession to a murder for which I already have someone in custody. The note mentions you, Miss Gordon, a couple of times. I also have a note found in the girl's waste-paper bin which seems to be a phone message saying you intended to call on her after seeing Miss Callaghan. All this suggests to me that you've been pissing about with things which are none of your bloody business. Am I right?'

Lindsay shrugged. He looked expectantly at her, but when he saw there was nothing more forthcoming, he went on. 'I've one or two questions arising from the confession. You have read it, I take it?'

Lindsay nodded. 'I have, but Miss Brown hasn't.'

'For your sake, I hope I'm not going to find your fingerprints all over it. Quote: "I know they were messing about with scaffolding this morning." Unquote. Now, I want the explanation, please.'

Lindsay looked up. 'It was clear to Miss Overton that since you had already made an arrest that fitted the circumstances, you wouldn't be looking for alternative solutions. So she asked Cordelia and me to take a look at this business to see if we could come up with anything that would help clear Paddy Callaghan, whom all three of us believe is innocent.

'I have been a journalist for some years now,' she went on, finding her stride. 'I've done a fair number of investigations, a couple of which have resulted in arrests. I have qualifications both in English and Scottish law, and I know quite a bit about the burden of proof. If I didn't, I'd be too expensive a risk for newspapers to employ. I'm not as much of a fool as you seem to think, Inspector. And neither is Cordelia. I thought we might just manage to come up with one or two things that you and your experienced team had missed, especially since people seem to find it easier to talk to us. As for messing about on the kitchen roof with the scaffolding – it was testing a theory which seemed to cover all the salient facts.'

'Spare me the speeches,' he said caustically.

She ignored him and continued. 'I don't particularly expect you to believe this, but all week I've had something nagging away at the back of my mind. I had a feeling it was important, but it just wouldn't come to me. I only remembered what it was in the early hours of this morning.'

Then she explained the sudden realisation of what she had seen so briefly the week before. She went on to relate the events of the morning. When she came to the end of her tale, he looked aghast.

'God preserve me from amateurs,' he said bitterly. 'And just how many fingerprints, footprints and other forensic traces do you think you obliterated this morning? What in heaven's name possessed you to take the law into your own hands to this extent? Answer me, woman!'

'I didn't think there would be anything on the building site. After all, the workmen have been there all week. As far as the rest of it is concerned, I supposed the criminal would have been wearing gloves. It wasn't a spur of the moment crime, and everyone knows about fingerprints these days. And Chris Jackson made sure she didn't do any damage to the paintwork. There weren't any marks on it before, anyway. I checked early this morning when I realised what it was I'd seen last Saturday.'

'Your stupidity is staggering,' Dart groaned. 'That corpse upstairs is a bloody monument to your stupidity. I suppose it never occurred to you to come to us with your information? If you'd done that, I can guarantee Sarah Cartwright would still be alive. Instead, you have to do things your way, and now she's just a lump of dead flesh. You say the girl lied in her statement. She admits that in her confession. If, instead of phoning to put the frighteners on her, you'd come to me, she'd still be alive. I've known that girl since she was in her pram. Now I've got to go and tell her father that not only was his daughter a murderer but that because of the sheer stupidity of a couple of so-called amateur detectives, she's dead.' He shook his head. 'Congratulations, ladies. It looks like you've got your friend off the hook. I just hope you can live with the price.' He got to his feet and walked to the door. Before he left, he turned to them and said, 'Don't leave the area before the inquest. I think I'll be wanting you to tell your story to the coroner.'

The policemen left the two women alone. Lindsay stared unseeingly out of the window. After a few minutes, Cordelia got up and put her arms round her. Lindsay half-smiled and said, 'One of us better ring Gillian and get her to set the wheels in motion to get Paddy freed. Why don't you do it? I don't think I can face it right now. I should have listened to you.

'I'm really sorry about all of this. I've not done

you any favours, have I? Not to mention that poor, tortured kid. Me and my big ideas. I've made a right balls-up of this from start to finish.'

Cordelia kissed her forehead. 'Don't blame yourself. She chose to kill Lorna. You didn't make her. Everybody seems to be forgetting that side of the story. And she chose to kill herself rather than face up to the consequences. She'd have sat back and let Paddy be destroyed if you hadn't acted. And in spite of what Dart said, I'm not so sure they'd have taken you seriously if you'd gone to them. They'd probably have accused you of wasting police time. So don't go blaming yourself.'

Lindsay sighed deeply and turned her face away. 'I can't help feeling responsible for the way things have turned out. That's clearly what Pamela Overton thinks as well as Dart. And Cartwright. How's he going to feel? She was all he had. Oh shit . . . why does everything have to be such a mess?'

19

There was no champagne to welcome Paddy
Callaghan back to Longnor House on Sunday
morning. After the due process of law had been
carried out, Gillian drove Paddy back from the
remand centre. Cordelia had cooked a lavish
Indian meal, and when Paddy walked through
the door she was greeted with hugs, kisses, tears,
cold lager and the aroma of curry spices. After
the emotional reunion, Lindsay walked over to
the main building to tell Pamela Overton Paddy
was back. The headmistress hurried off immediately to see Paddy in her rooms and Lindsay, who
now felt even more uncomfortable in her presence, took the opportunity to file an exclusive
story on Paddy's release, complete with interview,
to the *Clarion*.

After she had dictated the story, she spoke to
the newsdesk. 'Lindsay here, Duncan. The copy
for my exclusive on the girls' school murder
should be dropping on your desk any minute now,

I've left a number where you can reach me if there are any queries.'

'I've just got it in front of me now, kid. Not a bad piece of work. Mind you, you've taken long enough over it; it should be good. When do I get you back working properly again?'

'If you gave me a job instead of shifts, you'd know the answer to that. I'm supposed to be in on Wednesday at one o'clock. So I'll see you then.'

'Give you a job? I'd never see you then! I must be paying you too much as it is if you can afford to spend a whole week gadding about in England.'

Lindsay laughed. 'I'd rather be suffering from an old slave driver like you than doing what I'm doing right now. I've not had a proper night's sleep since I left Glasgow.'

Duncan's voice had a chuckle in it. 'That was always your problem, Lindsay, mixing business with pleasure. See you Wednesday.'

Lindsay sat in the headmistress's study, smoking quietly and turning over the events of the last week yet again. She forced herself to think about the horrors of the previous day. Now that the first shock had subsided she was able to think more objectively about Sarah's suicide and her confession. It struck her that the confession was remarkably bare of essential detail. There was nothing about Paddy's duffel-coat toggle, something known only to the murderer, the handful of people who had actually seen the body, Paddy and the police. In itself, that was hardly world-shaking, thought Lindsay, though it would have made sense for Sarah, in the flow of her confession, to have said something like, 'I made the garrotte with the cello string I took from Music 2 in the morning when I was there with Miss Callaghan, and a toggle I took from someone's coat in the cloakroom at Longnor.'

Lindsay began to feel faint stirrings of disquiet. The girl hadn't explained how the window catches could easily be opened. It was Lindsay herself who had fleshed out the method of the crime to the police; ironically that would render Sarah's 'confession' all the more credible to them. Also, of all the people who had fallen under Lindsay's suspicion, Sarah was one of the least likely to know how long Lorna was to spend in the music room before she went on stage, for she had no involvement with the musical life of the school.

Supposing Sarah hadn't killed Lorna, Lindsay speculated. Supposing she believed her father had killed Lorna – leaving aside for the moment whether he had or not. If she had reasons for thinking he was guilty, and that he was close to being discovered, would she have killed herself to protect him? That was the sixty-four-thousand dollar question, Lindsay realised. Considering what she knew of the girl's character, from her own observation and from the comments of others, she thought it was a distinct possibility. The girl worshipped her father. The only other anchor in her life was the school and her relationship with her fellow pupils, which had been dealt a hard blow by events at the craft fair. Most girls would have shrugged the matter off then and there, but Sarah had reacted rather extremely. She seemed, by choice, to be a very isolated girl. So it might well have been that she would rather have sacrificed herself than see her father arrested for murder.

Lindsay sighed deeply. Part of her said, drop it, leave it be. Paddy was free, free and cleared. But the other part of her refused to let go. Her newspaper training had heightened the tenacious determination in her to get to the bottom of things and not to be fobbed off with half an answer. Now doubts had wormed their way into her head and she was afraid they were going to give her no peace.

She shook her head vigorously, like a dog emerging from a stream, crushed her cigarette out and walked briskly back to Longnor, hoping that diving back into the celebrations would drive her doubts away. Pamela Overton had gone by the time she returned, and Gillian Markham was standing by the door with her coat on.

She turned to Lindsay and smiled. 'I'm glad you're back,' she said. 'I'm off now to let you get on with your celebrations, but I wanted to thank you for all the work you've done on Paddy's behalf. I know this business has been pretty terrible; on the positive side, however, Paddy's name has been cleared, and that's largely due to the efforts of you and Cordelia.'

Paddy interrupted. 'That goes for me too. If we'd relied on the police to clear this business up, I'd still be rotting in jail. So thanks, both of you.'

Lindsay blushed and shook her head. 'Maybe we did do that. But I cocked the whole thing up in the end. I was so excited by what we'd found out that I ignored Cordelia's good sense, and I have to accept responsibility for what happened to Sarah. It'll stay with me for a long time. Maybe it will make me stop and think twice about some of the stunts I get up to. But the people who deserve at least as much thanks as me and Cordelia are Pamela Overton and you, Gillian, yourself. If Pamela hadn't been so convinced of your innocence in the first place that she demanded our help, I don't think it would have occurred to Cordelia or me to get involved in the way we did. And you've been pretty exceptional too, Gillian – I can't think of many lawyers who would go along with the unconventional routine we've been pulling over the last week. End of speech. Now, will someone give me a beer?'

Gillian said goodbye and left the three of them sitting round the fire with their meal. They ate in a companionable silence for the main part, and it was only after they sat back with coffee that Paddy demanded to know the full story of their investigations. Between them, Lindsay and Cordelia managed to give her a full rundown.

There was a hush while Paddy took in all they

had to tell. 'What a waste!' she sighed at last. 'So much loyalty. So much love. And two horrible deaths out of it. And what for? A bunch of bloody playing fields, which Cartwright will almost certainly pick up since I can't see us raising the money now. Oh God, I think I'll get a job in some grotty inner-city comprehensive where nobody cares that much about anything, let alone a few acres of green.'

'You'd hate that, and you know it,' Lindsay retorted, 'so what about some inner-city comprehensive where people do care and need what you can give them?'

Paddy burst out laughing. 'I'm hardly out of prison and already you're lecturing me. I give up, Lindsay, I give up!'

Their general laughter was interrupted by a knock at the door. Paddy groaned. 'Sounds like everything's back to normal already.' She called, 'Come in!'

Caroline's head appeared round the door. 'Sorry to interrupt,' she said. 'But we just wanted to tell you how pleased we all are to have you back with us. We all knew you didn't do it, and we missed not having you about the place. It just wasn't the same having Sherlock Holmes and Watson keeping an eye on us. I say, Miss Callaghan, you should have seen them in action. Extremely tough cookies.'

'That will do, Caroline,' said Paddy, smiling. 'Thank you for your kind words. I'll do the rounds later on, so you'll be able to check for yourselves that I'm still in one piece.'

'Okay, Miss Callaghan. We've all been a bit worried about you. It's good to see prison hasn't ground you down.'

'Caroline – on your way!'

The girl grinned and vanished. 'I swear her grin hangs around after her, like the Cheshire Cat,' Cordelia muttered.

Caroline wasn't the only visitor. As the afternoon wore on, most of the members of the staff popped in briefly to congratulate Paddy on her release. But the atmosphere remained muted, for no one could forget that a girl had died. After a couple of hours, Paddy suggested that they all go for a walk up the hill behind the school. As they set off, Lindsay spotted Jessica Bennett walking through the trees from the main building. On an impulse she said, 'You two go ahead, I'll catch you up. I just want to have a few words with Jessica. Nothing important, just a little point I want to clear up for my own satisfaction.'

Cordelia shook her head with an air of amused tolerance. 'You're never content, are you? All right, but don't be long or you'll never catch us up.'

'Don't be so sure of that,' said Paddy. 'After a week's incarceration, I feel totally flabby.' They walked off, leaving Lindsay to wait by the door for the girl.

When Jessica spotted Lindsay, she smiled broadly, 'Hi,' she said. 'I hear Miss Callaghan's been released. It's wonderful news, isn't it? I'm so glad you were able to find out what really happened.'

Lindsay smiled wanly. 'I'm glad she's back. But I seem to have done as much harm as good. Listen, Jessica, can you spare me a couple of minutes? There's something I want to ask you, just to settle something in my own mind.'

The girl frowned slightly. 'But I thought it was all cleared up now?'

'Come in a minute,' said Lindsay, leading the way into Paddy's sitting-room. 'There are a couple of details I was wondering about. It's being a journalist. I'm like a dog with a bone.'

Jessica sat down. 'All right. Ask what you want and I'll try to answer.'

'It's my own fault. I should have asked you this when I spoke to you before. But I let myself be sidetracked when you told us where you found Miss Callaghan and what frame of mind she seemed to be in. Daft of me – because I asked everyone else what I'm going to ask you now. I had a feeling it might be important. All I wondered was if you saw Sarah at all on Saturday night, and if so, when and where.'

'Is that all?' she said, sounding relieved. 'I actually saw her a couple of times. When I went to get my coat to go across to Main Building to get Miss Callaghan, Sarah was just going out of Longnor. She had her anorak on and she was wearing track suit bottoms and trainers.'

'What time was that?'

'It must have been about a quarter past seven. I remember looking at my watch and thinking that was good because I'd be able to find Miss Callaghan before the concert started. Then, when we came back, I went back into the cloakroom to hang my coat up. That must have been just after half-past seven – say, twenty-five to eight. Sarah was sitting in the cloakroom, just staring into space, I tried to talk to her, but she just shrugged me off and I saw her going back upstairs. I suppose she was going back to her room. It's terrible to think of it now – she must have just come back from killing Lorna then, mustn't she?'

Lindsay was non-committal, trying not to show that what the girl had said was significant. She thanked Jessica for her help and as gently as possible got rid of her. She sat at Paddy's desk with her head in her hands. What she had just been told made her thoughts race furiously round her head. How could Sarah have killed Lorna between seven fifteen and seven thirty-five? Although that part of the school grounds over-looked by the music-room windows was normally dark and deserted at that time of the evening, on the night of the murder it had been busy: cars were being parked and people were walking to the concert. It would not have been feasible to have carried out that murderous climb until the area had been quiet again – in other words, till seven thirty. And Lindsay couldn't believe the murderer would have taken any chances till the concert was under way, to muffle any sounds coming from the music room.

So that left her two choices. James Cartwright. And Anthony Barrington. If she had to pick one on the basis of what she already knew, she would have opted for Cartwright every time, but it wasn't that simple. If she went to Inspector Dart with her latest suspicions, she was sure she'd get extremely short shrift. And approaching Cartwright himself on the day after his daughter had killed herself was something she couldn't face. She thought back to her first few weeks as a journalist, when she had discovered how much she hated the ghoulish task of talking to bereft relatives, trying to collect pictures from them. Now she would do almost anything to avoid those assignments. She knew journalists who could cope in that situation, but the grief of strangers was something she still found painful and embarrassing, especially after Frances' death. She asked herself how, carrying the extra weight of responsibility for this death, she could walk into Cartwright's house and start asking the questions she needed answers to.

That left Anthony Barrington. It could do no harm to talk to him, she reasoned. If he was innocent, she could eliminate him – which would leave her virtually certain of Cartwright's guilt. And if he wasn't innocent she would have avoided a crass encounter with Cartwright.

She made her decision then and there. She glanced at her watch. If she drove fast, she could be at Barrington's Welsh home by six. She grabbed a piece of paper and wrote, 'Had to go out on business. Sorry – back about nine. If the office rings, tell them I'm on the road and I'll phone in later.' She didn't want either Paddy or Cordelia to know that pursuit of the truth was still gnawing at her like a maggot.

But luck wasn't on her side. Just as she was leaving the building, Cordelia jogged back down the path. 'I came back to see what was holding you up,' she said. 'Paddy's nattering to one of her colleagues so I thought I'd collect you. Coming?'

Lindsay shook her head. 'I've got to go out,' she muttered. 'I've left you a note.'

'What do you mean? Don't be so mysterious! Where are you off to?'

Lindsay sighed. 'If you must know. I'm going to see Anthony Barrington.' She looked like a sulky child caught stealing chocolate.

'Oh Lindsay,' Cordelia groaned, 'why can't you just leave it alone? Look, Paddy's free. Sarah has confessed. The police are satisfied. Why can't you be?'

'Because it doesn't seem right to me,' she replied stubbornly. 'You didn't read that suicide note. I did and I don't believe Sarah killed Lorna. For a start, the note was too long. It's as if she was trying to convince us that she'd done it. But it was also short on detail. There was nothing in

302

it that wasn't common knowledge. I'm convinced that she killed herself because she thought her father had done it and she couldn't face living with that.'

'But if Sarah killed herself because she thought her father was guilty, why not go to see him? Why go to see Barrington?'

'I'm going to see Barrington, because that's what we were intending to do as the next logical step. Besides, it's a softer option than Cartwright just now.'

'You're crazy,' Cordelia retorted angrily. 'Can't you just accept that it's all over and you've made a mistake? You don't have to be perfect, you know. No one expects you to be infallible.'

'I wasn't wrong, damn it,' Lindsay exploded, 'I'm bloody certain Sarah didn't kill Lorna. It's not enough any more just to clear Paddy. Not for me, anyway. There's someone walking around out there who committed murder. I don't think that's a very healthy state of affairs, do you?'

'No, but why should it be you that's got to put it right? Call the police, tell Dart what you think. That's how you should do it. Haven't you learned anything from what's happened?'

'Oh yes,' said Lindsay, her voice heavy with sarcasm, 'and Dart's going to pay a lot of attention to me, isn't he? No, I'm going to talk to Barrington. That's that.'

They stood glaring at each other. Cordelia broke the silence with a sigh. 'Well, I'd better come with you, hadn't I? We don't want you walking into a potential murderer's front room on your own, do we?'

But Lindsay, thoroughly roused, was in no mood for olive branches. 'I don't need a minder,' she stated. 'I've been looking after myself in dodgy situations for a long time now. I think I'll manage it on my own. See you later.'

She turned on her heel and walked over to her car without looking back. When she glanced behind in her rearview mirror, Cordelia had gone. Lindsay smacked her fist against the steering wheel.

'Why do I do it? Why the hell do I do it?'

20

Just before six, Lindsay left the main trunk road she'd been following through Wales and turned north up a terrifying single-track road with a series of hairpin bends and sheer drops down the mountainside. Lindsay was only glad it was twilight and she couldn't see the extent of the precipitous slopes. Eventually the road climbed to a tiny village consisting of a post office, a pub, a chapel and a handful of cottages. Other houses straggled up the hillside. Lindsay pulled up and took another look at the scrap of paper with Barrington's address. Plas Glyndwr, Llanagar. No wonder the Welsh got fed up with the English and their weekend cottages, thought Lindsay. The invaders even pinched the best Welsh names.

She set off slowly, trying without success to find the house. Carrying on up the road, however, as she came round a particularly awkward blind bend, she found Plas Glyndwr. Lindsay braked sharply. This was no weekend cottage. It was a four-square, large family house, set behind banks of rhododendrons with a fair-sized lawn and big kitchen garden to one side. A dark blue Daimler was parked in front of the house and an elderly Ford Cortina sat outside the side door. 'Oh well, in for a penny, in for a pound,' she muttered to herself as she reversed the MG up the drive.

She got out and rang the bell by the front door. A full minute passed before it was opened by a woman in her fifties wearing a voluminous wrap-round apron. She had flour on her hands and smudges on one cheek. She looked surprised to see Lindsay.

'Can I help you?' she inquired, her Welsh accent evident even in those few words.

'I'd like to see Mr Barrington, if he's at home,' said Lindsay.

'And who shall I say is calling?'

'My name is Lindsay Gordon,' she replied. 'He won't recognise the name, but I know his daughter Caroline. I won't take up much of his time.'

'Wait here a moment,' she said and disappeared, shutting the door firmly behind her. She was back within thirty seconds. 'Come in,' she said, leading Lindsay in.

As they walked through the hall, Lindsay noticed that the only distraction came from framed Ordnance Survey maps of the region hanging on the walls. The woman showed Lindsay into an airy sitting-room, furnished unpretentiously with large chairs upholstered in well-worn William

Morris Liberty prints. Anthony Barrington was sitting at a big roll-top desk by the window, a tumbler of whisky in his hand. He looked remarkably like the photograph in Caroline's room. He was wearing a baggy Aran sweater, old corduroy breeches, thick socks and sheepskin slippers. His eyebrows were raised quizzically as he rose to greet Lindsay.

'Good evening, Miss Gordon, is it? Do sit down. My housekeeper tells me you're a friend of Caroline's. What has my mad daughter been up to this time to drag you out into the middle of nowhere?'

'Thanks for seeing me, Mr Barrington. Caroline hasn't been up to anything she shouldn't have. It's not exactly Caroline I wanted to talk to you about, though she's involved indirectly.'

His eyebrows shot up again in surprise. 'Oh?' he said speculatively. 'You do know my daughter, I take it?'

Lindsay smiled. 'Oh yes, I know Caroline. She's a remarkable girl. You must be proud of her. She'll go far with that lively mind. But it's more to do with the school. Last week, Pamela Overton asked me to do something related to the murder of Lorna Smith-Couper.'

Lindsay's words seemed to hang grimly in the air. Anthony Barrington remained completely unmoved at the sound of a name that must have taken him by surprise.

'And what exactly do you imagine that has to

307

do with me?' Lindsay found him distinctly intimidating as he towered above her.

'If I could just explain. Last week the police arrested Caroline's housemistress for the murder. Miss Overton asked me and another friend of Miss Callaghan's if we would make some inquiries into the matter, since she believed Paddy was innocent and she knew that I felt the same way. I don't know how much you know about the events of the last few days?'

He studied her carefully before answering. 'I read in this morning's papers that a girl at the school had killed herself and that the police were investigating a connection between her and the murder. I rang Caroline this morning about it, since I was naturally concerned, and she told me that Sarah Cartwright confessed to the murder. As a result, Miss Callaghan has been freed. Or so the school gossip goes. I would have thought that meant an end to it. I don't quite understand what you are doing here.'

Lindsay sighed. 'I'm not completely convinced that Sarah was responsible for Lorna's death. I know the police are satisfied, but there are nagging doubts at the back of my mind. I suppose now that Paddy's free I should be satisfied. But I want to be sure there's not still a killer on the loose. Forgive me if I seem melodramatic. Now, I only discovered a couple of days ago that you were about on the day of the murder and I wondered if you had noticed anything out of the ordinary?'

'What on earth can you mean by that?' he said, a note of vexation in his voice.

'This week, I discovered that the murder was committed in such a way that it required certain preparations to be made in advance, made, in fact, at about the time you were dropping Caroline off after your afternoon out . . . Obviously the police have questioned most of the people who were around at the time but I don't think they've gone to the lengths I have because they were sure they had the person responsible. I just wondered if you had seen anything unusual.'

'I see,' he said, seeming to relax. 'By the way, I'm not being very hospitable. Would you like a drink?'

'No thanks, I've got the car,' said Lindsay, glad of the excuse not to accept a drink from a man she still feared could be a murderer. 'Now, when you dropped Caroline off, what exactly did you do, can you remember?'

'We got to Derbyshire House about half-past five – quarter to six – that sort of time. I drove her up to Longnor House in the Daimler. I got out with her and went up to her room to collect some family photographs and came down more or less right away, because it was nearly time for her to have dinner. Then I drove back to my hotel.'

'Did you go straight back to the hotel?'

'Of course I did! When I got there, I sat in the car for about half an hour listening to the end of a Bartok concert on the radio.'

'You misunderstood me,' said Lindsay, congratulating herself that she was beginning to get somewhere on establishing opportunity. 'I meant, did you come straight down the drive the way you came in, or did you by any chance drive round by the building site?'

'The building site? Oh, you mean where they're putting up the squash courts? No, why on earth should I have? They're way beyond the trees. I suppose it might have been logical to turn left and go round the back of the house to rejoin the main drive but I simply went right, back the way I'd come. It was more or less dark by then and there were quite a lot of girls going off to dinner. I didn't want to chance hitting any of them with the car so I avoided the back of the main building as far as possible. Does that answer your question?'

'Yes, thank you. You were aware of what was happening at the school that night, weren't you?'

'Caroline had mentioned the concert, yes.'

'I'm surprised you didn't stay for it, since you seem to enjoy music enough to sit in the car on a cold night listening to the end of a piece of Bartok,' said Lindsay casually.

He looked sharply at her. 'I had a lot of work to do. And besides, the programme didn't appeal to me,' he retorted.

Never give two excuses when one will do, thought Lindsay. The mark of the lie. 'The programme or the soloist?' she coolly asked. 'I know a certain amount about your relationship with Lorna, you see.'

'If you know anything about it at all, you will also know that it finished a long time ago,' he replied, anger giving his voice a sharp edge.

'Caroline has spoken very freely to me about the affair and your reactions to it,' said Lindsay, keeping calm.

'How dare you question my daughter about a family matter!' he exploded, 'I'm damned certain Pamela Overton gave you no brief to subject her pupils to such disgusting prying.'

'Caroline volunteered most of the information. She seemed to think that uncovering a murderer's identity was rather more important than personal feelings. Don't think it gives me any pleasure to rake up the sordid details of people's private lives.

'And I have to tell you, I think your daughter is a damn sight more honest than you are. You've given me a version of events that I know isn't strictly true. You were seen in your car at Derbyshire House at about twenty past seven. Now, you weren't at the concert and your car was gone fifteen minutes later. The police don't know this yet, but it's made me wonder what you were up to – and I'm sure they'll wonder too. While you claim to have been listening to Bartok, you could have been killing Lorna. You may find this outrageous, but it seems to me that there's a stronger case against you than ever there was against Paddy Callaghan – and they arrested her.'

Throughout this speech, Anthony Barrington had looked profoundly astonished. In any other circumstances, his expression would have provoked laughter, with his open mouth, his bewildered expression and his raised eyebrows. The silence was almost tangible, but before it could become oppressive, he found his tongue.

'How dare you!' he roared. 'My God, you've a nerve. First you interrogate my daughter – and you haven't heard the last of that, I can assure you. Then you walk into my house as bold as brass and accuse me of murder, with no evidence whatsoever to support some crack-brained theory. Do you think the police are fools? If they're satisfied, maybe it's because they've got evidence. Evidence! Do you know what the word means? It means something more substantial than accusing a man of murder just because he changed his mind about going to a concert.

'Pamela Overton must have taken leave of her senses, letting an idiot like you loose on something like this. Now, get out of here before I call the police and have you arrested. And if I ever hear you've repeated this insane accusation to anyone else I'll have a writ for slander on you so fast your tiny mind will go into a flat spin. Just take yourself out of my house – and don't ever go near my daughter again or you will be truly sorry.'

There was nothing for it but to go. She piled into the car, all dignity gone, and found that her hands were shaking. She glanced back at the house to see Barrington silhouetted in the doorway, shouting and waving his fist at her. She shot down the drive and hurtled back down the narrow road with scant regard for the tortuous bends. Once on the main road, she stopped at the first lay-by and lit a cigarette.

She tried to sort through her impressions of the hair-raising interview. She realised she had mishandled the situation and wished she'd brought Cordelia along for moral support. As far as eliminating him was concerned, there had been nothing offered in the way of proof. But unless Anthony Barrington was a first-class actor, Lindsay would stake her life on his innocence. It suddenly dawned on her that that was exactly what she had done by bowling up to his front door alone. It sent a chill through her. 'I really have been bloody stupid from the very start over this,' she thought. 'Still, I'm further forward than I was. I don't believe that outrage was faked – and it says something that he admitted to having gone back to the school because he'd changed his mind about the concert. I wonder what made him feel he couldn't go through with it once he'd steeled himself to coming back? Oh well, I guess I'll never know.'

She set off for the long drive back to Derbyshire, stopping only to check with the *Clarion* newsdesk that there were no queries on her copy. While she was in the phone box, on impulse she decided to phone Cordelia and tell her she would definitely be back by nine.

She got straight through to Paddy and was immediately bombarded with questions. She refused to supply any details of her humiliation, promising to fill them in when she returned. Once she got Cordelia on the line she said, 'Don't say anything to Paddy yet, but I've just come from an extremely heavy scene with Barrington.'

'I'm not surprised,' she replied stiffly. 'What exactly happened?'

'I'll tell you later.' She sighed. 'Suffice it to say that it never happens like this in books. Your fictional detective never gets thrown out of rich men's houses with threats of slander. I think in future I'll stick to being a journo. At least journalism more or less lives up to its own mythology.'

Cordelia laughed softly and said, 'You mean you really are a promiscuous alcoholic who spends her life running into crowded newsrooms yelling, "Hold the front page"?'

'But of course,' Lindsay replied. 'Pour me a drink, pass me a woman and a cigarette while I knock out a world exclusive. I'll see you later, okay?'

She made better time on the return journey as there was little traffic about. Two hours of hard driving with Joan Armatrading blasting out of the stereo had made her feel better. She got out of the car singing and noticed with surprise that a police car was drawn up next to Paddy's Land

Rover. As she walked towards the door of the house, two uniformed officers got out of the car and intercepted her.

The elder of the two, a sergeant, said, 'Miss Lindsay Gordon?'

'That's right. What's the problem?'

'Inspector Dart has asked me to bring you along to the police station. There are one or two things he wants to have a word with you about.'

She forced a taut smile to her lips and said in a voice that struggled to stay casual, 'I don't suppose I have a great deal of choice?'

The sergeant studied her, saying nothing. She shrugged and said, 'Very well. Shall we go?'

They travelled the short journey to the police station in silence. The car pulled up by a long, low building above the town centre. Lindsay followed the policemen inside to a large hallway with a reception desk closed off by partitions of frosted glass. The sergeant left her to wait with the constable and disappeared through a side door. From the reception area she could hear the low murmur of voices. Lindsay wondered what Dart could possibly want with her now.

A couple of minutes passed before the sergeant reappeared. It felt longer. 'Come with me, please,' he said. 'The Inspector's waiting for you.'

They walked together down a long corridor. Even on a Sunday evening the station seemed busy. There were lights on throughout the building and people appeared in doorways and bustled along the corridors. They stopped before an unmarked door and the sergeant knocked. It was opened by Dart's silent young sidekick. He stood back for her to enter and the two uniformed men departed.

Inspector Dart was sitting behind a cluttered desk. He glanced up at her, shook his head wearily and said, 'Some coppers get to spend Sunday night at home with their feet up watching *Dirty Harry* on the video. Other poor sods get dragged out because they happen to get tangled up in cases that throw up right stupid bastards. Guess which category I come into, Miss Gordon?'

Lindsay said nothing. Her silence clearly exasperated him. He went on. 'I could say, I suppose you're wondering why I had you brought here tonight. But that would be a pretty silly thing to say to someone who thinks she's smarter than the whole of Derbyshire Constabulary. I think you know very well why you're sitting here tonight.

'I've had a complaint about your activities. A very strongly worded complaint from a very irate gentleman who alleges that you virtually accused him of committing murder. Not even an unsolved murder, at that. A murder to which an eighteen-year-old girl confessed before she killed herself in an extremely unpleasant and painful way. Now I don't know what the hell you think you're playing at, but this gentleman told me a great deal about your little chat. I presume you know what I'm talking about? Or are there some more people scattered round the countryside that you've been accusing of murder? Well?'

'I suppose Anthony Barrington's been on the phone,' said Lindsay resignedly. She was thankful that her journalistic experiences over the last few years had destroyed any awe and respect she had ever felt for the police. It made the interview a little easier to deal with at the end of a draining day.

'He has indeed, Miss Gordon. And from what he says, you really have been playing silly buggers this time. Isn't it enough to drive one girl to suicide? Don't you think that's sufficient mayhem for one weekend?'

'That's unfair. Sarah did what she did for her own reasons, which I suspect had little to do with me. But I managed to work out what really happened last Saturday night – which is more than you and your men achieved.'

They glowered at each other across the desk. When Inspector Dart spoke again, he sounded calmer, 'I'm at a loss to know what you're playing at. I want an explanation.'

'If you treated people in an adult and reasonable way, you might get explanations more often. But every time I've spoken to you, all I've had is hostility and aggression. That, together with the fact that you locked up my best mate for a crime she had nothing to do with, means you shouldn't be surprised that if I've got any ideas at all about this business, I want to check them out myself before I entrust them to you.'

He got up from the desk and walked round behind her. She refused to turn round to face him. His voice sounded tired. 'The last thing the police want is to be made fools of. In this force, we're not stupid and we're not bent. We are, by and large, a bunch of honest coppers doing our damnedest to clear up the messes that the inadequate, the criminal and the plain bloody stupid leave behind them.

'If in the process we upset the likes of you then that's tough luck. You can look after yourself; you're not some pathetic little wimp. So don't expect us to fall over ourselves being nice.

'But you've proved that, even though you've done some incredibly stupid, naive and dangerous things over the last week, you've got a brain. So I'd like to know what happened tonight, and why.

'And before you start, just let me say again how bloody naive and stupid you've been. Just suppose Anthony Barrington *had* been a killer. You went off there on your own. You might like to think you'd have been able to deal with that situation, but I'm not so sure. A person who has killed has broken a fundamental human taboo. Once broken, the taboo loses all force. The next kill is easier. And if your life lies between a killer and safety, it's not worth much. This is real life, you know, not some kind of game. You could have been as dead as Lorna Smith-Couper by now.'

Lindsay nodded slowly, feeling an enormous weariness sweeping over her. 'It occurred to me afterwards. I'm afraid that I get carried away when I get gripped by an idea. However, I think I've reached the point where I have to tell you what I think happened last Saturday night.'

21

Lindsay walked out of the police station and breathed the cold night air deeply. It tasted clean after the stuffiness of Inspector Dart's office. She sighed profoundly, knowing that she still had work to do before she could sleep. The interview had been trying and far from satisfactory. She walked across the deserted market place to a phone box and dialled Paddy's number. It was Cordelia who answered.

'Where are you?' she demanded. 'Do you know what time it is? You said you'd be back by nine. The police have been here looking for you. I've been worried sick.'

Lindsay allowed herself a lopsided wry smile. 'You sound like my bloody mother,' she replied. 'I got caught up, that's all. I'll tell you about it later. I've got one more thing to do, and I'm not sure how long it'll take me. Will you wait with Paddy till I get back?'

Cordelia caught the serious tone in Lindsay's

voice. 'Are you all right?' she asked anxiously.

'Yeah, I'm fine; just a bit tired, that's all. I only rang so you wouldn't be worried. See you later.'

'All right. Take care, now. I'll wait up for you.'

Lindsay put the phone down quickly. The concern in Cordelia's voice hurt too much. She didn't want to do what she was going to do but she couldn't see any alternative. That didn't take the fear away, however. She left the phone box and quickly walked the half mile to their hotel. She ran upstairs to their room and let herself in. She pulled out her miniature tape recorder from her holdall and checked the batteries. She broke open a fresh pack of tiny cassettes and inserted one. Finally, she did a check for voice level with the machine in her jacket pocket. Satisfied that her equipment was working properly, she took a last look round the hotel room. She thought of writing a note to Cordelia in case anything happened to prevent her safe return, but then dismissed the idea as melodramatic, turned on her heel and marched back downstairs. It took her a couple of minutes to get her bearings, then she set off to walk to James Cartwright's house.

The street was quiet and empty except for a few parked cars. Lindsay shivered when a strong gust of wind caught her face as she turned into Cartwright's drive. There was a light burning in the hall, and a smudge of light on the lawn at the side of the house which Lindsay guessed came

321

from the ground-floor office where she and Cordelia had interviewed Cartwright before.

On the doorstep, she set the tape recorder for voice-automated recording and rang the doorbell. Some time elapsed before it opened, framing Cartwright against the strong light from within. He looked tired and dishevelled, as if he'd gone to seed overnight and as he spoke, his sour gin breath hit Lindsay. 'What the hell do you want?' he demanded angrily.

'I want to talk to you. About Sarah,' said Lindsay quietly.

'You? What the hell do you think you've got to say that I would want to listen to? My daughter's dead, thanks to you, and now you want to talk to me about her? You can piss off.' He moved to close the door, but Lindsay was quicker and pushed her body into the gap.

'That might be what the police have told you, but you and I know a different story, don't we? If anybody drove Sarah to slash her wrists, it wasn't me. I know the truth, Cartwright, and I want to talk to you about it. You can take your pick. Either we talk about it now or I go to the police and talk about it with them.'

He looked suspiciously at her. The blurred look left his features as comprehension drove the effect of the drink away. 'I don't know what you mean,' he replied belligerently. Lindsay said nothing. 'Oh, for Christ's sake, you'd better come in. I don't want a scene on the doorstep,' he sighed.

'You've got a bloody cheek,' he complained bitterly as he led her down the hall to the office. Once there he rounded on her. 'Sit down. Now what's all this crap about the police?'

'I thought I'd like to put a proposition to you,' said Lindsay. 'Forget about blaming me for Sarah's death. It'll go down fine with anybody else, but it won't wash with me.'

His expression was calculating. 'And what's that supposed to mean?'

Lindsay managed to maintain the tough façade she had adopted, though inwardly she was quaking with fear. 'Last Saturday night. Saturday's not been a lucky day for you lately, has it? First Lorna, then Sarah.'

A flash of genuine pain crossed his face. 'You're not fit to speak her name,' he spat.

'Leave it out, Cartwright,' Lindsay replied. 'I know how Lorna was murdered, which, thanks to the conversation I had yesterday with Inspector Dart, is getting to be common knowledge. But only you and I know who murdered her.'

A new wariness appeared in Cartwright's face. 'Sarah confessed, you know. Not easy for me to believe, but my daughter did that to try to save my business.'

'Save it for the funeral oration, Cartwright. Though, funnily enough, those are the first true words you've spoken in this whole sorry business. Sarah did just that. She confessed to save both your business and your neck. She was bright enough to know that alive her "confession" wouldn't stand up to a five-minute police interview. There were too many details of the killing she simply didn't know. And the reason for that is that it wasn't Sarah who killed Lorna. It was you.'

He sat and stared at her, his hands balling into fists on the desk top. 'You must be mad. I've got an alibi. The police have checked. It was Sarah, God damn it, it was Sarah!'

'I've checked it out too. And it's not tight enough. Lorna was killed between half-past seven and twenty to eight. You could just have done it on the basis of the times you were actually seen in the two pubs. Sarah couldn't have done it, though. By twenty-five to eight she was in Longnor. That only leaves you with the necessary knowledge and skill to assemble that scaffolding and kill Lorna.'

'You can't prove that. If you could, or thought you could, you'd be telling the cops, not me.' He got to his feet and started pacing about the office restlessly.

'I can prove that Sarah couldn't have done it. I've got a witness who will swear to where Sarah was at the crucial time. You've had it, Cartwright. So listen to my proposition.'

His lips curled in a sneer. 'You're talking rubbish. But let's hear this so-called proposition. If it's blackmail you're after, forget it. I haven't got a bloody penny.'

'I got involved in this business because Paddy Callaghan was arrested. Since then, a lot of people have had a very shitty time because of you. I think it's only fair that you should make it up to them in some small way. So all I'm asking is a written undertaking that you will withdraw from all negotiations concerning the purchase of Derbyshire House's playing fields. When I get that, I'll forget everything I ever knew about Lorna's murder. Do we have a deal?'

He continued to pace back and forth. 'If I pull out, which I might say is because of the way I feel about my Sarah's death, what guarantee do I have that you're not going to go around spreading these slanderous lies about me?'

'Why should I say anything? I'll have got what I want.'

'And what's to stop you coming back any time in the future and making more demands?'

'You'll just have to take my word for that.'

His seemingly aimless striding around had brought him to within a few feet of Lindsay's chair. Suddenly he lunged at her. Caught by surprise, she could only struggle feebly as his weight overturned the chair and pinned her to the floor. His hands were round her throat, squeezing. She could feel the bursting pressure in her chest as her lungs fought for air. Just as she felt her head start to swim, his hands came away as he jerked her to her feet and pulled his arm round her throat in a half-nelson. She gulped air desperately as he pulled her back so hard that her toes scrabbled to stay on the floor. With his free hand, he picked up a stiletto paper knife from the desk top. He held it to her temple and growled, 'That's what I think of your lousy proposition, Miss Gordon. Now I'm going to let go of your neck. And you're not going to move a muscle. One move and this goes straight into your smart little brain. If you're clear about that, say yes.'

Lindsay swallowed hard and croaked, 'Yes,' through a dry throat. He let her go and moved surprisingly quickly round in front of her.

'Walk backwards towards that other desk. One step at a time.'

She stumbled backwards until she backed painfully into the metal edge of the desk. He moved so close she could smell the combination of stale gin and sweat. She could feel bitter vomit rising in her throat and swallowed it back with effort. He reached beyond her and picked up a roll of coloured plastic tape. 'Now turn around and walk slowly to the chair by the wall. The one with the arms.' Lindsay obeyed, bewitched by the knife that was now pricking into her neck just below her ear. When she reached the chair, he punched her roughly into it and handed her the tape. 'Use your left hand to tape your right wrist to the arm of the chair,' he told her. 'And make a good job of it.' Lindsay did what she was told like an automaton. Only now was her numbed mind beginning to come out of shock and beginning to reason. Not that that was much help, since she couldn't think of anything that could be effective against this animal with the knife.

He watched her carefully, and picked his moment well for the next part of his operation. His hand darted out and grabbed her left wrist. Without breaking the tape he swiftly taped her free hand to the chair, throwing the knife on to the floor.

Lindsay tried to kick him as he bent over her, but her foot only glanced off his shin. He started with the pain and reacted swiftly with a hard slap to the head that Lindsay felt the length of her spine. 'Bitch,' he spat. 'Try that again and I'll kill you here and now. And don't think I'm bluffing. That was Lorna Smith-Couper's mistake.' He moved to the side of the chair and pushed it away from the wall. He came round behind her and started going through the pockets of her jacket. He removed the tape recorder triumphantly. 'I thought you might have one of these,' he crowed. 'I'm not daft, you know.' He opened the machine and pulled out the cassette. He walked over to a metal bin and began to draw the tape viciously out of its plastic cassette. When he reached the end of the tape, he took a cigarette lighter from his desk and set fire to the tape, which blazed briefly then died.

'Thought you'd got me, didn't you?' he gloated. 'Well, you were wrong. Now I've got you. And you're not going to live long enough to tell your little tale to anybody else. This bloody land was worth killing once for. It's got to be worth killing twice for it.'

Lindsay found her voice. 'Make that three times. You as good as killed Sarah as well.'

'Don't say that,' he almost screamed. 'I know why Sarah died. It was because of your meddling. If you'd kept your nose out of this nobody would have ever known anything about that bloody scaffolding. It was you that killed my daughter, you bitch.'

'Keep thinking that if it helps. But one day you're going to have to face the fact that Sarah preferred to die rather than live with a murderer.'

A cunning look crept across his face. 'You're trying to make me lose my temper, to give you a chance of coming back at me. Well, it won't work. Where's your car? Is it outside?'

Surprised by the change in tack, Lindsay blurted out, 'No, it isn't.'

'Where is it then?'

Lindsay couldn't work out why the question was being asked, but some instinct for self-preservation made her keep her mouth shut.

He moved back to face her. 'I asked where your bloody car is.'

'Find out your bloody self,' Lindsay retorted. Before the words were out of her mouth, his hand slashed at her face again. Pain blotted out her consciousness for a moment. When she could sense anything again, she tasted blood and felt her mouth beginning to swell. Her left eye felt on fire. She shook her head to clear it.

'Where's your car?'

He grasped the little finger of her left hand and began to bend it backwards. Lindsay gritted her teeth as the pain flooded through her arm. 'It's at the school,' she gasped.

He let go. 'All the better. No one will have noticed it here. We'll go and collect it a little later on. You're going to have a nasty accident. Driving away from the school. There's a lot of really bad bends up on the Cat and Fiddle road. Somebody who doesn't know their way around and likes to drive fast could easily have a fatal accident up there. Don't worry, you won't feel a thing. A bump on the head, that's all. I'll drive you up there in your own car and we'll send it over the side. Shame you don't like wearing a seatbelt, isn't it?'

Lindsay stared at him with pure hatred. 'You bastard,' she said, her words slurring slightly.

He moved towards her again. But before he could reach her the door burst open and Inspector Dart ran into the room followed by half a dozen uniformed officers. 'Police!' he yelled. 'Stop right there, Cartwright. Okay, lads, take him.' They rushed towards him in a body. Cartwright picked up the fallen chair Lindsay had been sitting on previously and hurled it at the approaching policemen, then threw himself through the window. He'd reckoned without Dart's foresight. He dived, bleeding, straight into the arms of Dart's sergeant and another group of uniformed men. He thrashed out blindly but it was only a matter of seconds before they overpowered him, hand-cuffed him and hustled him off to a waiting police van.

While the struggle was going on, Dart crouched behind Lindsay's chair and picked the tape away from her wrists. She felt herself close to tears and collapse, but she was determined not to give way in front of the policeman. 'You took your bloody time,' she complained weakly. 'I was beginning to think the radio mike had packed in when he jumped me.'

'You did well,' Dart said as he helped her to her feet and lit a cigarette for her. 'We picked it all up loud and clear. I took the precaution of having a shorthand writer take it all down as well as taping it, just in case. We wanted to let him hang himself good and proper, since he seemed reluctant to make anything amounting to an admission. Probably because he guessed you were wired. That was a good idea of yours to take your own tape recorder. It put him right off his guard after he'd disposed of that. Now we can probably get him for attempted murder on you as well.'

'Terrific. That makes me feel it's all been worth-while,' said Lindsay ironically. 'Now, could one of your lads take me back to Derbyshire House? I've had enough for one day.'

'We'll need a full statement from you. But that can wait till the morning. Don't you think you should go down to the hospital and get checked over?'

Lindsay shook her head. 'There's nothing broken. I'd know if there was. I'm just bruised and shaken. Nothing a good night's sleep won't put more or less right. But thanks for the belated concern,' she added. She walked out of the room on very nearly steady legs.

A few minutes later the police car drew up outside Longnor House. Lindsay glanced across at her car. It seemed many hours since she'd left it. She glanced at her watch and was astonished to see it was barely past midnight. 'I'll never feel the same about that car again,' she said to the policeman with her. 'If that bastard had had his way, it would have been my coffin. Tell the Inspector I'll see him tomorrow about noon.'

The door into the house was locked. Lindsay's shoulders sagged. It was the last straw. She leaned against the wall of the porch and studied the bells. Housemistress. Senior Mistress. Junior Mistress. She pressed the top bell and prayed for Paddy.

PART FIVE:
CODA

22

It was just after nine the following morning when Paddy pulled back the curtains in her bedroom and turned to look at the waking figure in her bed. Lindsay's sleep-rumpled hair suited a disreputable appearance that included a black eye, a split and swollen lip and a badly bruised jaw. She opened her eyes and winced as the pain hit her. Paddy brought her a glass of orange juice and smiled anxiously. 'How are you feeling?' she inquired.

'Like I've been run over by a truck,' Lindsay replied crossly. 'I'm sure that bastard Dart deliberately let Cartwright work me over.'

'I don't know what you're talking about, you know,' Paddy complained. 'You staggered in here last night looking as though you'd been mugged, told us everything was all right, demanded a large Scotch and a bed and refused point-blank to tell us a bloody thing more until you'd slept. Cordelia has been going out of her head with worry. I couldn't get her to bed till gone three. Really, Lindsay, you are the pits.'

Lindsay attempted a scowl, then thought better of it. 'Sorry. I had just had more than enough for one day. Anyway, shouldn't you be teaching? Isn't that what they pay you for?'

'I've managed to off-load my classes for today on the grounds that I'm nursing an invalid journalist. So if Pamela Overton comes across, try to look sick.'

'That won't be hard. Where's Cordelia?'

'Upstairs, I presume. I've given her the guest room. She was sufficiently anaesthetised by the time she went to bed to sleep half the morning if we let her.'

'Where did you sleep, then?'

'On the sofa. After prison comforts, it seemed like the Ritz.'

'Sorry I spoilt your homecoming.'

'Never mind that. Just tell me what the hell has been going on!'

'When I've had a shower and Cordelia's here. Not till then. I'm not going over the whole thing twice.'

Paddy wasn't happy with this answer, but Lindsay was adamant, insisting on washing and dressing immediately. Paddy left to fetch Cordelia, and Lindsay winced her way to the bathroom, where she let the hot water soothe away some of the aches from her battered body.

When she emerged, Cordelia was pacing the

living-room. She rushed to Lindsay and hugged her. For the first time since she'd woken up, Lindsay forgot her pain. 'Don't ever scare me like that again,' Cordelia murmured. 'Thank God you're all right.' Paddy looked mildly astonished, then discreetly exited to the kitchen to brew more coffee.

When she returned, the two lovers were sitting together, Lindsay with her bruised head on Cordelia's shoulder. She sat up to relate the events of the previous evening. Just the telling of it was enough to make her shiver with horror. And the effect on Paddy and Cordelia was no less chilling.

'You must be crazy, Lindsay,' Cordelia cried. 'Going in there on your own. You could have been killed. You should have taken me with you.'

Lindsay shook her head, 'No, this was one thing that had to be done solo. There's no way Cartwright would have opened up at all if there had been two of us. He wouldn't have fallen for the line I took. He'd simply have tried to brazen it out. So I had to trust Dart to take care of me.

'He'd fitted me out with a very good radio microphone, so that was transmitting everything said and done in the room. The cops were sitting outside in a troop of unmarked police cars with a van parked in the next-door neighbour's drive behind the shrubbery. And for extra security, Dart's sergeant was outside the office window with one of those limpet microphones.

'Dart was very quick at getting the operation

together once I'd convinced him it was the only way to do it. He wouldn't hear of it to begin with, but I told him if he wouldn't help me, I'd do it on my own and the only way he could stop me was to throw me in the cells. He finally relented when I pointed out that eventually I'd be back on the streets again, and I'd go straight to Cartwright and confront him. At least when the case comes to trial I'll have a wonderful exclusive to flog – How I Caught The Girls' School Killer.'

'Yes. The scars will probably have healed by then,' said Cordelia drily.

'I'm sorry to be a bore,' said Paddy, 'but you'll have to bear with me. Don't forget, I've not been party to all these discussions you've had in the course of the past week. Someone has yet to explain to me exactly what has been going on. Starting from the murder.'

Lindsay took a deep breath and began. 'I now know how precarious James Cartwright's financial position was. He admitted last night he didn't have a brass farthing. Inspector Dart told me he'd made some bad property deals lately. He had already raised a lot of capital on the strength of his time-share scheme and it was absolutely crucial that the playing fields deal succeeded. Had he not pulled it off, he would have been forced into liquidation and bankruptcy. He couldn't face that prospect; he enjoyed his lifestyle too much. And he was worried about losing Sarah's affection

338

and respect if he couldn't give her the life she was used to.

'He tried to bribe Lorna not to play that night. Even though the tickets had already been sold, if Lorna had pulled out, a lot of people would have been looking for their money back. And it would have completely discredited any further attempt to raise the money. But Lorna wouldn't hear of it. She was enjoying herself far too much watching people being upset by her presence. Also, in spite of herself, I think she did care about the school. And she had sufficient integrity as an artist not to let her public down. So she refused, and in deeply insulting terms. He was thwarted and also very angry. That's when he thought of trying to murder her. He had reached the end of his tether, something Lorna couldn't have known. He was desperate enough to be dangerous.

'He knew the school layout very well. So, when everyone was at dinner, he went to the music room and helped himself to a cello string. He was probably wearing his driving gloves, because the police haven't found any prints. He probably also checked that the window catches were still easy to manipulate. Then he fetched the scaffolding and set it up.

'He dashed back to the Woolpack and bought a pint. He must have downed it in a oner, because by about twelve minutes past seven he was back at the school. He went to Longnor – I guess because he knew the cloakroom was near the door and it would be quieter than the main building – and helped himself to a toggle, presumably having realised by then that the string was sharp enough to cause bad cuts even through gloves if he used it on its own. That's almost certainly when Sarah saw him. I think she was probably coming downstairs to go for a walk at the time, or to go down to the gym to do some exercises, perhaps.

'I'm guessing a bit now. But I think she followed him, catching up with him as he was preparing the garrotte or climbing up the fire escape to the scaffolding. He sent her back telling her to forget she'd seen him.

'Then, of course, he killed Lorna. He had to leave the scaffolding on the kitchen roof because he was running out of time to keep up the alibi he'd set himself. Of course, once the murder was common knowledge, Sarah must have realised her father was implicated. The girl must have been under colossal strain all last week. I suppose your arrest made things even worse for her, Paddy. Then when she heard about our experiments with the scaffolding, she must have felt sure the net was closing around her father.

'She must have realised that the lie she'd told the police about you in the music room would be found out. Incidentally, I don't think she lied out of particular malice – at that stage, after all, it wasn't clear that the police were going to arrest you. I think she was just trying to cloud the issue in every conceivable way possible. I think what drove her to commit suicide was a combination of factors. She knew her father was a killer and she couldn't bear it, but she still wanted to protect him, and the only way she could do that was to kill herself. Just confessing wouldn't have been enough. She'd never have been able to make up a story that would have satisfied the police. And she probably felt that if she gave herself up to the police, the very thing that she was trying to avoid would happen – her father would give himself up to protect her.

'As it was, I'm not altogether sure he would have done. He was happy enough for her to carry the blame after her death. That's what I find most inhuman about him.' She paused to pour out more coffee. 'God, my throat is sore. I'm amazed there are hardly any bruises on it. I thought he was going to kill me.'

Paddy looked puzzled. 'But everyone seemed to be satisfied after Sarah's death that the whole thing had been cleared up. What made you think you knew better?'

'Apart from a general sense of superiority, she means,' said Cordelia with a rather grim smile.

'I finally got on the right track when I asked Jessica Bennett a question we should have asked her when we first interviewed her. When I saw her yesterday I wanted to ask her if she'd seen Sarah at all on that Saturday evening – just for my own satisfaction, I suppose, though I did have one or two doubts about Sarah's confession. It seemed so superficial, so lacking in feeling and detail. But Jessica's answer put Sarah out of the running. She said she'd seen Sarah going out of Longnor at about quarter past seven.

'And at the crucial time when the murder must have been committed to avoid any comings and goings, Jessica saw Sarah in the cloakroom. She tried to talk to her. But Sarah went straight upstairs. Jessica didn't see her again that night.

'That removed Sarah from the list of suspects. But it put her father right back into the frame. However, Anthony Barrington still seemed a possibility, and I thought on balance I'd prefer to talk to him. Barrington gave me such a hard time, I was convinced he was innocent. He was too outraged to be guilty. And then, of course, he called Dart and I was hauled off to the nick.

'And the rest you know,' she said, closing her eyes as a wave of tiredness hit her.

She forced her eyes open again. 'I've got to go and give the police a statement at noon. And then, if you don't mind, Paddy, I want to go home. I've got work to go to on Wednesday, and I could do with a day's sleep.'

'I understand,' said Paddy. 'I'll never be able to pay you and Cordelia back for what you've done for me. But come back soon and see us again, promise?'

Lindsay grinned but said, 'Ouch! I must stop

doing that. I'll come soon if you guarantee no hassles.'

'I guarantee it.' They smiled at each other, relaxed again after the upheavals of the last ten days.

'I'll drive you back to Glasgow,' said Cordelia, 'you're far too tired to hammer up the motorway on your own. Besides, I think we've got one or two things to talk about.'

Paddy's eyebrows had shot up. 'Well, well, well,' she marvelled. 'I see some good has come out of all this.'

'Surprised?' demanded Cordelia.

'Before we get into all of that, I need to phone my newsdesk,' said Lindsay apologetically. 'Sorry. Since I've got to go down the cop shop this morning, if I don't put over a story nice and early my life won't be worth living on Wednesday. Can I use the phone?'

Paddy grinned at Cordelia. 'How does it feel to play second fiddle to a news story?'

Cordelia pulled a face. 'I don't think I want to get used to the idea. Maybe Lindsay could change her priorities . . . just a bit?'

Lindsay dialled the number. 'Yeah, yeah, okay, Cordelia. I'll work on it. But tomorrow, eh, please . . . Hello? Duncan? Lindsay here. I've got a real belter for you this morning . . .'

Common Murder

V.L. McDermid

A protest group hits the headlines when unrest at a women's peace camp explodes into murder. Already on the scene, journalist Lindsay Gordon desperately tries to strike a balance between personal and professional responsibilities. As she peels back the layers of deception surrounding the protest and its opponents, she finds that no one – ratepayer or reporter, policeman or peace woman – seems wholly above suspicion. Then Lindsay uncovers a truth that even she can scarcely believe.

'A well-pitched and topical mystery'   *Sunday Times*

'McDermid's snappy, often comic, prose keeps the story humming'   *Publishers Weekly*

ISBN: 0-00-719175-8

Final Edition
V.L. McDermid

When Alison Maxwell, a well-known Glaswegian journalist with an irresistible sexual attraction to both sexes, is found murdered the police look no further than the owner of the scarf used to strangle her. Lindsay Gordon, however, has other ideas. Maxwell was a serial seductress who kept a secret record of her encounters – including one with Lindsay herself. Recalling the threats that followed the end of the relationship, Lindsay knows all too well the feelings of rage, fear and passion that Alison Maxwell could invoke.

Soon Lindsay is embroiled in an investigation involving blackmail, stolen government documents and the vested interests of a group of people determined to keep her from finding the truth.

'Witty and corrosively unsentimental'   *She*

'A treat . . . gripping until the very last page'   *Pink Paper*

ISBN: 0-00-719176-6